T0381446

THE UNEXPECTED ENTRY

IN THE EYE OF THE BADGE

PEACHES DUDLEY

authorHOUSE®

AuthorHouse™
1663 Liberty Drive
Bloomington, IN 47403
www.authorhouse.com
Phone: 833-262-8899

Published by AuthorHouse 01/22/2025

ISBN: 979-8-8230-4147-8 (sc)
ISBN: 979-8-8230-4146-1 (e)

CONTENTS

AUTHOR'S PREFACE

Living in the high-priced famous luxury tower, in the big apple, Stephanie and her neighbors reveal secrets to one another as hidden drama unveils itself before their eyes. As tenants in the drama high rise building, can their tight knitted friendship sustain the criminal activity that has intensified itself in their place of residence. As Stephanie's family encounters tragedy from the hostile New York City streets, can one of her close friends handle the criminals that lurk around their home which endangers the welfare of her family. Joined together by the commonality of a sport, can this group of friends who love the downward rush of the ski slopes handle the drama of the New York City profession. Will the young teen love affair be affected by the overprotected Ness of professionals. Can the Elder of the church be of any assistance amid the buildings criminal mischief. This eye-catching entertainment out of New York City reads like a thriller.

Peaches Dudley resides in Harlem, New York. She's an author, poet, song writer and respected singer. Her unique voice and true style exhibit her activeness in the community. Being well-traveled, there is no place in the United States her feet haven't touched. She is known as a great storyteller.

ACKNOWLEDGEMENTS

To my sister Tracy Miller, I love you dearly

Wanda V. Addison thank you for always being there for me throughout the years

Richerdeen Chisolm "Big Mama" thank you for always listening to my stories

Chyna "Jane Doh" your creativity inspires me to achieve goals

Lashera Upson Naomi Dickerson Jessica Robertson, I appreciate all that you do

Christine Dudley Steve Dudley Matthew Dudley Michelle Clarke A.J. Jones Dawn Dudley Julia Dudley Hattie Williams Canara Price Your constant love motivates me to reach goals

Avraam Barlow thank you for taking time out of your busy schedule to listen to my stories

Kevin Miles, I appreciate your friendship Governor, you keep me laughing

Jake Langley Tracy Jones ReadyRockDee Vera Fields, thanks again and again

Pastor David Wright Karen Lindstrom Davon Moore you've brought out the winner in me

Terri White Lynn Easter Jean Wormley Veronica & Jessica Green thank you for the support

Eric Morgan YoYo Morgan and my heart David Morgan, I love you very much

DO NOT COPY

CHAPTER 1

THE SURPRISE KNOCK

"Girl I can't talk to you right now; George is in town I'll call you back later" Tiffany shouted as she ended the telephone conversation with Stephanie. As Stephanie slowly placed her cell phone down on the marble kitchen counter while continuing scrambling eggs mixed with pepper jack cheese in the frying pan that her grandmother Lucille gave to her as a housewarming gift ten years ago when Stephanie moved into the apartment the doorbells rhythmic chimes began to ring. As her pet dog, a Shar-pei mixed named Brownie, ran through the penthouse apartment loudly barking making his way to the door to alarm the neighbors on that floor, there is a visitor that has unexpectedly arrived at the apartment door Stephanie quickly turned off the flame on the stove.

"*Who is it*" Stephanie Yelled! As she placed a lid on

1

top of the frying pan covering up her favorite breakfast meal scrambled eggs with spicy cheese. *"Brownie quit all that loud barking I can't hear who it is standing at my door"* Stephanie shouted as she exited her penthouse kitchen quickly making her way through the large duplex apartment towards the apartment front door.

"Who is it?" Stephanie loudly asked again as she walked closer to her apartment door.

"It's Brad Steph I have a package for you" the male voice loudly shouted from the hallway, standing on the other side of the door.

"Why didn't you just leave the package at the door Bradley" Stephanie yelled as she began to unlock the huge locks on her apartment door.

"I wouldn't have the pleasure of seeing your warm smiling face on today and would have missed out on your radiant aura which you brightly send" Brad shouted as he patiently stood on the other side of the door in the empty hallway awaiting his neighbor Stephanie to open her penthouse apartment door. Opening the thick penthouse apartment door Stephanie turned the brass doorknob slowly as she pulled the door towards her with a half-smile on her face. *"Morning Stephanie, this is why I couldn't leave this heavy box at your door. I believe it was delivered yesterday afternoon because when I arrived home and stepped off our elevator this large box along with a few small packages was stationed here in our hallway. When I saw your name on the box, I honestly took it into my penthouse apartment and on my way outside for some fresh air I repeatedly rang your doorbell yesterday evening. When I rang the doorbell, I didn't*

2

hear Brownie barking and there was no answer" Bradley cheerfully said with a huge grin on his face. As Brownie quickly maneuvered around Stephanie dashing through the now cracked door, running into the hallway towards Bradley wagging his curled tail, Stephanie took in a long deep breath and widely open her mouth, exhaling, blew her breath into the hallway. While Bradley, who remained smiling slowly bent himself over, reaching down to rub his four-legged friend Brownie on his fur, Stephanie opened the penthouse door wider.

"Thank you, Bradley, for finally giving me my package" Stephanie spoke.

"Steph you know there's nothing I wouldn't do for you. Not only are we neighbors but I consider you, my friend" Bradley loudly responded. As Brownie begins to sniff around the large box that was on the floor next to the pairs of sneakers and boots lined up against the side wall in front of Stephanie's duplex penthouse apartment the elevator arrival chimes rang. As the elevator doors quickly opened Brownie began to loudly bark once again. Stepping out of the apartment buildings elevator was a young tall Slim muscular built Armenian gentleman in a tight fitted doorman suit.

"Good morning, everyone! Hey, Brownie, how's my good boy?" The doorman loudly shouted as he stood tall in the hallway by the penthouse floor elevator while Brownie jumped up and down on the bottom of the tall doorman's pants leg.

"Morning Aram we're fine. Hungry! But doing well" Stephanie loudly replied with a huge smile on her face.

"Yeah, everyone here is great this morning buddy. How about yourself?" Bradley answered as he quickly squatted down to the floor clapping his hands signaling for Brownie the Shar-pe mixed doggy to run back towards him.

"I'm adjust greatly sir. I know today going to be a good day for everyone" Aram loudly answered. *"That's just good to know and great to adhere"* Bradley sarcastically responded.

"Yes sir. And I came upstairs to make sure that Ms. Stephanie received her delivery from yesterday" Aram loudly said. Bradley then slowly removed his eyes off Brownie who was now playfully being rubbed by his own hands shifting his eyes onto Aram while slightly tilting his head upwards staring at Aram directly into his blue eyes. Stephanie took in another long deep breath and exhaled with her mouth wide open blowing her breath into the hallway.

"Yes, I have it now Aram. This is the box that's stationed here next to Brad. Thank you for checking up on my delivery status Aram" Stephanie answered.

"Glad to know. Well, I'm going back downstairs to work if anyone needs anything don't be afraid to let any of us know" Aram said as he quickly turned around pushing the elevator button located on the apartment buildings penthouses floor wall panel before he immediately got back onto the elevator.

As the apartment building elevator doors closed, Stephanie stepped out of her apartment into the hallway, quickly balled her fist and punched Bradley on his muscular shoulder. *"You don't have to be a jerk Brad! You know his English is not very good. He hasn't been in this country long as you and I have, and English is not his main language"* Stephanie said.

As Bradley slowly stood up now facing Stephanie in the hallway *"that's a pretty good punch you have there. Have you been taking boxing classes at the gym you attend?"* Bradley asked.

"No, I haven't Brad. I know how to fight and defend myself from mean characters like yourself" Stephanie replied.

"I'm not a bad guy Steph. Once you get to really know me, you'll enjoy my company the same as your good dog Brownie here always does" Bradley responded while bending over once again to play with Stephanie's pet dog.

"I thank you for personally bringing my large package to the apartment door and I'll take it from here Brad. It's breakfast time and my fully cooked meal is waiting for me inside of my apartment inside the kitchen on the table for me to indulge Brad" Stephanie softly said.

"I understand Steph. It was a real pleasure seeing your beautiful face this morning. As I now repeat what Aram clearly said "now it's going to be a great day"" Bradley shouted as he started walking backwards across the hallway to his penthouse apartment door.

Stephanie purposely leaving the box in the hallway returned inside of her apartment shutting and locking her duplex penthouse apartment door.

Finally sitting at the dining room table eating her favorite breakfast meal Stephanie's cell phone began to ring. It was her brother Ezra who had just returned home from Switzerland with his girlfriend where they celebrated her twenty first birthday. Quickly picking up her cell phone *"Welcome home stranger I'm so glad to hear from you on this morning"* Stephanie said while softly chewing on the scrambled eggs with pepper jack cheese.

"Hi big sis. What an experience this has truly been. I'm back! Feeling better than ever Steph. I must admit. I'm glad to hear that you missed me" Ezra answered.

"So how was the trip to Switzerland? I mean the secret honeymoon, stinky butt" Stephanie inquired. *"Did you not hear me Steph? Feeling better than ever!"* Ezra loudly replied.

"You don't have to shout in my ear, stinky butt" Stephanie responded.

"I'm not shouting. And I didn't go on any honeymoon. Hey Steph. What's going on with you this early morning?" Ezra inquisitively asked.

"Little brother this creepy neighbor bothers me at times. I know I shouldn't let him get under my skin or into my head. At times he just annoys me. I left him in the hallway not long before you called me so I'm probably still tripping over his overbearing a noxious personality" Stephanie honestly responded.

"Oh, that Brad dude! He is still flirting and trying to get to intimately know my big sister. You want me to come over there and beat him up for you?" Ezra asked.

"That would have been great if only you knew how to fight, stinky butt" Stephanie humorously replied.

"I really don't understand how anything as minuet as that

Brad dude's mannerism can get to you. As long as you have been living in big busy New York City. I know you must be well adjusted by now to the different aggressive behavioral patterns of New Yorkers. Even if they're way different from the calmer or slower behaviors we were raised around as Mormons living in Ogden, Utah. You've been a resident in that building now for ten years so nothing or no one should be creeping my big sister out. Not at this early morning hour" Ezra said.

"You're right Ezra. But the guy just bothers me, and I can't get used to that feeling. Specifically, when I'm not feeling the creep" Stephanie answered as she continued chewing on her plate of scrambled eggs with pepper jack cheese.

"I hear you Steph. You need to go visit Switzerland, there so much to do and see there it would take that Brad dude, off your mind. I loved every minute of that trip" Ezra loudly said.

"You mean you loved every minute of being next to the birthday girl and her dirty little pin up secrets" Stephanie responded.

"Don't make fun of my playboy bunny. That's my cupcake of the month" Ezra said.

"Yuck, don't make me throw up, stinky butt. You probably need to throw her away or throw her back into the dirty pond where you fished her up out of and go shop around to get another one" Stephanie quickly responded.

"Don't hate on us Steph. We're destined for greatness. There are big things in stored for us. Our future is humongous Ly set. And I'm not talking about cosmetic surgeries either" Ezra responded. *"You know you're a sick kid"* Stephanie loudly said as she laughed.

"Listen Steph, what are you going to do about this Brad dude that keeps on knocking?" Ezra asked. "I'm going to continue to leave him in the hallway just like I left my very large box that he voluntarily delivered to my door" Stephanie answered her younger brother.

"Wait! What? You actually left your package in the hallway because of a friendly crush? Come on sis! That's just dumb. Ignoring your gift over some Bumb. I'm surprised at you, Steph. This is not my sister I'm hearing from right now. I might need to hang up from you and try calling you back later" Ezra loudly said.

"No, Ezra I simply wanted to eat my breakfast and Brad interrupted me because he wanted to personally deliver a box that already had been delivered to my door. So, I simply left it where he originally found it. Right in front of my penthouse door!" Stephanie shouted while finishing up eating her favorite breakfast meal.

"Listen Steph. You don't have to yell into my ear. The dude likes what he sees. Maybe you need to bring another dude into your apartment so that Brad can see that you're off the market. Maybe then he will ease off you" Ezra suggested. "I'm just saying, that's a very large apartment with a great balcony view of New York City. I couldn't see anyone turning you down for a nightcap. If you seem to can't think of anybody, I have a nice contact list of eligible bachelors for you to use" Ezra said as he started laughing.

"No Ezra I don't need any of your young hoodlum friends scurrying around in my well-kept apartment. It's bad enough that you don't like to bathe your dirty little butt. I can only imagine what your so-called friends smell like" Steph

8

sarcastically responded while drinking her juice as she finished eating her favorite breakfast.

"How's my Brownie this morning I know he missed his favorite uncle" Ezra calmly asked as the loud sound of pure tone beeps started echoing through his cell phone in the background signaling that a large motor vehicle was moving in reverse.

"Ezra where are you?" Stephanie curiously asked her younger brother because of the loud back-up beeper coming from a truck whose sound was now blaring loudly through the cell phone directly into her eardrum.

"I'm on my way to the post office to mail some things off to Kenny." Ezra honestly replied.

"Are you still sending that piece of crap money Ezra? You need to stop taking care of that fool. He's a Bumb! If he can't take care of himself by now at this time of his life that is not your problem little brother. If he is foolish enough to repeatedly make the same financial mistakes again and again that is not your worry! Let him find another solution to his foolishness. You have enough on your plate. You have that pin up playboy bunny constantly hanging around you now in which you must attend to not his hungry horses he can't feed" Stephanie said.

"He asked me for some information so I created a little package for him that I know he will benefit from and I'm now on my way to the post office to send it to Kenny, Steph. That's all" Ezra calmly replied.

"Lies! Stinky butt! You're sending that jerk your hard-earned money! If that was the case, then you would have done what seventy percent of the world is doing and that's send him a text loaded with the information he needed. Or attached the

downloaded file to an email and pushed the button send, on the bottom of the email and he would have received it ten seconds. Don't give me that crap stinky butt. He's been sucking the life out of your pockets far too long, and it must end somehow. I want it to end now" Stephanie loudly said as she backed her chair up from the dining room table and stood up making her way to the kitchen to place her now empty plate in the kitchen sink.

"I'm not a sucker Steph! Kenny is not a fool either. He's a truly good friend who I love. That's my buddy. We've been through a lot together Steph. You need to have a little bit more respect for my friends and stop worrying about who I associate myself with and concentrate on your own friends starting with that gentleman neighbor across the hallway from you who is so kind enough to bring your mail to your door" Ezra said.

"He brought me mail that was already delivered to my door by someone else. Another guy who the parcel delivery services pay well for him to do" Stephanie replied as she opened the kitchen cabinet to pull out the canned dog food for brownie her Shar-pei mixed dog to eat. *"Brad is a creepy neighbor who annoys me. Kenny is a fool who is draining my brother's pockets for money to feed his hungry horses. I personally feel if the man can't afford the expenses of his ranch, then he needs to sell it to someone who can handle the very costly expenses and move on to another career. Not have my brother roaming the loud streets of the busy city, early in the morning stressing himself to help cover a foolish man's problem"* Stephanie continued to say.

"I'm not taking care of Kenny's barn or his livestock and I'm not taking care of Kenny's problems Steph. I'm just

overnighting my good friend some good information that's all. Plus, I just got back from a very expensive vacation in Switzerland, so my pockets are empty. My wallet is bare, and my accounts are negative. My playboy bunny is going to have to carry us for a little while until I've financially recovered" Ezra said.

"Good boy Brownie. Eat it all up like a good boy. Enjoy your meal Brownie because you know mommy takes care of her good boy" Stephanie said as she placed the canned dog food into the doggy dish on the marble kitchen floor by the kitchen sink. "Ignore your uncle Brownie who thinks I'm not aware of what is really going on" Stephanie continued to say. Leaving the kitchen and walking towards the balcony Stephanie stopped by the coffee table and picked up the remote to turn on the flat screen television that was mounted on the wall.

"Steph. You need to stop worrying about me so much and go outside in that hallway to retrieve your box. I know you want to see what's inside. That's crazy that Brad dude has you, paranoid in your own home. What's the sense of having a beautiful penthouse apartment if you can't live comfortably. You need to overcome your fear of the Brad and get to the box Steph" Ezra loudly said as he walked up the steps of the post office.

"Did you bring me back any souvenirs Ezra? What did you get for mom and dad?" Stephanie loudly asked, trying to change the course of the conversation as she changed the channel on the television by the remote that was in her hand.

"Well, I brought back from Switzerland something nice for

Tiffany. I know that beauty queen is going to love the souvenir I purchased for her" Ezra loudly replied.

"Tiffany is very much occupied at the moment George is back in town" Stephanie quickly replied. *"What! Is her baby father here now? Wow real madness! Both of you woman are having problems with creepy city men on this morning. It looks like I came back into town at the right appointed time. Came back to the United States in time to stop the creepy madness"* Ezra shouted out as he burst into laughter. *"Steph. Have no fear super Ezra is now here"* her younger brother Ezra continued to say as he stood online positioned inside of the stanchion ropes awaiting a teller inside of the crowded post office.

"Are you going to share with me what souvenirs you brought back from Switzerland for me stinky butt or are you going to surprise me?" Stephanie kindly asked her younger brother again as she put the remote to the flat screen television back down on top of the dining room coffee table while slowly walking towards her large penthouse apartment balcony that overlooked the busy city.

"No, I'm not going to tell you anything until you share with me what's inside of that box that you frighten Ly left outside of your door in the hallway because of my dude, Brad" Ezra replied. *"Plus, if I was to, tell you what the gifts are that I brought back from Switzerland for our parents you would spoil the surprise by running your mouth"* Ezra added as the line moved closer to the post office counters inside of the busy post office.

"Are you calling me a snitch stinky butt?" Stephanie loudly asked as she stepped outside onto her penthouse

balcony checking the leaves on the plants that are arrayed on the balcony.

"*You labeled yourself a snitch when you told daddy about the trip to Las Vegas Kenny, and I took that weekend we were supposed to be at his grandparents' house. You made it official that you are a snitch when you told daddy about the racetrack betting Freddie, and I was involved with, out in Erda, Utah. Steph. you have a big mouth and when you told mom about me sleeping over Courtney's house on Friday nights that established your, label as a snitch. That's probably why the twins don't call or speak to you as much as I do*" Ezra said as he walked to the end of the stanchion ropes becoming first in line waiting for the post office tellers that were occupied servicing other customers to be available.

"*I have matured since I graduated from high school Ezra. I have even matured since I graduated from college. I sincerely apologize if I hurt you, Ezra. So, what wonderful souvenirs you brought back with you from your honeymoon with the playboy bunny in Switzerland stinky butt?*" Steph asked as she leaned her slender body over the railing of the balcony of the penthouse apartment.

"*I liked the towels in the hotel, so I packed three of them up in a beautiful white plastic bag from the hotel gift shop downstairs that was in the hotel lobby especially for you. You'll enjoy the flush cotton as it presses softly against your smooth skin soaking up all the water from off your body as you enjoy your long two-hour showers Steph.*" Ezra sarcastically said, followed by an outburst of laughter. "*You are really a sick kid. Do you know that? A sick puppy*" Stephanie spoke.

"*Just relax your fearful nerves sis. I brought some wonderful*

13

souvenirs from my wonderful trip in Switzerland with my wonderful snow bunny back home for my wonderful family. I will call you later Steph. I'm about to walk up to the post office counter now" Ezra loudly said as he started walking in the direction towards the next available post office counter which was labeled numbered eight.

"Ok Ezra welcome home and thanks so much for calling I now feel much better" Stephanie shouted as she disconnected the cell phone call from Ezra her younger brother. As Stephanie calmly inhaled the New York City morning air taking in a slow relaxing deep breath Brownie started to loudly bark again. As Stephanie exhaled slowly blowing her breath into the breeze of the morning air on her penthouse balcony, she could hear the doorbell ringing over Brownie's loud barking. *"Wow! Who is it now? Will I ever obtain peace somehow? Busyness please go, ahead and take your bow. The crowd just won't let up this morning my quietness is like, wow. Whoever it is, I'm coming now"* Stephanie rhythmically spoke to herself out loud as she walked back inside of the very large duplex penthouse apartment towards the thick front apartment door to see who was currently standing at her apartment door.

CHAPTER 2

THE POST OFFICE SCUFFLE

Following the direction of the blinking green arrow on the computerize display board inside of the crowded post office that directed Ezra towards the unoccupied post office counter that was numbered eight, Ezra moved swiftly. Approaching the available postal worker, Ezra placed his large package envelope on top of the post office counter.

"Good morning how can I you help you" the muscular Hispanic gentleman who had a smile on his face kindly asked Ezra.

"I would like to send this large envelope priority express mail please" Ezra loudly said while taking his wallet out of his favorite extra-large red and white hoodie sweatshirt pocket.

"Is there anything flammable or hazardous inside of the envelope?" The muscular Hispanic gentleman

15

postal worker asked Ezra as he continuously swayed the stool, he was sitting on behind the post office counter, left and right with a smile remaining on his face.

"No there isn't" Ezra quickly responded. *"Okay, well my name is Ronald and I'll be the one that is helping you on today"* Ronald replied as he took the large envelope and placed it on the scale with the smile remaining on his face. *"You have some challenges I see because you're supposed to use one of the priority envelopes or boxes located on the counters over there by entrance doors but today must be your lucky day cause I'm going to continue to assist you. No need to go anywhere else but here as we get acquainted"* Ronald, the muscular Hispanic gentleman postal worker said with the smile still on his face as he continued to swerve the stool with his butt muscle, he was sitting on left to right.

"Pardon me! What are you talking about?" Ezra curiously but loudly asked as he tightened up his facial muscles giving the postal worker a puzzled look.

"Well, I do see you here often at this post office location, and from my recollection I have served you at my station a few times. So, now we have the chance to get to know each other a little better" Ronald boldly said as he typed into the desk computer the information that was on the large envelope Ezra had given unto him.

"That's okay guy, I'm not into making any new friends these days" Ezra quickly replied as he took a step back from the post office counter.

"Okay not a problem, I'm still going to assist you" Ronald spoke.

"Well, that's what I came here for Mr. Ronald" Ezra

replied stepping forward once again closer to the post office counter.

"I also do full body massages and other types of massages on my leisure time. I run a successful business. I'll give you a few of my fliers with the contact information on it and you can even pass them out if you would like. I'm extremely good with my hands. I have a lot of credible references. My work speaks for itself" Ronald boldly said as he started printing out the detailed information onto the correct label of the large package envelope Ezra was planning to send to his friend Kenny.

"No, that's okay. I don't do that stuff. I think you have me mistaken for someone else guy. I just came here to mail the envelope and that's all I want to do today" Ezra abruptly spoke.

Ronald stood up tall from off the swivel stool as he placed the new printed label on the large envelope. A loud noise the sound of an argument busted out behind Ezra, first Ezra tried to ignore the loud bickering because it sounded like two guys but as the sound of a woman loudly using profanity escalated and the sound of crashing all suddenly followed Ezra quickly turned around. *"Don't talk to her like that you lost your mind man that's my wife you are talking to like that I will hurt you in here!"* The large bearded bald head man screamed out.

"You're not going to hurt anybody. Not me! Not today. I will smack fire out of you on today!" the slim, thick Rastafari man said with a medium size box still in his hand as he faced the large bearded bald head man.

"You need to get a hold of her before I punch her skinny

self directly in the face, I'm not the one! Miss, you need to shut your mouth now! You about to learn today, Miss," the thick black woman said who had been responsible for knocking over the stanchion ropes which made that loud crashing noise inside of the crowded post office that alerted Ezra's attention.

"I'm calling the police!" An elderly lady loudly yelled out who was standing in the line directly behind the African American woman, while dialing her keypad on her cell phone.

"Call the police I don't care. You don't disrespect my wife!" The large bearded bald head man screamed out and said as his wife kept on using profanity and started moving her skinny body closer towards the African American woman.

"We going to need security in here" a young Asian man jokingly spoke as everyone around him who was standing online inside of the stanchion ropes began to laugh.

"You have one more time to speak that filthy language to me and you going to get popped!" The African American woman shouted out.

"You're not going to pop anybody sister" the large bearded bald head man loudly replied.

"Mr. Listen nobody over here is talking to you! You need to shut that anorexic cat of yours all the way up! Put a muzzle on that sick cat over there!" The African American woman loudly responded.

"Nobody shutting me up! Him, you, no one!" The skinny woman yelled out as she then started slowly pacing herself back

in forth positioned outside of the stanchion ropes being the only person who was not standing in line.

"*Listen Miss, I'm telling you I'm not the one! Your bout to catch it today! I've already warned your disrespectful nasty self!*" The African American woman loudly shouted out. That's when the slim woman wildly charged herself towards the African American woman with both her hands lifted high in the air. Two young guys, who were originally positioned in the line inside of the stanchion ropes directly between the slim thick light skin Rastafari man and the African American woman quickly moved themselves to the left out of the neurotic slim woman's path of attack. The African American woman immediately tightened up her fist and quickly threw punches back at the slim woman who was now charging at her. As the two-woman started fighting one another throwing fist, grabbing hair the bald bearded man attempted to grab the African American woman by one of her arms, pulling her away from his wife but the Rastafari man immediately dropped his own box on the post office floor and swung his fist at the bald bearded man striking him in the left eye intercepting him from grabbing the African American woman. Fighting back the solid bald bearded man then rushed the Rastafari man knocking them both into the stanchion ropes located on the other side of the line and as they both stumbled over the ropes one of their elbows hit the elderly woman with the cell phone in the head knocking her onto the postal floor. Hitting her head hard on the cold brass pole located on the

19

base of the stanchion ropes the elderly woman laid completely still. As people who were originally in line started screaming, panicking and scattering away from the ruckus Ezra along with another customer started moving towards the other end of the post office. As Ezra quickly maneuvered towards the window labeled one two large male post office workers came running out from behind the locked door by window one, one of them knocking hard into Ezra pushing him back in the direction towards the woman as they fought each other. The African American woman then swung her fist hard into the slim woman's nose knocking her onto her knees. She then unhooked the stanchion rope from the pole and begin to wrap it around the slim woman's neck as the two large postal workers tried their best to stop the men from wrestling who were now on the ground by the elderly woman. Ezra seeing the thick stanchion rope placed around the slim woman's neck immediately stuck out his right arm reaching over towards the African American woman, placing his right hand on the African American woman shoulder began to put pressure in attempt to stop her from strangling the slim woman. Then without hesitation the African American woman leaned her mouth into Ezra's right hand and started biting him as her hands continued to squeeze the stanchion rope around the other woman's neck. As Ezra loudly screamed cause of the sudden pain in his hand, out of reaction he then quickly grabbed the African American woman by her curly hair pulling on the hair with his left hand trying to pull her teeth from off the flesh on the top of his right hand. The bald man glancing over in the direction of the woman seeing the Stanchion rope around his wife's neck as one of the large postal workers tried to constrain him, the bald man then immediately reached into his pants leg, pulling his jeans upwards, reached into the strapped leg holder pulled out a large knife and started slashing at the postal workers. He then charged towards Ezra stabbing him in his collar bone area in attempt to free his wife who was now being chocked and strangled by the other woman with the stanchion rope. The bald bearded man started knocking the African American woman in the side of her head as Ezra stumbled backwards before collapsing onto the post office floor. As blood begins to shoot out onto Ezra's red and white hoodie from the knife wound, Ronald quickly came running out from behind the post office counters and started punching at the bald man striking him hard directly into his left eye simply because the knife was still stationed in his customer Ezra's collar bone area. Ezra, who was lying on the post office floor covered in blood from the knife and bite wounds on his entire right upper side, was in excruciating pain. He slowly lifted his head upwards fixating his eyes onto the post office clerk, Ronald, as he continued punching his fist hard into the bald bearded man's face as the other large post office worker tried to intervene in the fight. As the sound of police radios and running shoes suddenly came into the post office Ezra, in severe pain finally lay flat on his back closing his eyes.

"*Hey, stop break it up! Hey, let go! Mam, let go! Hey, stop break it up now, that's enough!*" The male New York City police officer loudly yelled as he and three other police officers quickly entered the crowded chaotic post office yelling as they ran towards the two women and Ronald. "*Let the rope go now!*" The male New York police officer loudly yelled as he grabbed the African American woman's arms attempting to loosen her grip of the stanchion rope. "*Break it up now, that's enough! Hey, stop now sir get down on your knees*" another New York police officer loudly yelled immediately reaching for Ronald the Hispanic post office clerk's muscular arms trying to stop him from constantly beating the bald bearded man. "*Please stop! Break it up now! Stop now sir get down on your knees!*" The male New York police officer loudly yelled again as he and another female police officer grabbed Ronald tossing his muscular body down to the cold post office floor.

"*Back up now! Disperse the area. Everyone please clear, out of the post office now!*" Two female New York police officers together in union started loudly yelling trying to get the crowd of people who were once waiting customers to leave the post office as more police officers quickly came running inside of the post office to contain the now dangerous hostile situation.

"*Sir down now! Back off! Back off! Get down now!*" An undercover male officer loudly yelled as he and two of his undercover partners, who were also plain clothe wearing police officers together quickly grabbed the light skin Rastafari man roughly tossing him down to the cold post office floor.

"They started it! I'm innocent! I didn't do anything!" The Rastafari man yelled as his entire body hit the cold post office floor hard with his arms stretched out behind him as the plain clothe officers apprehended him.

"Mam, are you okay? Can you hear me? Mam, are you hurt?" The female New York police officer yelled to the elderly woman who was stretched laid out across the cold post office floor directly next to the pole of the post office Stanchion ropes unresponsive.

"We need medical attention here at this location now! Multiple victims have sustained severe life-threatening injuries police officers are on the scene and the situation is under control. However, we are in need of medical assistance here" the Sergent authoritatively spoke loudly over her police radio as she walked around the perimeter inside of the post office. One of the ranking New York City police officers carrying a medical duffle bag quickly entered inside the post office and in haste ran towards Ezra who was laid down flat on his back stretched out on the cold post office floor as two other New York police officers were kneeled over him. *"Sir, can you hear me? We have paramedics on route! Sir, are you able to open your eyes?"* The male police officer loudly spoke as he checked Ezra's vitals. The senior ranked New York police officer carrying the duffle bag approaching Ezra kneeled over his right side as he immediately opened the duffle bag pulling out the wound care packages to help control the

bleeding that dampened Ezra's favorite red and white hoodie sweatshirt.

"Tell Steph. To help me please. Super Ez. Is in pain. Steph help me please I'm hurt badly" Ezra softly whispered as his eyes remained shut. *"Super Ez. Can't save you today, Steph. Please hurry here and help me because I need you the pain is too severe"* Ezra continued to softly whisper.

"Where does the pain hurt you sir? And can you open your eyes to me? I need you to try" the male police officer loudly spoke as he continued to check Ezra's vitals.

"Whose Steph. Sir? May I ask who's Steph and super Ez.?" The senior ranking police officer asked as he maneuvered his hands around the hoodie trying to get inside of the sweatshirt to the punctured wound around the knife that was sticking out of Ezra's collar bone area with the wound care cloths he had removed from the police emergency duffle bag. Trying to stop the bleeding another police officer took some wound care cloths out of the package as well and immediately started applying pressure to the affected area in attempt to stop the bleed.

"She's my older sister. I'm the youngest boy but I have two younger sisters who live in Colorado, but they really don't speak to her like I always do. She could help me. Sir Steph. Will take away the pain" Ezra whispered as he then fell unconscious.

"Sir paramedics should be arriving here any minute, but I need you to stay alert and talk with me. Can you do that for me? Sir! Sir! I ask if you can open your eyes and do that for me. Can you talk to me sir?"

The male police officer loudly shouted as Ezra became unresponsive. The police officers then frantically started pressing down on the wound applying pressure around the knife with the wound care clothes while they continued to monitor Ezra's vitals.

"So, I need to know who started this fight?" The female Sergent loudly asked as she approached the only large male post office worker who was not apprehended by any police officers that was standing idle overlooking the horrific scene which took place inside of his workplace in shock of disbelief. Specifically at Ronald, his muscular Hispanic coworker who was now also on the cold post office floor presently in handcuffs and surrounded by New York law enforcement agents.

As the Emergency Medical Technicians entered inside the post office wheeling a stretcher carrying their medical equipment, one of the female New York police officers directed them towards Ezra because of the blood and the police officers that were nervously surrounding him. Another team of Emergency Medical Technician medical professionals entered the post office followed by a team of New York police officers. As more of New Yorks finest the NYPD entered inside of the post office the second team of EMS workers worked on the unresponsive elderly woman. Another team of Emergency Medical Technicians workers slowly entered the now crowded post office full of law enforcement agents, and the female New York police officer directed them to an Asian man who was also on the floor and had also got caught up in the scuffle between the bald man and the Rastafari. Trying to escape the Asian man fell along with them when the two gentlemen stumbled over the post office stanchion ropes towards the cold post office floor. He had suffered from a severely sprained ankle and couldn't stand up on both of his feet. Another Emergency Medical Technician team arrived at the downtown post office and when they slowly entered the now busy post office full of law enforcement agents the other female New York police officer escorted them over to a young white woman who was dressed in business attire who was also down on the cold post office floor that seemed to had suffered a mild heart attack as she stumbled to the floor sometime during the brawl between the four individuals inside the crowded post office. As the Lieutenant arrived with a few NYPD deputies, the female Sergeant updated them with a current report of the early morning horrific event. As all the post office workers begin to file themselves along the windows, the Emergency Medical Technician workers along with several police officers transferred Ezra unto the stretcher who remained unresponsive. A few more plain clothe police officers quickly entered inside of the now busy and crowded full of law enforcement agents downtown post office. As another team of Emergency Medical Technician workers quickly entered inside of the post office one of the male police officers signaled for them to walk towards their direction to check on the bald man whose eye was swollen and blood pouring down his face from what seemed like a broken nose.

"Get off me, I'll kill that witch! Let me go" the African American woman yelled out as police officers had her handcuffed and pinned down on the cold floor of the post office.

"Officers this is not right that couple started it!" The Rastafari man continually yelled out while law enforcement agents surrounded him as he remained handcuffed on the cold floor of the post office. Another team of Emergency Medical Technician workers arrived who immediately ran over to the slim woman as her hands were on her neck area as she continually coughed and choked gasping for air while down on the cold floor of the post office surrounded by New York police officers.

CHAPTER 3

THE FRIEND ZONE

Answering her thick apartment door as the doorbell chimed rhythmically sounded, while Brownie continued his loud barking, Stephanie looked through the peephole located on the thick apartment door to see who was again ringing her musical doorbell.

"Praise the Lord sis. I don't have much of a voice this morning" the thick African American woman softly spoke standing in the hallway next to the large box that her neighbor who lives directly across the hall, Brad, had personally delivered earlier to Stephanies penthouse door.

"Hey, Melonie how are you feeling this morning?" Stephanie loudly spoke as she once again pulled on the brass doorknob opening her thick apartment door.

"Good morning sis, I just came from church and wow did we have an awesome praise time in Brooklyn early this

morning. So glad I arose and shined with God this morning sis. So, what's in the box?" The thick African American neighbor softly inquired.

"Oh, Melonie I was meaning to bring that inside, but I had to first enjoy my favorite breakfast meal" Stephanie loudly replied.

"um-hmmm" Melonie loudly hummed. *"Well, come on sis. I'll help you bring this very large box inside of your house so we can see what you brought the both of us"* Melonie loudly replied. As Stephanie burst out in laughter, she opened her thick apartment door wider so together the two ladies could bring the large box inside. Suddenly the elevator chimes sounded, sending a personal invitation to Brownie to again start his loud barking alerting everyone that someone was now arriving onto his penthouse floor. While dashing his four legged self-straight into the penthouse floor hallway, running pass Melonie towards the elevator as the elevator doors opened. Soon as the elevator doors opened, Aram the doorman quickly stepped off with a sheet of white paper in his hands and a huge smile on his face. *"Hey, ladies are everyone okay?* Aram the tall Armenian doorman loudly asked.

"Are you stalking me handsome? Melonie softly asked as she positioned herself along one side of the large box.

"I'm not sure Aram, If we're exactly okay. I still must get this heavy box inside of my apartment" Stephanie warmly replied.

"Sure, I'll be glad to help everyone out. That's why the building management hired me" Aram loudly spoke.

"Because your handsome or is it because you're helpful?" Melonie asked.

"Because he's helpful Melonie! Isn't that right Aram" Stephanie asked.

"Yes! I've been working here for two years and as the main doorman in this building between the hours of eight in the morning to four in the afternoon, I have always helped everyone" Aram loudly replied as he squatted down and with both his hands, he scooped the box up bringing the delivered package inside of Stephanies duplex penthouse apartment.

"Get back Brownie! Watch it!" Stephanie yelled as she reached for her dog's collar trying to stop him from running in between of Aram's legs.

"Yes, he's very helpful. Aah, handsome, you can leave that box over there by the banister of the staircase Aram" Melonie cheerfully said.

"Melonie! Yes, over there where she just told you is fine Aram. Thanks so much Aram. Oh, wait let me get something for you" Stephanie said as she quickly ran towards the living room pass a loveseat and sofa that was close to a door which led to a small room. While Stephanie was inside of the small room, Melonie quickly shut the front apartment door securing everyone inside.

"We really appreciate this Aram. Now I know you're stalking me. I've only been in this building for fifteen minutes and your handsome self is the only smiling face I've seen besides my good neighbor Stephanie" Melonie said.

"No, mam I'm just doing my helpful job Ms. Watkins. This right here is me doing my extra duties Ms. Watkins"

Aram loudly answered as Stephanie came back jogging across her large living room towards the staircase banister in her duplex apartment.

"Thank you, Aram, for all of your help on today" Stephanie said as she handed him a fifty-dollar bill.

"You're welcome, ladies anytime" Aram said as he slowly walked back towards the penthouse apartment door that Melonie had shut. As Stephanie hurried to the door to let Aram out of her apartment, Aram slowly reached out his right hand towards Stephanie. She paused standing completely still for a minute. Stephanie stared looking at his hand, then slowly lifting her head upwards she looked directly into his blue eyes before extending her right hand to Aram. They eventually shook hands as if an agreement to a business contract had just been established.

"Okay, you two enough of this! Now come on Sis. Let's open this box and see if everything has arrived" Melonie raised her raspy voice to say.

As Stephanie turned the Brass doorknob, pulling the thick door open Brad was standing there on the doormat in front of her door with no shoes on his feet.

"Bradley what are you doing standing here at my door?" Stephanie busted out loudly asking with a look of concern on her face.

"Oh, I apologize I didn't know you had company. I was having a little trouble with my washing machine, and I was wondering if you may have experienced the same problems" Bradley, Stephanie's only penthouse floor neighbor quickly responded.

"You could always call downstairs to the front desk, speak to the concierge where they could assist you with that matter Bradley. Specifically, if you don't have Chong, the handyman supervisor's cellphone number saved in your phone contacts" Stephanie loudly spoke.

"Hi again, Mr. Bradley sir. If you would please excuse me" Aram said as he exited Stephanie's apartment placing his right hand on his doorman cap tilting his head slightly downward giving Bradley a salute as he walked past quickly moving his tall slim body towards the penthouse floor elevator.

"Get back Brownie!" Melonie shouted out as she clapped her hands signaling the Shar-pei mix pet dog to stop from following the doorman Aram outside of the apartment and for him to quickly come running his four-legged fury self towards her direction.

"That voice sounds familiar is that my God sent Angel Melonie, that I hear so clear this morning" Bradley inquired stepping his bare feet back onto the nicely decorated doormat in front of Stephanie's door after moving out of his doorman's way as Aram proceeded to the elevator.

"Yes Brad, it is I beloved, Praise the Lord! His Mercy endures forever and ever" Melonie shouted out standing by the bottom steps banister inside of Stephanie's duplex penthouse as Aram Quickly hoped on the elevator returning to his doorman duties inside the tower lobby.

"Sounds like you're on your way to church neighbor" Brad spoke.

"Correction Brad, I'm just coming home from a five o'clock in the morning prayer service at my church that turned into an

extra hour of praise service followed by an awesome word that was delivered from our pastor. Oh Jesus! I just felt a quicken right there. Halleluiah! Oh, God the presence of the Lord is still stirring my spirit up this morning. We had an awesome time this morning in church" Melonie loudly said as she slowly moved towards the front door of the apartment.

"Was that your brother that was hollering, hooping, reared back and preaching early this morning that blessed you'll with a good word" Bradley asked as he rocked back and forth standing barefoot on the mat in the hallway.

"No that was not my brother today. He's not a member of my church. You know my eldest daughter joined his church two weeks ago. I guess she's reaching that age where she's trying to separate from mommy and daddy. She wants her own, but my baby is still not that grown. Plus, my brother had spoiled her since she was born, so now a days, that's her favorite uncle who my daughter loves to stay up under. My husband may be a little bothered by her absence from the family as we supposedly worship together. However, I get it. I'm not even upset as long as she's in church praising God than I'm pleased. But today, Brad. Bright early this morning we were praising God with my pastor under the mighty hand of God where I just danced, dance and danced" Melonie replied standing directly next to Stephanie.

"Well, I hope you've been saying prayers in those services at your church to your God for me Ms. Watkins and for the whole world that seems to be just falling apart. If it's not the wildfires, storms or wars it's the viruses and serious illnesses that destroying our civilization." Bradley said as he remained standing in front of the door while Stephanie continued giving him an awkward stare.

"Brad of course I prayed for you! I pray every day for my girl Stephanie too. Specially my girl Danielle, I send God up little extra for her with a whole lot of dancing. With this busy city, where we live, where anything is possible, I go extra hard, and I will shout for an extra length of time. But if you are having problems with your washer and dryer, do you need for me to send a text to Chong, so he could come upstairs here to check out your appliances inside of your apartment?" Melonie asked.

"No, don't trouble yourself Ms. Watkins, I'll do as Steph. Suggested and call downstairs to the concierge." Bradley replied with a smile on his face.

"Yes! You do that Brad. Have a good day" Stephanie said as she slowly closed her huge apartment door leaving Bradley standing barefoot on her doormat.

"Are you okay Sis. Now what was that" Melonie asked as the two-woman walked away from the door headed back towards the large box that was positioned at the bottom of the duplex apartment staircase.

"He just creeps me out! For real girl! Super annoying and creepy. Ezra was right I'm going to have to bring a dude up in here quick to get rid of him Melonie" Stephanie spoke.

"Jesus! Oh God that was not in my prayers for you girl" Melonie immediately responded.

"No Melonie, I'm really, serious. Maybe another man inside my penthouse will keep that buzzard away" Stephanie spoke as she tore the white envelope off the top of the very large box with her hands slicing the envelope open with her fingers, to read the items listed on the invoice inside.

"*Steph. What is going on with you today. I know you have spoken of Brad in a negative tone before but not like this. You just slammed the door in the poor man's face. He has a crush on you, neighbor*" Melonie said, followed by a burst of laughter. "*I understand he's not as handsome and gentleman like Mr. Aram downstairs. Nobody can compare to the tall Armenian stallion fitted tightly right dressed all the way down girl, neatly modeling the building uniform in the eyes of Ms. Stephanie*" Melonie continued to say sarcastically.

"*Melonie No. Aram doesn't need to be insulted by that creepy man with no shoes standing at my door all morning. That's just weird. I'm not into weirdos*" Stephanie responded.

"*No cause you're into that tall handsome doorman located downstairs posted in our lobby. That's why you're so defensive when it comes to Aram*" Melonie clearly spoke.

"*Melonie, please! Even as famous and popularly known as this condominium tower is here in New York City, as well as in real estate, there are still thousands of doormen across the city that daily, properly wear their buildings uniforms and make the lobby entrances look costly.*" Stephanie responded as she turned away walking towards her high ceiling marble kitchen to get a butcher knife so she can slice open the delivered large box.

"*Girl, I didn't say anything about building status, property or rent prices. Neither did I say anything about the building workers that labor in them. I spoke of that undeniable smile plastered on your face when our Aram is around. That's probably the reason Brad. Gets so jealous of Aram. Your warm facial expressions you always show, when our morning doorman is on duty. All that warm, soft, buttery attention you show to* our morning building worker. Not only the defensive behavior girl, but the butterfly feelings you must feel inwardly for Aram, because it sure comes out in your behavior Steph. Now pause! Now, freeze! Strike a pose. There's no breeze! Aram is on his post, and everybody knows yes, they are close now watch Stephanie cheese" Melonie jokingly rhythmically spoke as she burst into laughter while showing Stephanie her teeth.

"I'm surprised you allowed your daughter to go to another church" Stephanie said attempting to change the direction of the conversation, pulling the large butcher knife out of the wide kitchen drawer.

"Yeah, my husband is not happy about that decision Steph. That's daddy's little girl but she's older now. That seems to be a challenge for my big strong teddy bear. She's now out of daddy's sight on Sundays as well. Even if there's a love interest at my brother's church. I'm sure my brother will eventually hit me up and give me the full information of her desired attendance at his place of worship. We have two more little girls and two boys, even one son a year and a half directly behind her. So, for me that's one less eye I must keep checking on during church service. The less stress, the harder I can bless" Melonie responded gripping the large box with her thick hands, while Stephanie started slicing through the seal with the butcher knife across the top of the box desiring it to open.

"Melonie you and that blessing! I'm surprised your family sits with you in service the way you're always stomping, jumping and running around the sanctuary" Stephanie sarcastically replied.

"That's right Steph. I will dance, for him dance, for God dance, for sure dance, praise him dance, girl you got that right, in the daylight or throughout service at night, on the spot when the word of God is being preached as the atmosphere becomes hot, I just send it up and dance" Melonie rhythmically replied while clapping her hands and stomping her feet on the flush carpet by the staircase as Stephanie reached inside of the now opened large box.

As the rhythmic doorbell chimes sounded, and Brownie once again started loudly barking running his four-legged fur self towards the apartment door Stephanies cell phones ringtone also began to alert her of an incoming call while Melonie slowly walked towards the door.

"You want me to answer the door Steph? So, you can answer the phone and don't have to encounter the Brad" Melonie spoke.

"Eeesh! Gives me the creeps!" Stephanie yelled out as she quickly ran back across her large penthouse duplex apartment towards the table with the TV remote to the flat screen TV, where she had placed the cell phone earlier, while answering the door for her neighbor Melonie. As she quickly picked up her cell phone to answer, checking the caller ID, Stephanie saw that it was Tiffany returning her phone call. Melonie continued to slowly walk to the apartment front door giving Stephanie time to answer her cell phone and make her way back over to the front door.

"Hi, Tiffany, I guess it's safe now for you to talk" Stephanie said answering the phone call as she walked

across her carpeted duplex apartment back towards the huge door to see who was ringing her doorbell. Opening the huge apartment door, it was the third-floor, east wing section of the tower, their neighbor Danielle standing on the nicely decorated welcome doormat with a large dish in her hand.

"Morning Dee Dee, what's that in your hands?" Melonie cheerfully asked.

"Are we babysitting Brownie today" Danielle loudly asked Melonie as she quickly came inside of Stephanies penthouse apartment. *"Morning all! I have something hot you'll must taste"* Danielle loudly said while power walking over to the marble kitchen.

"Girl, what did you chef up now? Looking at the hour of the time of day that it is, someone must have been up all night watching one of those cooking channels again" Melonie spoke as she closed the thick apartment door turning the huge locks securing the ladies inside of the apartment.

"You'll must taste this" Danielle shouted out again as she placed the hot dish on top of Stephanie's marble kitchens stove. *"Okay Stephanie what's going on with the butcher knife? What are you chopping up here for breakfast"* Danielle sarcastically said as she turned around and saw Stephanie walking towards her with the butcher knife in her hand while talking on the cell phone with her best friend Tiffany.

"Girl, bye! We were opening this box that the Brad, from across the hall delivered to her door personally with no shoes on his crusty feet earlier this morning" Melonie said pushing pass Stephanie walking over to the kitchen sink to wash

her hands with the full bottle of dish detergent that was on the marble kitchen sink counter. Melonie then quickly reached up to the overhead kitchen cabinets to collect some small plates for Danielle's homemade cuisine.

"Oh, the secret admirer penthouse neighbor who doesn't have a chance over Aram the lobby hunk that greets everyone at the door" Danielle replied. *"Wait, why he had no shoes on his feet?"* Danielle quickly asked.

"Exactly Danielle! Creepy! He's too weird for me" Stephanie loudly replied as she dropped the Butcher knife in the sink, turned on the hot water faucet again to also wash her hands.

"Because he lives directly across the hall. Technically he's still in his house. I walk around my apartment and at times in the hallway with no shoes on my feet. And I have way more neighbors on my floor than she does. Matter of fact a drafted New York knicks basketball player, moved in yesterday five doors down from me. I saw him talking to one of the night security guard workers in the hallway with his white socks on late last night. What's the big deal" Melonie loudly, replied

"Yeah, but you have a house full down there. You're excused from looking awkward. Plus, you're the big United Nation Ambassador in this place. No one is going to question a UN official definantly about her footwear. Neither mess with the hefty judge's wife. As for the new jock on the block he might have been modeling athletic footwear. They tend to do that" Danielle replied as she removed the lid from her hot dish as the steam in the form of a cloud immediately shot up into the air.

"I have told you'll before about talking about my husband's belly fat. We're working on that! Those few extra pounds my teddy bear picked up around his waist the last three years, together with a personal trainer we've missioned to combat" Melonie replied placing three small saucers on top of the stove next to the smoking hot dish.

"Tiffany said tell the judge to stay away from the snacks he's much too fat" Stephanie yelled out as she burst into laughter pulling open the smaller drawer to collect some forks and a large spoon for the hot dish Danielle brought to her apartment.

"Amen sister!" Danielle yelled out as she started clapping her hands and dancing around in the marble kitchen.

"Tell Tiffany I said keep her eyes off my man chic, I'm a jealous woman" Melonie responded with an outburst of laughter.

"Doesn't the aroma smell delicious, wait until you taste it" Danielle said as she took the large spoon from out of Stephanie's hand as Stephanie disconnected the phone call from Tiffany.

"Tiff is on her way over here so we're going to need another plate. Now what is this morning masterpiece that you've brought upstairs to my crib Dee Dee, that supposedly smells wonderful?" Stephanie softly asked as she placed the silverware down on top of the stove next to the hot dish.

"Well, I know you're into your yoga Steph. With your deep breathing exercises, your late-night Pilate sessions and very intense workouts. As well as your strict dietary regiments *that I'm sure you cheat on every now and then. But you must taste this fatty seafood dish. I attended a dinner party over a year ago while I was upstate in Vermont, the week Tony took me to his Airbnb villa in those snowy mountains. You remember when I shared with you guys about that horrible plane experience I had on my skiing weekend with Tony. As much as I enjoy skiing and I love snowy slopes, we could have stayed our asses here in New York City and just went upstate to one of the ski lodges in New York and had a better time. The flight from John F. Kennedy airport to Maine was extensively delayed before we even boarded the plane. I can remember telling you ladies that aggravating evening at the airport almost as if it happened yesterday. Then the plane, after we had finally boarded, sat on the runway for I don't know how long because of the runway traffic. I remember the pilot kept apologizing over the overhead intercom system for the delay. I just wanted a drink, martini, shot of scotch, anything to calm my nerves. Mainly because we still had a connecting flight to catch. When we finally arrived in Maine, the connecting flight to Vermont was overbooked because of all the extensive delays it was a complete nightmare. But that airplane taxi ride to Vermont was the worse airplane ride I have ever flown. That little, tiny airplane of 18 people and we were crouched in the back like sardines in a can, was an air disaster in my memory bank. Every dip, air bump, turbulence, plane shake, repeatedly every three to five minutes was horrific. That was a miserable connecting flight. I was furious!"* Danielle loudly explained as she continued to scoop the cuisine from out of the hot dish unto the small plates on top of the stove with the large spoon.

"*Girl, what did you expect from a small plane. They don't go but so high in the air and you were riding across the mountains of the northeast coast just below in between the Canadian mountains. I can even remember telling you back then, "what did you expect from riding in a small plane between mountains in the highest elevations of the United States""* Melonie spoke.

"*What's the name of this dish Dee Dee*" Stephanie asked again with an inquisitive look on her face.

"*Yeah, but Melonie, that was too much bumping in the air for me. By the time we arrived in the middle of the night at that Airbnb I was exhausted, and my head was throbbing. My neck was tired because my head kept on bobbling like a bobble head doll during that connecting flight to Vermont. So, Tony tried making it up to me during the week with that dinner party at this famous British rock stars home. Someone he knew in Vermont connected Tony with the party invite. The party was nice I do have to admit, he got brownie points for that. But this dish at the dinner segment of the party was the highlight not only of that night but the whole damn trip*" Danielle continued to share. "*It was so delicious guys I was all in the kitchen trying to get the name and ingredients from the caterers. At that point I didn't care if Tony was embarrassed by my unprofessional behavior. The taste of this seafood dish is exquisite*" Danielle said as she wiggled her hips around the stove inhaling the aroma coming up out of the steam from her morning cuisine.

As the doorbell chimes rhythmically sounded again and Brownie started his daily routine, loudly barking once again dashing off to the door, Stephanie inhaled a deep breath and slowly exhaled her breath, blowing it into the smoke from the hot seafood dish that hovered the stove area.

"That's Mike Steph. I had called and told him I was on my way upstairs to your place" Danielle said as she handed Melonie the small plate of her hot seafood cuisine to taste. Stephanie marched her way through her large apartment once again getting in her daily power walk warm up exercises at home this morning because of all the friendly neighborhood traffic bombarding her private penthouse space. As Stephanie opened the huge door it was her neighbor Mike, along with his two buddies Freddy and Alonzo also tenants of the famous apartment tower that was now standing in the hallway on her nicely decorated welcome doormat. Mike is an actor, singer, dancer, comedian and part-time cocktail waiter who has lived in the building with his lover for eight years. Freddy is a single fashion designer who works in the garment district. Alonzo is a student in law school and shares an apartment with other college roommates. The women in the building label them the three amigos because you always see the three of them traveling outside in the streets of New York City together. Loudly entering the apartment, they all made their way into Stephanies dining room area around her kitchen table, laughing and holding different conversations as Danielle played host serving everyone a sample of her fresh out of the oven seafood dish on Stephanie's small saucers. Melonie poured and served everyone apple juice that she found in Stephanies large refrigerator.

"*You need to let me have a party here Steph. I will turn this place all the way up! I will have celebs all up and through here. I will have my haters Gagging gal!*" Freddy loudly said as he crossed his legs showing off his platform sneakers.

"*You said that to me before Fred*" Stephanie quickly answered as she crossed her legs sticking the fork into the small saucer of the seafood cuisine that was placed on her dining room table.

"*And I'm going to keep on suggesting and bringing it to your attention gal unto you give me a date when the event can happen. It will be the best runway fashion show ever! The liveliest show this building has ever seen in its dull existence*" Freddy dramatically said.

"*Girl, there is nothing dull about this building. Especially this penthouse floor. Isn't that right Steph?*" Melonie spoke as she pulled up a chair to the table.

"*Oh, Ms. Steph is holding out on the top floor drama. Someone please do tell, what my nosey body has obviously missed*" Mike said as he bit into the hot seafood cuisine.

"*I'm still waiting to hear what the name of this dish is. Why the secret Dee Dee?*" Stephanie loudly asked.

"*Child, they are serving us secrets upon secrets up on this penthouse floor this morning*" Alonzo said as he crossed his legs showing off his bunny slippers.

"*Brad. The barefoot beast seems to be the biggest secret of them all, honey! You, better believe it*" Melonie loudly shouted out as she sampled her neighbor Danielle's hot seafood dish.

"*Oh, Ms. Preacher woman please do share because I know your sanctified bones got all the care*" Mike loudly spoke as he uncrossed his legs and then crossed them once again showing off his sneakers as Brownie brushed his four-legged fur self by the sneakers heading under the kitchen table to beg for food.

"What's the name of the dish Dee Dee?" Stephanie loudly asked again.

"Don't block my blessings Stephanie honey! Mama Watkins about to oil us down with something heavy" Alonzo said as he waived his fork in the air rolling his eyes at Stephanie.

"The man has a serious crush on our girl Stephanie. Honestly, he has had it for some time now. Today isn't any different than any other day around this apartment building when it comes to the conversations between Stephanie and Bradley" Danielle spoke.

"Yeah, but Aram is the catch of the day that Stephanie has her eyes on" Melonie said.

"Girl, who doesn't! That man is Fine! My heart just skips every time he's at the door" Mike spoke.

"You are correct with that one Mike. Who doesn't. A whole lot of eyes on Aram, particularly the young models. Even the new single quiet ones in Danielle's East Wing side of the tower" Alonzo said.

"Oh, wait a minute girl it is getting steamy up in here. Steph, you may need to crack open a window or slide open that balcony door to cool down because you'll serve hot mess up in this runway penthouse. Oh, wait a hot minute. Whose catwalk paws got their eyes on our kittens' doorman?" Freddy loudly inquired uncrossing his legs as he stomped his platform sneakers on the kitchen carpet before crossing his legs again.

45

"*Yeah, that new batch of fish that recently moved into the studios on your East Wing Danielle are very pretty. My roommates are all over them, day and night. Them thirsty boys been trying to sex them since they entered our tower*" Alonzo spoke as he kicked his bunny slippers into the air.

"*So has Aram!*" Mike softly responded.

"*Speak up Mike, don't whisper now child*" Alonzo loudly replied.

"*Really? Well, isn't that some breaking news this morning. Girl, so you telling me that Aram has been making new friends*" Melonie inquired.

"*NO! I think what Mike is saying is that Aram been attempting to share the camera spotlight with the new centerfolds*" Freddy replied.

"*He's fine! A real heart throb. I mean, his English can improve but to the eyes he is desirable! Like I said, who wouldn't want to sample him. From what I'm seeing and hearing she's even enjoying the taste*" Mike revealed.

"*Oh, really! And Danielle, you didn't tell us this bit of important information! You are living right on the buildings section with them new hot tamales, and you couldn't let your girls know about our doorman's secret stash*" Melonie loudly asked.

"*Secret smash Melonie! Girl, secret smash!*" Freddy loudly responded bursting into laughter stomping his platform sneakers on the kitchen carpet.

"*You may need to stick with that barefoot beast that lives directly across the hall Steph.*" Danielle loudly suggested as she remained standing in the kitchen by the stove eating her seafood cuisine.

"Listen Aram is a nice guy. His respect grew on me. I'm sure whoever he's supposedly dating is happy being with him because of his charming mannerism. Stephanie innocently replied.

"Girl bye! You know it's all about Aram in your eye" Melonie rhythmically shouted out

"Girl, you need to let me have this event here in this penthouse of yours this week. With my creative eye you'll have him by your side. My events are always the buzz of the community. And Steph. This place is large enough to house the who's who in the community. I'll have so many male models up in this apartment by the end of the night you will have Aram all to yourself Steph. When he attends my penthouse party, he'll forget all about the newbie hottie." Freddy rhythmically said as he quickly stood up, standing on his platform sneakers while he sashayed across the dining room towards the penthouse balcony.

"I know that's right! Let them know how we move Freddy!" Alonzo shouted out, kicking his bunny slippers up in the air.

"Listen here Freddy, this is a respectable community. Girl, this is a family building with descent men, women and a whole lot of children" Melonie spoke as she scooped up her final bite with the fork of the seafood cuisine.

"Oh, wait listen to Evangelist mother Hubbard serving us the community board guidelines of the tower from her expensive sanctified shoe" Alonzo sarcastically said as he kicked his bunny slippers up in the air once again.

"Well, I don't know about Ms. Watkins personal views of the ten commandments. However, I do know her oldest daughter

been tipping out of that shoe into that Acura downstairs with the overnight garage attendant in their late-night joy rides to the other parts of the city. Seems like someone's descent child isn't feeling the tight bible lessons from the blessed mother's high heel" Mike spoke cutting his eyes at Melonie.

"Is that the love interest you were speaking earlier to me about?" Stephanie responded, cutting a smile.

"Shut up Steph, not funny" Melonie quickly replied.

"Oh, wait they are serving secrets upon secrets in this penthouse! Stephanie girl, I must open this Balcony door for an immediate breeze cause it's too hot here now. I can't take it anymore! Child, they are spilling all the tea. I'm gagging gal! You'll let us have it in this apartment this morning!" Freddy loudly dramatically yelled out as he continued to sashay around Stephanies apartment. "It's over the judge about to start sentencing drivers to life. Here comes the slamming of the gavel, Death by legal injection!" Freddy continued to loudly speak.

"Shut up Freddy, I keep warning you'll about talking negatively about my teddy bear" Melonie quickly replied.

"Guess you was correct Melonie; this building is not dull at all. Thanks to your home lively entertainment" Stephanie spoke.

"Shut up Steph." Melonie quickly replied.

The door intercom started buzzing. The distinct sound of the ring-initiated Brownie to sound off his loud barking as he dashed out from under the table running again towards the door. As Danielle walked over to the Apartment intercom phone, which was located on the kitchen wall, to answer the intercom call from the building's lobby front desk concierge, Stephanies cell phone also started ringing.

"Hello" Stephanie said, quickly and purposely answering the call in a mild tone, changing the trajectory of the conversation.

"Hi, little sis. It's Gordon. Where are you?" Gordon, Stephanies older brother inquired.

"Hey big brother, I'm fine and I'm at home. I have company now but I'm here in my house eating some delicious seafood. Why? Where are you at?" Stephanie replied.

"Sis, I'm here in Denver and was about to hit the slopes before I spoke to Sergeant Edman of the New York Police Department over there in your neck of the woods" Gordon responded.

"Say what? Gordon what are you yapping about now?" Stephanie loudly asked, as her best friend Tiffany, who had finally arrived, came walking through the apartment door.

"Little sis. Something bad just happened to Ezra. I returned his call just a little while ago from when he contacted me yesterday. But little sis. I was out all-day cross-country skiing and by the time I returned here to my house I went to sleep" Gordon explained.

"What happened to Ezra Gordon!" Stephanie shouted.

"Oh no! Something happened to Ez." Tiffany responded as she sat down in the same kitchen chair alongside her bestie Stephanie.

"What's the matter with your little brother Steph." Melonie asked.

"I'm getting to that Steph. When I called him a police officer answered his cell phone, informing me that Ezra had gotten stabbed inside the post office and has lost a tremendous amount of blood. He seemed to be unconscious when the local authorities arrived on the scene. He's in the emergency room at the hospital now. When the Sergent asked me of the relation to the victim I told him I was his brother but I'm in Colorado" Gordon nervously explained.

"Oh God, what hospital did the police Sergent say that Ezra was in Gordon?" Stephanie frantically asked.

"The Sergent said to me he was transported to Lenox Hill Hospital and right now he's in the best of *care. He assured me that as they professionally treat him, he's in capable hands"* Gordon nervously explained.

"What the hell does that mean?" Stephanie frustratedly shouted out.

"Jesus Steph." Melonie calmy whispered.

"Oh God, Steph" Tiffany nervously spoke.

"Stephanie, it means the Sergeant trust the doctor and his team who is working on our brother" Gordon softly replied.

"They don't know my little brother like I do. I must go over there to the hospital now. Gordon, I was on the phone with Ezra not too long ago, while he was inside the post office. The only reason we disconnected is because he was more concerned about sending that money to that damn loser, Kenny, and his hungry animals. Let those scrawny horses starve! If he can't afford that money pit neither can any of us. I got on him this morning about cleaning up Kenny's mess. It's been going on too long Gordon. Oh, my baby brother, bleeding till you lost consciousness" Stephanie softly cried out as her eyes

began to water filling up with tears. Tiffany quickly put her arm around her bestie.

"Jesus, we call on your divine healing power now" Melonie softly whispered.

"We're here with you Stephanie" Tiffany softly whispered as the tear started falling on Stephanies cheeks.

"Were here Steph." Melonie softly whispered.

"Wow, that's horrifying" Danielle softly spoke.

"I Know little sis. I can imagine how you're feeling at this moment. As for me, I was shocked. I really didn't expect this. I don't have his new girlfriend's cell phone number. I suggested to the officer that he stay close to that phone until a family member arrives because she's going to contact him eventually wanting to know his current location" Gordon nervously explained.

"I'm sure" Stephanie quickly replied wiping the tears off her face with her hand. "I don't have her cell phone number neither Gordon. I never even thought about having it in case of an emergency." Stephanie softly said.

"So, when you get to the hospital, if she hasn't made contact by then, hopefully they will release Ezra's personal items to you or at least his cell phone and you can scroll through his phone to get in contact with her. Wow! Steph. This is bad! Mainly because he was attacked! Until we get full information on what has happened to our younger brother, we can't make any assumptions or panic. No sudden moves. I'm glad I followed my gut instincts and reached out to call my brother. Little sis. I need you to be strong and collect as much information as you can. I know you want to call dad and mom

right now. Stephanie, don't. Go to the hospital, show, your face and collect info! You are our only true blood representative amid a tragedy. Ezra needs you with him now and eyes over his shoulders looking out for whatever care he will need. I'll call them as soon as we hang up. Stephanie, don't! Just go and let me talk to our parents" Gordon spoke as he quickly disconnected the call.

"No, he didn't just hang up on me! He has his nerve. I'll call whoever I want, whenever I want to" Stephanie loudly blurted out as she stared at the cell phone.

"What happened girl" Melonie politely asked.

"My older brother who lives in Colorado reached out to Ezra and the police had his phone because he was just violently attacked in a stabbing incident inside the post office. Ezra is in the emergency care unit at Lenox Hill hospital so I'm heading over there now" Stephanie explained.

"I'm sorry Steph" Mike softly spoke.

"Me too, girl I'm lost for words. I know you're in pain as well" Freddie softly said.

"I'm sorry this happened Steph. But we can go with you if you like" Alonzo quietly suggested.

"Yeah, Steph, I'll drive you over there. That's horrible! And he doesn't need to be alone in that large public place" Danielle said.

"Come on let's get you over to the hospital" Tiffany said as she immediately raised herself up from the chair and rushed to one of the downstairs guest bathrooms.

CHAPTER 4

THE CONEY ISLAND KISSES

Squeezing her breast ever so gently, her hands reaching for the thighs their lips came together for one more kiss. Putting his top lip over her bottom lip as she sweetly sucked on his juicy top lip enjoying the gentle feel of her delicious lips as their tongues slowly made their way to one another lips the kiss lasted longer than a few seconds. With her lips resting nicely in between his lips as he furthered his tongue inside of her, she quickly grabbed his face, pulling his head closer towards her until she could feel his cool nose pressed up against her flesh. As the parked car remained idling with the Bob Marley Reggae classic hit song loudly playing in the background while the windows continued to be fogged due to the intense body heat coming from both of their intimate bodies intertwined with the heat blowing from the Acura's car radiator, neither of them could hear each other's intense moans over the loud music. As she continued to inhale long breaths causing her chest cavity to expand, capturing the attention of his eyes, he unlocked his lips from hers and slowly moved his head downward towards her voluptuous breast. Taking his hands and gently lifting her tight shirt over her C cup size breast, with his tongue now easing inside of her bra, with his lips surrounding her areola he then pulled her nipple outside of the bra and began sucking with intense force. Both now taking in deep breaths making the moaning sound even louder as she reached her hand down towards her bra pulling her other breast out so he can suck on that one too.

"That's it, stay right there because you feel so good on me" she softly moaned as he continued to suck on her breasts.

"Yeah baby, mmm, you like this? You like the way I make you feel" he repeatedly said as he continued to suck on her nipple.

Chirp, Chirp, her cellular phone ring tone continuously sounded, alerted her of the voicemail message that someone had left. As spontaneously anxious as she is now to respond to the cell phone alert the feeling of his wet desire for her loving is too good to ignore. Entertaining his hands as they worked their way down off her breast towards the black jeans she was wearing, her button fly, already popped open, he raised his eyes locking eyes with her in a direct stare as he began to kiss her lips all over again.

"You ready for me like I'm wanting you? You just do this

to me. My penis is so hard for you right now" He softly spoke as his tongue and bottom lip sucked on her top lip.

"Jamal, you have me so wet for you right now, I'm probably going to have to ring out these panties when we're through" she softly replied.

"I do that to your body for real my luv? You're so sexy I must be the luckiest guy on the planet to be having this moment with you" Jamal softly said.

"My phone keeps chirping, I want to answer it, but I'm caught up in your moves all over me Jamal. I don't want this feeling to stop" she honestly replied.

"Answer your phone my luv.

I'm not going anywhere.

The taste of you is like honey, tasting you is heavenly sent from God above.

Why should I skip out on you to chase a bag of money.

Why should I disappear. I'm craving for you my luv.

My luv, these feelings I got for you cause me to stay as you can clearly see, today my luv I'm right here. I'm not going anywhere. You got me. I want to taste your lips every day.

I want you. I want to feel, you. And I want you to feel me. I want you to want me like I'm feeling you right now that's how I want us to always be" Jamal rhythmically said as he slowly placed his fingers around the opened button moving them inside of her black jeans.

"Damn Jamal, don't stop" she softly whispered to him

"Monica, I got you. I'm not going to let anything, or anyone hurt you" Jamal softly whispered as he thrust his tongue in between her lips making Monica's toes curl. Relaxing herself, Monica then opened her legs wider

as Jamal's fingers slid behind her panties. His knuckles, also the top of his hand, now gently resting on Monica's skin as he very softly moved his hand up and down her flesh.

"Jamal, yeah. I want it Jamal" Monica very softly whispered as her cell phone continued Chirping. Jamal, being a little irritated by the annoying sound of the phone's alerts, suddenly stopped his fingers from gently moving around Monica's pelvis.

"Nah, my luv I need your undivided attention for what I'm about to give you. It also may be important. I don't need the judge to panic, fearing you are missing or upset with you. Monica, I got you. Go ahead and check your phone" Jamal suggested. Monica, listening to her boyfriend's advice, slightly lifted her body up off the butter soft heated leather back seat, reaching across his slim body into the front passenger seat of Jamal's new car and snatched her purse. Quickly looking inside the Luis Vuitton style purse, Monica pulled out the blinking phone. Speed dialing the keypad on the screen lock display screen of the designer cellular phone, Monica immediately went to the voicemail icon to check her multiple messages. As she started listening to the messages Monica slowly turned her head towards Jamal looking directly into his eyes.

"I meant every word I said, my luv" Jamal spoke. Monica taking her left hand and placing her fingers around his hard penis that was now erected sticking out of his unzipped designer pants started gently massaging it. Quickly disconnecting the call. Monica put down her phone.

"What happened" Jamal inquisitively asked placing both of his hands on top of her left hand as they both now embraced his erected penis.

"You're right. It's my mom. Something tragic has happened in our building and she needs me to pick my brothers and sister up from school and the daycare program. She mentioned that she was calling my school to give permission for me to leave after the lunch period has ended to handle the family errands that she has just assigned me to do" Monica sadly replied.

"Will your school tell Ms. Watkins that you're absent today?" Jamal responded.

"That's the problem Jamal, I'm not sure. But if they do and daddy finds out then he will be upset with me" Monica sadly responded.

"No problem my luv. I'm not going anywhere. Like I told you Monica, I got you. We'll pick up where we stopped later. I'm not going to work tonight, it's my two days off. Let's get you back to Manhattan to school now and hopefully I'll see you tonight outside of the tower's cameras. I'm not even upset. If anything, I'm happier now than ever. You've given me enough in this moment to jumpstart my day my luv. What class are you supposed to be in now" Jamal asked.

"Looking at the time, Global Studies and by the time we travel from Coney Island to my high school in Manhattan it'll be economics" Monica responded.

"Cool, lets bounce Dr. Watkins" Jamal loudly shouted removing her hands off his bodies private part as he put his erected penis back inside of his unzipped pants. Monica slowly placed her breast inside of her bra. Quickly zipping up her designer black jeans, as

Monica buttoned up her fly, she took in a deep breath squeezing in her stomach muscle for her to close the tightly fitted black jeans. As Monica's chest once again expanded because she was sucking her gut in, the rise of her breast inside the bra captured Jamal's attention and he quickly leaned towards her chest area kissing her again. As Jamal continued kissing, licking and now sucking on her chest area, Monica, taking both of her hands and putting them on his face, thrusted Jamal's head closer to her body. As his head was now plastered onto her body, Monica slid further down into the butter soft heated leather backseat. Jamals tongue now moving faster around the top chest area, his lips never lifting off her beautiful soft skin, started sucking harder as his jaws caved in.

"Keeps this up you're going to give me a hickey boo" Monica softly said as she widened, her legs once again, while Jamal slowly rested his hand between her legs on Monica's crotch area.

CHAPTER 5

I WANT TO KNOW WHO
HE REALLY IS

Stepping off the crowded elevator into Manhattan's semi busy tower lobby, Danielle immediately turned to the right walking towards the other four elevators which are only designed to reach the floor of her apartment that was in the east wing section of the very expensive luxury apartment building. Danielle, a CEO, of her own company, where she mainly works from home, living alone in a studio apartment that's on the lower floors of the Manhattan luxury tower that only contains studio apartments. Being a single divorced business entrepreneur, Danielle loved cooking, for her friends, tasting deliciously new foods and being entertained by her many male acquaintances. Walking up the long hallway ramp that led to the east wing section of the luxury apartment tower Danielle ran into Chong the buildings handyman supervisor.

"Good morning Ms. Silverstein how are you today" Chong loudly inquired.

"Not good Chong. Not good at all!" Danielle loudly replied. *"Something bad has happened to Steph. I must help my girl Stephanie out. This is so unfortunate Chong. But listen, I'm very upset with you! Chong, you really let me down this week. I was shocked! I'm very much surprised that would you even do that to me, and I thought we were on good terms"* Danielle loudly responded.

"What happened now Ms. Silverstein?" Chong loudly asked.

"No! It's not what happened now? As if I'm a complainer! Do you know who you're messing with. I've been a tenant here before you even had this job. I even vouched for you, to the building Super when he was hinting about promotions. I'm surprised that you would even speak to me in that manner. As if I'm an annoyance!" Danielle loudly replied.

"They didn't address the leak in your bathroom Ms. Silverstein?" Chong politely asked.

"So, then you already know why I'm completely disgusted with you Chong. You even gave me your word this week when I spoke to you about the flood. It was more than a leak!" Danielle loudly shouted.

"I remember Ms. Silverstein us discussing the leak in your bathroom when you contacted me on my cellphone one whole day later, after you discovered the leak. Your words to me were "Chong they never showed up." I apologized for the whole mishap and most likely miscommunication to you, Ms.

Silverstein. *However, I do remember explaining to you in detail after you directly told me over the cell phone that you contacted the front desk concierge, that they are not maintenance. When it comes to serious building malfunctions that you feel require experienced, certified plumbers and electricians that you contact my office directly not the front desk. I even gave you my personal cell phone number as I've given to most of the tenants in this building. When I provided you with my number, even back then, Ms. Silverstein, I explained this important information to you. Yes, you have been living here longer than I've been employed in this building. I really do appreciate your input almost four years ago when the super promoted me to supervisor. But none of that means I owe you special service. There are hundreds of units in this high-rise tower that I oversee daily. So, to handle serious challenges like what has occurred in your apartment's bathroom ceiling, Ms. Silverstein, I have implemented a plan that does work for those challenges when my instructions are followed."* Chong explained.

"My ceiling! The water was pouring out of my bathroom electrical outlet as well as my ceiling" Danielle loudly replied.

"Yes, that was on the next day. You didn't report that problem to me when you called me on my cell phone, and we briefly talked. You reported that serious problem of the leak in the electrical outlet to the front desk after we spoke to each other on the phone. Am I correct about that Ms. Silverstein? Am I correct about the fact that the sudden panic coming from you is because, your apartment bathroom now had multiple leaks of running water the following day after you discovered the original leak" Chong loudly asked.

"Listen, don't get technical with me Chong, as if I'm some

school child. I don't care what exact time is documented that I reported the leak. The issue is that I reported it. And I'm not pleased with the response or the responding time that I received of the flooding in my bathroom. Yes! I point the blame at you Mr. supervisor" Danielle loudly yelled as they stood in the long walkway that leads to the four east wing elevators. *"Yes, I blame you, Chong! Because no one came upstairs when I initially made the call. The water ran outside of my bathroom and into other areas of my apartment. Yes, Chong I'm very much pissed at you. I spent the entire day mopping up water as if I'm employed with a cleaning service agency. My feelings hurt, because I pleaded for help! No one came to my rescue. I'm a very good tipper in this building and I make sure during the holiday season that I look out for everyone. My Cards that I distribute to the staff around the holidays are never empty. And this is the thanks I get. This is how you'll repay me. You are the head person in charge. So, yes Chong, I'm totally disgusted with you. And I'm not pleased with how it was handled on this week"* Danielle loudly spoke.

"Ms. Silverstein, let me ask you this question then. Is the water still running in your bathroom?" Chong politely asked.

"No! around seven o'clock that night after we spoke the leaks stopped." Danielle answered.

"Leaks, so how many bathroom leaks were there inside of your apartment?" Chong politely asked.

"Listen I don't have time for this interrogation my girlfriend Stephanie needs me, and I have to leave the building" Danielle loudly said as she turned and continued walking up the long walkway towards the elevators.

"*Ms. Silverstein do you mind me walking along with you to go upstairs to your studio apartment and take a look at your bathroom ceiling*" Chong loudly asked.

"*At this point I don't care what you do Chong*" Danielle loudly responded. Walking along with Danielle towards the four elevators that lead to only the studio apartments in the east wing of the towers. Phillip, the senior staff handy man, was waxing the huge brass columns inside the walkway.

"*Morning, Ms. Silverstein*" Phillip said in a raspy tone.

"*Hey Phillip! Listen, I needed to have a word with you. It's something I've been meaning to discuss with you for a while*" Danielle softly spoke.

"*What's on your mind Ms. Silverstein? Listen, that's a nice turquoise two-piece jumpsuit you're wearing. You've been shopping on thirty fourth street again, without me Danielle*" Phillip jokingly said.

"*Oh, you like this? No, I've been shopping daily on the home shopping network. They have some great buys*" Danielle quickly replied.

"*Well, you look great, Dee Dee*" Phillip politely commented.

"*Thanks Phil. That's mighty kind of you. You know with my clientele growing as it has been lately; I've been staying at home more these days. So, I do most of my shopping right upstairs inside of my studio. I've also been watching the cooking channel late at night, some of these chefs are very entertaining. Speaking of late nights. Phil, what's going on with Monica Watkins at night here in this building?*" Danielle asked, the buildings senior handyman while placing her right hand on her hip.

Phillip throwing his rag down near the commercial janitorial cleaning cart on wheels that he was using to clean the hallway columns, gently placed his right hand on Danielle's left shoulder ushering her to step away from Chong who was patiently waiting for Danielle to go upstairs to her apartment and check the possible water damage from the leaks earlier this week. *"Dee Dee, Monica been creeping with that black thug that's on the overnight shift for a little while now. But I heard he's a member of her brother's church. Now that's what I heard. Can't tell you if it's true or not. Him in church I don't know all about that. That Skeleton is a lot of trouble, if you know what I mean. That's why the super's wife is his little building playmate. Like I said that bag of bones downstairs that works in the garage is not the church going type. He's also good friends with the former talk show host and everyone living in the building knows that guy is a creep"* Phillip responded in a raspy tone.

"Speaking of creeps. What I've been wanting to share with you Phil is my girlfriend Stephanie penthouse floor neighbor, that is terrifyingly spooky. His creepy ways are coming across as a stalker. She's completely grossed out by him. What's happening on the penthouse floor?" Danielle inquired.

"Mr. Bradley is a busy one I've got to admit. He and I have had our days. I'm not sure if I'm on any of his guest list any time soon. Specifically, his Christmas card list" Phillip loudly replied.

"Thanks Phil, you've been extremely insightful this

morning. I must run and take Stephanie to the hospital because something awful has happened to her younger brother Ezra. I must go upstairs and get my heavy jacket and use the bathroom if it's not flooded" Danielle loudly said as she rolled her eyes. *"I cooked delicious seafood pasta earlier. It's called "Lobster will claw your tongue" and it is simply delicious. Mike and the fellas were upstairs in the penthouse sampling the cuisine, and their tongues enjoyed the taste. I told Stephanie I would call when I'm ready"* Danielle continued saying as she turned and continued walking to the east wing elevators.

"Ok, Ms. Silverstein you stay warm and be safe out there. Let Steph. Know I'm praying for her" Phillip said as he walked back over to the commercial janitorial cart on wheels to finish his cleaning. Walking to the east wing lobby elevators, Stephanie pushed the landing button to signal the elevator so she could quickly go upstairs to her studio apartment.

"Mr. Bradley has a serious crush on your friend. He's a very possessive individual" Chong said as he came and stood next to Danielle.

"You need to be attentive to the plumbing emergencies that occur in this building when folks like me contact you in desperate need of assistance. My floors were soaked Chong. I couldn't imagine where the water was coming from. I'm very disappointed with your work performance this week. That flood left a negative impression with me." Danielle loudly spoke. *"The water was dripping onto the toilet tank, then onto the floor. The water started leaking from three other different spots off the ceiling, pouring down the wall onto the bathroom floor. The water was also pouring out of the electrical outlet*

above the sink. It was a mess" Danielle loudly shouted as the east wing elevator chimes sounded and they both stepped onto the elevator.

"Ms. Silverstein, the late afternoon that you telephoned the building staff to alert us of the bathroom leak, we also had received numerous calls all day long of serious apartment issues throughout the building. When someone says leak into their apartment, that indicates there is a problem outside of their apartment. Most likely the cause is from the apartment above them. I'm sure my staff was on the case knocking on doors above you trying to detect flooding. If it's not coming from the actual apartment, it could be coming from a leaky pipe. That gets complicated because the location of that particular leak possibly can be coming from inside the walls. If we were already busy serving customers, then only one staff member was walking around the east wing looking for a leak. The next day we received three more calls from tenants on the east wing about hearing loud dripping from inside the walls. The apartment underneath you reported they could hear the dripping in their kitchen. The reason the leak did stop was because I personally found the leak on the eleventh floor, on your apartment line" Chong replied as the elevator door opened on the sixth floor.

"Hi Danielle," the tall gentleman loudly said with bags in his hand.

"Morning Zack, this is a surprising face that's greeting me on my floor" Danielle replied as her and Chong together slowly stepped off the elevator.

"Yeah, my wife and I went shopping on yesterday, so I came downstairs here to the east wing to show my buddy Brian some of the items I picked up for our ski trip next month. You

know we'll all be leaving town for Christmas this year" Zack replied.

"That's nice. Where are you'll headed this year?" Danielle inquired.

"For Christmas the family is heading to the ski resort in Aspen. Brian is tagging along with us. Two of my wife's coworkers are also coming along with my baby brother. It'll be a blast. I'm super excited about the trip. As you can see, I'm stacking up on ski gear already" Zack explained.

"Speaking of Colorado, Steph's older brother spoke with the police sergeant here in New York a little while ago concerning their younger brother Ezra. Supposedly he was attacked in a post office this morning. He's in Lenox Hill now in serious condition" Danielle said.

"Oh, gosh! How bad has he been injured" Zack quickly asked.

"I'm on my way to take her now to the hospital's emergency room to see. He was stabbed repeatedly so it's not good and frightening for our neighbor Steph." Danielle replied.

"Yeah, she's a ball of fire. That Stephanie is a tough one. My wife and her twin sister attend Stephanies yoga class at that popular gym across town. My wife is always walking around the house doing deep breathing exercises because of Stephanie's class. I'm terribly sorry to hear this. Send her my love. I'll let my wife know immediately." Zack said as he quickly pushed the landing panel on the hallway wall to signal the elevator.

"Listen Zack, you always come home late nights, correct? Let me ask you. Who's the overnight parking attendant in this building?" Danielle loudly asked.

"During the week it's Jamal. At the weekends it's Stanley. Everyone likes Stanley, I say that's because he's a weekend parking attendant. Majority of the tenants are off at the weekends and return home late hours. I prefer Jamal because he's efficient. A real good kid. Good head on his shoulders and listens to a lot of Bob Marley. I listen to a lot of the Marley brothers' classic hits. He drives an Acura, and you always see him carrying a rag, washing his car. Why you ask Danielle?" Zack inquired, as he looked Danielle directly in her eyes.

"Just trying to get in my mind who's who in this building. The building staff is so large and many of them I never see because of the hours of their shift. But when I distribute my Christmas cards next month, I want to make sure I'm fair. So, Jamal is the week overnight guy's name." Danielle explained.

"Yeah, Jamal is good money. He's deserving of whatever it is you plan on financially giving him inside your Christmas envelope. Well, I know you must go, so please give Stephanie a hug for me and let her know Ezra is in my prayers" Zack loudly spoke as he pushed the button on the landing panel again as the elevator doors opened and he quickly walked on the elevator. *"Tell Melonie, I'll be praying hard for Monica as well"* Zack continued to loudly speak as the elevator doors closed.

Walking down the wide sixth floor hallway, Danielle and Chong the buildings handyman supervisor walked to her apartment door.

"This building is going to be empty after Thanksgiving Ms. Silverstein. A lot of tenants are either leaving on vacation

for the holidays or traveling home for the holidays." Chong said as he started texting on his cell phone.

"Yes, it always is a ghost town around here in the hallways come Christmas time. As for me it's my busiest work time of the business year, because there's a lot of parties and daily New Year celebrations, I must provide services for. So, I'll be extremely busy as usual from next week throughout the second week of January into the New Year." Danielle replied as she took her keys out of her pocket.

"Even Thanksgiving that's coming at the end of this month, a lot of the tenants here vacate the premises for various reasons." Chong said as he continued scrolling the display screen on his cell phone. *"With an empty building there are less eyes watching giving more opportunity for the creeps to play like you have just witnessed today"* Chong continued to say slowly lifting his eyes off the display screen on his cellular phone, as Danielle paused herself from placing her key into the apartment doors cylinder. Danielle slowly turned around and looked at Chong directly into his eyes.

CHAPTER 6

THE BUILDING FIST FIGHT

As Mike, Freddie and Alonzo stepped off the busy Friday morning Tower lower floors elevator, Aram was standing there speaking with another tenant.

"Good morning, ladies and gentlemen. Let me get the door for everyone" Aram loudly shouted as he suddenly dashed off in the busy lobby headed towards the front entrances huge brass door, leaving the young woman and her three dogs standing alone in front of the elevators. As the three amigos casually walked along with the morning crowd that exited off the elevators, because two of the other tower elevators' doors also opened simultaneously, filling the lobby up with tenants either going to work, exercising, doing daily routines or heading downstairs to the building's parking garage for their cars. Freddy stopped at the Lobbies front desk to speak to the concierge about his packages and laundry

cleaning services, before the three of them exited the apartment tower with plans on catching a taxi, to meet the ladies at the hospital.

"Morning Marisol, did I receive any packages yesterday I forgot to check? I'm expecting an important small package that should have arrived already. These buyers have been constantly blowing up my email about important items contained inside this package. I'm really getting annoyed. It's too early in the morning for their madness" Freddie asked the female concierge worker as she quickly walked behind her desk to the large rooms to check all the packages. *"Morning to you as well Max, let me ask you, did the cleaners service pick up my laundry bag yesterday? Because when you handed me the delivered dry cleaning, there are lots of clothes missing"* Freddy said to the male concierge as he placed his hand on his hip.

"Let me check the computer now and see what note, if any, is listed by your name sir" Max the tall athletic built concierge man loudly replied.

"Sir you have these two packages, here for you" Marisol the short female Hispanic concierge loudly spoke as she quickly returned to the front desk holding two small boxes in her hands.

"Yes, darling, you are definantly a life saver. My day has been rescued by Ms. Marisol" Freddy dramatically said as he placed his hands on his face shaking his head.

"She's the best Freddie" Alonzo loudly shouted.

"She most definantly is" Freddie quickly replied as he took the two small boxes from Marisol's hands. *"However, what's going on with my clothes? Why the missing*

pieces Mr. Max?" Freddy quietly asked. Leaning over the huge marble decorated front desk counter, looking at Max the male concierge directly into his face.

"I'm checking now sir. Let me call over to them now and see what the dilemma with your laundry services are." Max politely replied.

"Well, you do that Maxi" Alonzo quickly responded.

"Yes, Mr. Max, I will appreciate you doing that for me" Freddy quickly replied as he turned his body around to watch Aram at the front door.

"Good morning, Marisol, I want to put in a few services request for my apartment. My kitchen sink constantly drips all night long and it's annoyingly waking me up. The heating system in my apartment is also acting up, that might be a problem when those temperatures drop honey. Okay! I spoke to Chong about this before, but the lock on my door acts up at times. Now Chong said he would come upstairs and look at it. But until this day no one has checked my lock" Mike said as Marisol filled out the apartment service request form while standing over her coworker, Max who was still seated at the desk conversating on the buildings office phone. Aram slowly walked over to the front desk and took off his doorman cap.

"Gentleman, how are we doing this morning? Aram loudly asked.

"We're doing fine, Aram. You seem busy this morning" Alonzo quickly responded.

"Very busy Alonzo! Very busy. They keep us constantly moving here" Aram quickly replied.

"Oh, wait a hot minute! What's this my ears have just

heard, and my suspicious eyes have seen. First name basis I see. What's this Alonzo" Freddy sarcastically asked.

"Mind yours okay. Tend to the mysterious disappearance of your dirty silk drawers and leave the intellectuals to converse in privacy please" Alonzo quickly replied.

"Oh, you a shady queen! A shady one that I do see! Alright Ally cat, you go right ahead and meow on" Freddy replied as he quickly turned his body back around to face Max the male concierge who was still conversating with the building's laundry service receptionist on the telephone.

"So, Alonzo where are you'll headed to this morning?" Aram politely asked.

"We must make a hospital visit. So, whenever they're finished here with the concierge, we are going to need a taxi" Alonzo softly replied.

"that's not a problem, whenever you ready Alonzo I'll get taxi for you guys" Aram cheerfully responded as he put his doorman cap back on. Mike then turned his body around to look at Aram in his eyes.

"You're looking good in your uniform today as you do every day" Alonzo softly commented to Aram as Mike now stared at both. Aram quickly dashed off towards the huge glass brass doors yelling and screaming at a local delivery guy who stood outside of the lobby doors with a scooter.

"Hey, hey, you guys already know the rules here! All deliveries must enter the building at the security entrance! Get away from my door! You already know! Go! Go around the corner to the security entrance, now!" Aram loudly shouted as he ran to the huge brass lobby entrance door." Max immediately stood up quickly trying to end the conversation with the laundry cleaning service receptionist. As the argument escalated outside of the lobby between Aram and the local delivery person, one of the building security guards rushed through the lobby with his handheld radio swinging in his hand, to the front entrance door where Aram was standing. Aram was outside positioned directly in front of the door not allowing the delivery person to enter the building. As the local delivery person attempted to push past Aram, the heavy set African American security guard gently knocked on the huge glass door with his fist, alerting Aram that he was now standing at the door, so he could come outside to assist Aram and help deescalate the intense situation. As Aram turned around to pull open the door for the heavyset security guard, the unidentified local delivery man immediately tried to squeeze around Aram and boldly run into the building. Two more security guards came running through the luxury apartment tower lobby, from both directions of the giant spacious lobby also heading to the huge glass door, yelling, screaming, with their arms extended and handheld radios tightly gripped in their hands also trying to block the entrance of the glass door so the local delivery man couldn't enter inside of the building. A white car with a security logo on the side of the car door pulled up in front of the building, as an older white gentleman with salt and pepper hair, hoped out of the car wearing a long trench coat and having a handheld radio in his hand. As Max hung up the front desk office phone, he looked at Marisol the Hispanic concierge and she immediately went towards the back room. As the Mexican local delivery man refused to follow the security guards' building entrance instructions, a few more tenants entered the hostile lobby, from the apartment building elevators on both sides. Standing inside the lobby close to the huge brass glass door, the tenants all stopped, stared and watched the intense situation with the gentlemen escalating. The three security guards, the luxury towers doorman Aram, the older white salt and pepper haired gentleman dressed in a trench coat together started yelling at the very angry Mexican local delivery man. The Mexican local delivery man slammed his delivery bag onto the ground and started shoving the African American security guard with both of his hands. The apartment buildings doorman Aram, then started shoving the Mexican local delivery man pushing him back away from the heavyset African American security guard towards the curb in front of the building. As the Mexican local delivery man went to swing his fist at the luxury Towers doorman Aram, his right foot slipped backwards, down off the streets curb. The Mexican local delivery man, losing his balanced, stumbled himself towards Aram, his body roughly moving, knocking into Aram and the African American security guard simultaneously as the other two security guards quickly grabbed him. Another African local delivery person from another store, who was good friends with the

Mexican delivery man came running to the scene to aid his friend and quickly shoved the apartment buildings doorman Aram, pushing him away from what looked like a brawl between the grown men.

"I'm about to call the police" Max the concierge man spoke. *"Every day these same stupid guys try us. I keep saying one of these days, someone is going to catch it. What it's looking like, is today might be that day."* Max continued to say as Marisol the female concierge returned to the front desk. The building Super quickly entered the crowded tenant filled lobby because Marisol had notified him of the trouble Aram is having with a trespasser at the front lobby entrance door.

"Call the police Max! Call the police now" the stocky Italian Super loudly shouted as he moved quickly towards the huge glass door. As the Super went to push open the brass door, his faithful assistant Jimmy, the tall stocky young Italian man, immediately stepped behind the buildings Super, reaching his thick arms out over him, forcefully pushed the huge brass glass door open. Stepping outside Jimmy quickly grabbed the African local delivery man, pulling him away from his building's workmen. *"Hey, what's going on out here!"* The luxury apartment building Super loudly yelled. "I just notified the police, they're on their way! You guys know the rules! All deliveries must go through the security entrance of the building, around the corner." The building Super continued yelling, as he turned his head looking up the block for the police. Another African delivery man who was passing on his scooter

saw Jimmy mishandling the African local delivery man and sped his scooter towards the curb where the gentleman was tussling each other. Jumping off his scooter he immediately ran up to Jimmy swinging his arms towards him, in attempt to back him away from the African Local delivery man. "Get off of Him!" The tall African man loudly yelled at Jimmy. "You are no good, get off my brother! Let him go, you bad man!" The tall African man yelled as he swung his full-face helmet at Jimmy, cracking him in his right eye with the rigid outer shell of the full-face helmet, hitting Jimmy in the head very hard. As Jimmy stumbled back slightly, the Super quickly moved towards Jimmy, along with the older white gentleman dressed in the trench coat who then immediately dropped his handheld radio onto the ground and swung at the tall African man punching him in the side of his face with his fist. The local African delivery man seeing what he just did to his friend, thrusted his entire body forward, jumping on the older white gentleman and started punching him in the face. As he continued punching the older white gentleman in his face, his body, he then tried bringing him downward towards the ground. The Super kicked the African local delivery man in the side of his body with his hard construction boot. The force of the buildings Italian Supers boot knocked the African to the ground. When two other African delivery men who were walking in the area saw the African local delivery hit the ground from the kick of the construction boot, they immediately ran over in the direction of the luxury building Italian Super. Rushing him, the two African men grabbed the Super backing him away from the local African delivery man. Aram the Armenian buildings doorman then punched the Mexican local delivery man directly in the face as the two security guards, left the Mexican local delivery man and ran towards the two African delivery men who were around the Luxury buildings Super as the police patrol car came speeding up the block. Jimmy then started punching the tall African man making him loose grip of his full-face helmet as he too fought back. While the Mexican local delivery man and the heavyset African American security guard started fighting each other, throwing fist at one another, the police car immediately stopped in front of the building. It was now a brawl between the men outside of the luxury tower. While the men was physically fighting one another and loudly yelling at each other another police patrol vehicle came onto the block stopping in front of the brawl. As the brawl had escalated in front of the building, Max and a few of the building workers started escorting the tenants away from the huge glass doors out of the giant spacious neatly decorated luxury apartment building lobby for their own personal safety. Heading out of the side entrance of the building by the security guard station the tenants were escorted by the buildings staff. Stephanie and Tiffany stepped off the elevator with Brownie as he happily wagged his tail. Seeing all the commotion of her neighbors in the lobby as they stood by the upper floor elevators, she got nervous. Phillip the senior apartment building handyman stopped to speak with Stephanie and Tiffany as they together were enroute to walk Brownie outside around the apartment building for his daily bathroom stroll, before heading over to the hospital. Phillip informed the women of the incident currently taking place outside of the building with Aram and now the law enforcement agents. Mike, Freddy and Alonzo, being three of the first tenants escorted out of the building's security guard station, side entrance, picked up a New York City taxi that was stationed outside of the building. Stephanie's cell phone began to ring as they stood by the upper floor elevators conversing with Phillip. Checking the cell phone caller ID, it was Danielle letting her know that she was now ready to leave for the hospital and that she was making her way downstairs to the building's parking garage to get into her car.

CHAPTER 7

THE SCHOOL ENTRY

Pulling his new car up to the corner of the block where Monica's high school was located Jamal slowly turned off the Acura's ignition.

"Do you have a plan, my luv? Have you thought about how you are going to get into the high school building at this time of day" Jamal softly asked Monica.

"Sometimes students leave through the side exit doors of the school building before the lunch period. Sometimes students leave through the doors on the other side of the school building throughout the morning, specifically around lunch period. The reason is that the school safety guards are very busy trafficking students inside and around the school's cafeteria. Even if there's one school safety guard posted around any of those school exit doors, it's simply easier to maneuver around that one guard. My only problem would be waiting for someone to exit the school. I don't want to stand outside of the school door

and patiently wait, because then someone would notify the school safety agents of my intentions. I'm also not sure which side school doors someone is going to sneak out of" Monica quietly responded.

"My luv I can park my car closer, as we sit in hope and wait for someone to come out of the schools exit doors in which ever one you choose" Jamal suggested.

"Looking at the time on the clock, we have no choice" Monica replied as she nervously looked at her cell phone, to see if her parents were leaving anymore text messages.

"My luv, the longer I'm with you the happier it makes me. This is time well spent" Jamal softly spoke.

"Let's go around the corner and try the doors on that side of the school building" Monica suggested as Jamal quickly started up his Acura's engine and drove around the corner to the side of the High school where Monica had directed him. Circling the long city block in his new car, Jamal's cellphone started to ring. Monica slightly turned her head towards the new cars dashboard to see the name of the person displayed on the screen. Thanks to Jamal's new Acura's blue tooth connecting to his mobile device, Monica saw that the Supers wife Linda was calling him. Looking at the time of day, Monica suspected that Linda figured he wouldn't be with her because she's normally in class. Slowly moving her eyes towards Jamal, she noticed that he began fidgeting around, fixing his shirt and wiping his sweaty palms on his jeans stemming from the heated cars air conditioning system that was placed at high

speed. Monica then stared at Jamal while he pulled directly in front of the High school, putting the cars transmission into park.

"Why didn't you answer the phone" Monica asked as she turned down the warm air fan on his Acura.

"I'll talk to that person later. I'm not at work. It's my time off and I want to enjoy every minute with you my luv" Jamal softly responded as he wiped his sweaty palms on his jeans again.

"It's not like I don't know Linda. It might have been important. Like you said Jamal, you're not at work and you're not working tonight so she will not be seeing you at all in person on today anywhere inside of my apartment building. However, I'm sure Linda knows that already since her husband is the chief commander at your workplace. Plus, I would have loved to hear what you two talk about when you're not around me" Monica honestly said.

"My luv, don't worry about me giving anyone else attention besides you. You have my undivided attention day and night. I'm only focused on getting you inside that school building today, before your absence catches the attention of the judge. I don't need your mother's phone call to catch the attention of the high school principal. My luv, I really don't want you in any kind of trouble on today because I was in demand of your undivided attention" Jamal softly replied.

"I can't help how I feel Jamal. Maybe I shouldn't be feeling like that. But I'm curious to know what my buildings Super's wife and you are discussing. That's how I feel" Monica confessed.

"My luv, was you feeling about that earlier when we were

parked out there by Coney Island's board walk? Did you feel like that when my lips were resting on your nipples? Did you feel like that when my lips were kissing your gorgeous lips? Was Linda the topic when my lips were all over your chest" Jamal softly responded.

"You gave me a hickey on my chest Jamal. I hope mom doesn't see it. It felt good when you were doing it. I still feel good about your lips all over my body. But when mommy gets to rebuke the devil and binds up evil spirits, I sure hope she doesn't pick up on what we have done today. She left for church, at four o'clock this morning. That lady loves to praise God! So, today she is going to be on her super spiritual journey missions all day. Evangelism will be mommy's star role all day. Meaning her only conversation to us at home is going to be what God is revealing to his people. And how we need to celebrate God greatly for his many blessings that he freely gives." Monica explained while waiting for one of her schoolmates to exit out of the locked school doors.

"I can't help myself when I'm physically with you. You're beautiful, my luv. That's how bad, I want you. I enjoy tasting you my luv. The weather is getting colder so at least you can maybe hide the hickey with sweaters and long sleeve shirts. You brought that nice Shirling winter coat last week so I know that will help you publicly hide my feelings for you" Jamal softly replied.

"Yeah, but it's big Jamal. I'll try my best not to disclose your feelings for me. So is the size of your penis. I peep at it all Jamal! I saw on today how erect I can make you," Monica spoke.

"My luv, you're the only one I desire to pay attention

to" Jamal softly responded as the red school exit doors quickly swung open. Monica immediately jumped out of the car loudly begging the three students to hold the door while she sneaked into her high school building.

Quickly walking into the high-rise school building, Monica darted up the narrow staircase heading to the third floor. As she reached the bottom of the staircase from the third floor, the staircase door slowly opened. Hearing a two-way radio, Monica quickly turned around and with all her might, ran back down the narrow stairs toward the second-floor staircase door. Opening the door but not letting it slam Monica then ran down the hall darting to the left hallway headed for a classroom that she was familiar with. Seeing some students sitting together in the hallway, she quickly joined them. Sitting down on the floor, taking off her heavy jacket, she folded it up neatly and placed her purse on top of it. The students just stared at her because they were all Korean and were working on an art project together in preparation for a school assembly presentation in the auditorium, later in the day. Monica, ignoring them, kept her eyes fixed around the hallway for the school safety agents that were maybe patrolling the floor. Because she didn't plan on attending school today, Monica didn't have her school bag or tablet with her. Snatching the papers out of one the male students' hands because she could hear a two-way radio in the distance, Monica then pretended as if she was reading what was on the papers. As the sound of the two-way radio grew closer, Monica's heart pounded heavier. The short Hispanic female school safety agent slowly walked down the hallway towards the students. The Korean students begin speaking English one to another about their thoughts on Monica's notes. Monica, hearing the conversation, never lifted her head or her eyes off the papers. As the female safety agent walk past them, one of the Korean students snatched her coat from under Monica's purse. *"Monica, I keep telling you about putting your personals on top of my stuff"* the Korean student spoke. Monica finally lifting her head from the papers *"I'm sorry! But you didn't have to snatch it. Now can we please finish this presentation"* Monica replied as she slowly cut her eyes in the direction of the Hispanic school safety agent. As the school safety agent left that section of the school hallway, Monica turned to the Korean student and thanked him for helping her with the intense situation. *"Not a problem Monica. You're in my homeroom class. When I didn't see you in class this morning, and now you nervously appear sitting here with us, I knew what you were doing. You're also on the girls' volleyball team along with my girlfriend and she respects you a lot. I know your coach is extremely strict. So, if you were absent from school there would have to be a serious reason, you were going to miss volleyball practice."* The Korean student quietly said to Monica.

"Yeah, that's only half of my problems on today. I must get to my Economics class before my parents find out what I've done" Monica said as she leaped up and sprinted back down the hallway. Reaching the staircase door again, Monica darted upstairs to the third floor, attempting

to catch the last twenty minutes of her Economics class. Rushing down the hallway, as Monica entered the classroom there was another teacher standing in front of the assigned Economics classroom, teaching the lesson of the day. *"Hi, how can I help you?"* The heavyset white male teacher said to Monica. Monica slowly closed the classroom door. Walked over to her seat quietly. *"I apologize, the principal needed to speak to me there's an emergency at my home"* Monica softly replied. "Oh, Okay, speak to me after class" the substitute teacher quickly responded. As Monica sat down in the empty chair, another student that was seated behind her passed her a note. The note read: *girl, where you been all day. Ms. Mayo had to leave; her husband had been arrested for an incident at the post office earlier. Girl, text me.* Monica immediately turned around towards her bestie Cindy and shook her head.

Following class Monica and Cindy together approached the substitute teacher making sure he marked her present on the attendance sheet. *"Hi, Monica, that's not why I wanted to speak to you after class. I know who you are. Your father and I are real good friends. My wife is the court clerk in your father's courtroom. The Judge is a wonderful man. I'll be happy to tell him that you were one of the students in a class that I was covering today. I'm also an evening professor at the Borough of Manhattan Community College, where I've been teaching for years. My twin brother lives in your apartment building, and he speaks well of your parents all the time. What happened at home? Is everything okay with your family?"* The substitute

Economics teacher politely asked her. Cindy quickly pulled out her text phone, elbowing Monica in her arm, lifted her cellphone towards Monica's face.

"I'm sorry that's my brother, texting Cindy on her phone. He needs me to call him. My mother was trying to reach him earlier" Monica blurted out, as she snatched Cindy's cellphone and went out into the hallway. Walking down the crowded hallway filled with students shuffling to class, the cafeteria for lunch, the gymnasium for class or the auditorium for whatever presentation is being held, Monica quickly texts her mom, asking, "Have she spoken with the school?"

"This has been an unbelievable morning girl. Jamal took me out to Coney Island in Brooklyn, to make sweet love. My mom interrupts, leaves me messages that something has happened, and she needs me to pick up the kids. I wasn't planning on coming to school today. I knew I had to attend volleyball practice after school. Mom's call saved me from that problem before it arose. Jamal drove me back here to Manhattan" Monica said as they continued to slowly walk together down the crowded hallway. Bumping into one of their other girlfriends the three of them stopped and conversed. *"So how did you get into the school?"* Cindy asked. *"Jamal drove me around the South doors and when these freshman guys walked out, I quickly ran inside. Girl, these Korean kids helped me out downstairs and everything. Them guards were trying to hunt a sister down."* Monica explained, as she burst out in laughter.

"You were with Jamal so what was that like?" Cindy cheerfully asked.

"His lips were so juicy Cindy. Oh, I can still taste them.
He caressed my body with care.
I couldn't help but stare.
His words, so gentle. His lips, so gentle. His tongue gently
wet up my lips
It was nothing but love between us in the atmosphere.
All we could do was kiss. I felt his penis, yes it was there
Oh, I can still taste him, his lingering aroma of love, the
scent remains in my hair"

Monica cheerfully rhythmically explained.

"His lips sounds like they were working you out girl" Cindy spoke.

"Wow, girl that Jamal is a cutie, and he knows how to take care of a sister. That's what's up" Kaneesha loudly said. As the three of them slowly started walking down the hallway together. Approaching the staircase door, a white female school safety agent quickly came out the staircase helping to direct the crowd of students that were lingering around the staircase door, blocking the exit so other students couldn't go through. The three girls, seeing the school guard, turned around and started walking in the other direction. *"Hopefully Jamal can pick you up from school and take you to your sibling's school"* Kaneesha loudly said.

"Yeah, girl that would be cool. Then you could get some more of that good loving them lips serve you" Cindy said.

"Speaking of loving, what's going on with Mr. all-star? I'm surprised he wasn't waiting for you after class. Seems like every day you'll are joined to the hip" Monica inquired.

"You need to watch out for that new girl with those big

breasts. That freshman got all of them basketball players fighting over her." Kaneesha said.

"*Not Carlos. That's a dub! Only breast he is staring at are mines*" Cindy quickly replied to Kaneesha about her boyfriend Carlos.

"*I hear that girl! Exactly like Jamal. I made sure today his tongue was examining my areola in that smokey Acura*" Monica said.

"*I heard that freshman also been flirting with the team*" Kaneesh spoke.

"*That's probably why you'll two stays together all day*" Monica said.

"*No, it's not like that. And yeah, I heard those rumors too. But she isn't a threat to me. Carlos knows what he has got. That's why we're always together. That's why we're hot!*" Cindy rhythmically replied as she started dancing, moving her hips side to side.

"*No, what was hot was Jamals penis in my hands*" Monica said.

"*Yeah, Monica now that sounds hot! Girl, I know you glad on today he drove you there*" Kaneesha said as the three girls entered the other schools building staircase heading towards the music classroom on the fifth floor. They all shared the Chorus Class together before their lunch period. The music director Mr. Bowman was a former Broadway actor and had a great relation with the three girls. The three girls sang and sat together in the soprano section which happened to be a real treat for them. Entering the music room, the three girls made their way to the soprano section chairs inside the very large classroom.

"Honestly speaking I wish I was as strong as you Cindy. I'm not as confident with Jamal as you are with Carlos. I trust him. I love him. He confesses his love for me. We're together but not all the time. It's phone calls like the one he received in the car, before I sneaked into the school. That makes me feel insecure about our love. What makes it bad is I know the woman" Monica shared.

"The woman! What woman?" Kaneesha loudly asked as she crossed her legs throwing her sneakers up in the air.

"Linda, the building Supers wife. Girl, she be hawking my man like he's prey. At times I'm like chic fall back, you are playing me too close. He's my man not yours. When he's at work in the morning, downstairs inside the apartment building's parking garage, she is all over him. When I stop downstairs to see him before I go to school, I'm like girl, you need to fall all the way back. Their laughing and side conversations gets to me at times. Way too friendly for me" Monica continued to share.

"What this woman looks like Monica" Cindy inquisitively asked

"She's my height but older. She's an Italian blond-haired chic. She smokes a lot of cigarettes. Her and her husband. Every time I see them, they have a cigarette hanging out of their mouth" Monica loudly replied.

"Oh, men are flirts but so are woman, so I agree with your feeling because you do have to watch that carefully. Let me tell you about my neighbor. He's a fine, Puerto Rican cutie pie.

I mean fine! Girl I would love to see his penis outside of his pants" Kaneesha loudly said.

"Kaneesha!" Cindy shouted.

"I'm just being honest. I've seen him wrapped in a bath towel with no shirt on, standing in front of his studio apartment door, talking on the cellphone at times, when I arrive home. However, he lives next door with his girlfriend and their four-year-old son. She's very pretty. His girlfriend is Puerto Rican as well with beautiful blond colored hair. Very thin model shaped body. Ever since they moved into the studio apartment next door to us about three months ago her and I have been talking a lot. A lot of my neighbors don't speak to her for various reasons. I thought it was because most of the tenants in my building are Dominican but that's not entirely the reason for them not speaking. He's abusive! A real nasty dog! I'm in school all day, after school I'm in dance class every day of the week and then I'm hanging with my girls outside or I'm at the library working on a research project. At weekends I'm out of the apartment on dates with my girlfriend, if I'm not hanging out with either of you. So, I wasn't up on the smackdown going on next door. My Pitbull is up on it. But that's my brother's problem, not mine. I know now they give my pet dog a show during the day with all that yelling, screaming, and crying she does most likely during the day. Remember two weeks ago when I was absent from school because I had caught the Flu? One afternoon that boy knocked her head onto the wall so hard it knocked the pictures off our living room wall. I was so sick from that Flu virus, girl, I didn't have any television playing, radio or computer on because my sinus was seriously hurting me from the mucus of the Flu. I had a severe headache, so any kind

of noise irritated me. Girl, I heard the whole conversation next door, blaring through the wall! Amid all the silent quietness in our apartment, I overheard the constant arguing, the loud threats, punches of his fist into her, the smacks and the cries. I felt so bad I even cried. Then I remembered she always has sunglasses on even at night when I run into her in the lobby. Her glasses are stylish though. They hadn't been paying rent for the last three months. So, the original tenants of the apartment who were subletting the studio apartment came to collect the rent money from his abusive self. They are a real nice Dominican couple. She used to babysit me when I was younger, but they brought a very large house in Connecticut and secretly moved out of the apartment. They were arguing and cursing each other out. Girl, he said "You can't make me leave." That went on for about two days. The husband even came one Saturday afternoon from Connecticut while they were not home and took the doorknob off the hinges. Girl, I dyed" Kaneesha shouted as she busted out in laughter. *"I'm sorry you'll I know it's not funny for both families, especially the young Puerto Rican couple because they have a four-year-old son. Monica, you may need to get your mother to pray extra hard in her church for that little boy. She may need to put on some construction boots and go to stomping her church floor hard for that toddler. Dance and pray he don't end up an abusive bum like his father"* Keesha shared.

"Speaking of prayer services. Do you guys know my mom was leaving the house at four o'clock this morning for church. That's way too early for me. That's why I enjoy going to my uncle's church. Make no mistakes about it, his church is *spiritual too. However, they don't go the extra mile, doing all the extra for a blessing"* Monica said.

"I'm still shocked your mom allowed you to go attend another church service without challenging your decision." Cindy replied.

"It's her dad, she's going to have to worry about. Specifically, when the judge finds out Jamal is an active member of your uncle's church. And the two of you have been sipping on that communion wine together. Toasting it up, like newlyweds as a happy couple in the house of the Lord" Kaneesha said.

"Wait a minute, early this morning around five o'clock we heard these loud knocks at the door. I mean someone was banging hard. I thought it was for my younger brother because he's been selling dope along with my cousin that lives directly across the street. With my parents travelling together, promoting their business, more now than before we have less supervision in the house. My older brother is in charge. Anyway, girl they kept on banging hard on the door, the dog kept on barking, and I kept in my bed. Do you know it was ICE. Girl, the Dominican couple reported them. Payback for those two young Puerto Ricans, squatting in their apartment and refusing to leave. My older brother didn't answer the door at first. He went to the peephole to see who it was and when he looked, the agents had their badge in the peephole. ICE agents, whom my brother thought was DEA agents commanded him to open the door. He didn't want my younger brother to be arrested so my older brother stalled why my younger brother climbed out of the window onto the fire escape. I don't know where he thought his skinny butt was going, if they were inside the building and at the door, I'm pretty sure they were watching, our windows

from their cars. My Brother took so long they almost broke down the door. I finally got out of my bed and opened the door hoping that it would calm the officers down slightly. When I opened the door, girl, the whole hallway was filled with officers who even had their guns drawn. Immediately the ICE agent threw the white paper into my face asking me does the two suspects in the pictures on the paper live here. Girl, when I saw that abusive Puerto Rican couple faces on that paper, I wanted to slam the door on the officer's face. I blasted that man for that error. Girl, I went all the way off this morning inside my apartment! All of them guns drawn in the officers' hands, terrifying us that early in the morning and you're saying to me that you are at the wrong apartment. I fussed so bad my brother had to literally carry me to the room so they wouldn't arrest me for assault. How could they? They were in search of illegal immigrants. They quickly went next door and broke the door down to find nobody home." Kaneesha shared.

"Wow girl how terrified you must have been when you saw those guns." Cindy responded.

"Yeah, that's simply awful and heartbreaking for that child because he's growing up in an unstable, hostile environment" Monica replied.

"Speaking of children what is your mom saying about your siblings Monica?" Cindy asked.

"I'm not sure. I'm still waiting for her to reply to my text messages" Monica responded. "What happened to our boring Economics teacher? Why she left out on the day that I needed her?" Monica inquired.

"Like I said to you in the note, I was on my way upstairs to the Economics Classroom and she stopped me on the staircase *explaining that the desk sergeant from the precinct contacted her about her husband. He was arrested in the post office. Lot of people were seriously injured and taken to hospitals throughout the city"* Cindy replied.

"Wow, this is a day of craziness!" Kaneesha quickly responded,

"More like madness!" Monica replied.

"That was messed up! She was high tailing out of here! I like her too. Her Jamaican accent thick though, but I love her teaching methods. I missed her teaching us on today." Cindy said.

"Your boo going to meet up with you after school, girl?" Monica asked.

"You know she is. I'm trying to get her to join the girls' basketball team at her high school, but she likes working with children. After my boo walks me over to my dance school, she volunteers at an after-school program." Kaneesha said.

"You want her to join that basketball team so you can attend those school games and see your competition if there are any" Monica loudly replied.

"You lucky she's not a student at an all-girls high school" Cindy loudly spoke as the three girls busted out in laughter. As Mr. Bowman went over the class schedule for the remainder of the year and the chorus performance dates, Monica checked her cell phone one last time.

"Did you ask Jamal to drive you to your sisters' school?" Kaneesha inquired.

"I'm going to text him now and ask. I must pick my brother up from his school as well. Mom, must be busy because she's not saying anything." Monica softly replied.

"Let me ask you this Monica, are you absent in school on today? Having that Economic substitute teacher, marking you present in class is one thing. But not showing up to homeroom earlier this morning is a serious problem. Once, Mr. Buendia didn't see your pretty face he marked you absent on his sheet. That's the check in class! That attendance sheet goes directly to the administration office girl. It may have been entered on the computer system already. If your mom called or decided to call the office, then what are we going to do, Monica?" Kaneesha quietly asked.

"Maybe that's the delay, in why there's no response from your mom. I wonder what the emergency is" Cindy said as Monica slightly turned her head towards Cindy and stared at her.

"You young ladies are doing a lot of talking over here while I'm talking. All of us can't be talking at the same time. You should be preserving your golden voices for the set list of holiday songs we're going to rehearse on today" Mr. Bowman loudly said as he stood directly in front of the girls. "Christmas is just weeks away and I'm not going to be embarrassed this holiday season because somebody in this class has lost their voice due to excessive talking or someone in this soprano section is unsure of the notes to a song because they didn't pay attention to me in class, due to excessive talking!" Mr. Bowman continued to loudly discuss. Making his way back to the front of the classroom, Monica's cell phone begins to vibrate. Quickly glancing down towards her stylish black jeans, pulling the phone out from her pants pocket, Monica saw that it was her father calling, trying to get in contact with her. Jumping up out of the seat, Monica dashed out of the classroom back into the fifth-floor hallway to answer her father's phone call.

"*Dad, what happened? I've been trying to call mom, but she's not responding*" Monica frantically said.

"Hi, Pumpkin Spice. Your mom is in the emergency room with Stephanie and probably Danielle. But listen, why were you late to class? What happened at home?" The judge loudly asked.

"Huh? Dad, what are you talking about?" Monica softly responded.

"*Pumpkin Spice, I don't have time for this! I'm still in session. What happened in my house that caused you to almost miss Economics, some thirty minutes ago?*" The Judge loudly inquired.

"*Wait, Dad, why is mom in the emergency room? She texts me to pick the kids up after school. I've been trying to find out why?*" Monica honestly replied.

"*You don't need a reason to do what your mother asks! You don't need a reason to help your parents out! That's your family and you will look out for every one of them. Even your brother. He will have dinner when he gets home that you have cooked! I suggest you save your energy up because you're going to need all of it later this afternoon into the evening*" the Judge angrily spoke.

"*Dad, that's why I was calling mom about the exact times their school's end. That way I'll know whose school to go to first*" Monica replied.

"*You do the Economics and figure that challenge out!*" The judge angrily spoke as he disconnected the phone call. Placing the cell phone back into her stylish black jeans pocket, Monica slowly turned herself around heading back towards the large musical classroom when she saw, Paul the six foot seven inches, white male school safety guard, leaning on the wall staring at her with his two-way radio in his hand.

"Oh, Paul, you startled me!" Monica shouted out, as she placed her right hand over her chest.

"I'm not even going to ask why you're in the hallway. From that cell phone that you just shoved into your pants pocket, Monica that's evident" Paul spoke, in a raspy tone as he remained still while leaning on the fifth-floor hallway wall with his arms folded and his two-way radio in his hand.

"I've done something upsetting today. My dad seems to be furious with me about it. I heard it in his tone over the phone." Monica honestly admitted.

"Hide out on the second floor with a group of students in the hallway, who barley knows you, last period instead of being in your assigned class. Is that it?" Paul quickly responded.

"Huh, Paul, what are you talking about?" Monica asked?

"Monica, how long have you been a student in this school? How many times have I explained to you that nothing goes down under my watch, that I'm not aware of. When you saw my partner Evelyn patrol past you, at that moment Monica, you knew I was aware of your unproductive conduct" Paul said in a loud tone as he remained still while leaning on the fifth-floor hallway wall with his arms folded and his two way-radio in his hand.

"She didn't see anything" Monica loudly replied as she waved her right hand in a bye gesture.

"I sure did. The fact that you were not in homeroom earlier this morning" Paul, the six foot seven inches, white school safety guard loudly replied. Mr. Bowman swung open the door, marched directly up to Monica, stopped and placed his hand on his hip.

"Monica, what has gotten into you today? Are you going to sing or what? You have the whole class in here waiting for you, while you are in the hallway having conversations! That's not fair to your soprano section" Mr. Bowman loudly spoke.

"I'm sorry sir," Monica replied as she hurried back into the classroom. Mr. Bowman followed, closing his classroom door shut behind him. *"Girl, this won't due! Not before Christmas. You've done let that Jamal bring you down"* Mr. Bowman loudly spoke. Monica stopped, slowly turned herself around and stared at Mr. Bowman directly into his eyes.

CHAPTER 8

THE CHURCH MOTHER'S TESTIMONY

The sound of pure tone beeps loudly rang through the busy New York City Street, as the large truck which was blocking traffic slowly backed up into the small dock. Elder Jackson who was on his way to noon day prayer service, at the church where he's the associate pastor, slowly approached the large vegetable and fruit store. Seeing his buddy Malcolm, one of the stores' employees, standing in the middle of the street trying his best to stop the heavy flow of New York City, oncoming traffic, while the large delivery truck continued to loudly sound its back up beeper, slowly rear ending into the store's busy dock, Elder Jackson stopped to speak.

"Hey Malcolm, don't get your skinny butt ran over today

as those cars attempt to sneak around or sneak past you, scrub with your non dribbling self" Elder Jackson loudly yelled.

"Good day Pastor can't play ball! Whether I'm on the basketball court waxing your no skills playing self or I'm here in the streets guarding our fresh produce, no one is going to get one up on me" Malcolm, the tall vegetable and fruit store employee loudly replied.

"Yeah, alright scrub, don't let your lips get you in trouble out here in these city streets. It's too early in the day for all that rubbish you are standing out in the street talking" Elder Jackson jokingly responded.

"I haven't never said anything I couldn't back up, Pastor air ball. Instead of you out in these streets envying championship ballers like me, you should be somewhere learning how to shoot with your no net having self" Malcolm quickly replied.

"I told you before scrub, you name the place and the time I'll be there at the court" Elder Jackson immediately responded.

"Like I said, get your money up before you come for me Reverend. This is a big deal you are speaking with preacher man. All net, all day, baby! I hope those offerings you weekly collect, will be able to cover this hoop you are challenging" Malcolm loudly replied as the large delivery truck finally bumped the stores dock.

"Like I said, don't get your skinny butt ran over by those angry city motorists you out here boldly, holding up for your produce" Elder Jackson sarcastically replied.

"Hey, speaking of courts, let your brother Judge Watkins know I really appreciate what he did for my nephew. He's a good kid. Just caught up with the wrong crowd. My wife and I

vowed to help my sister out by spending more time with him. I honestly must admit some of that is my fault Reverend. I've been in my nephew's life since he was born. I ran the streets with the knuckle head that impregnated my twin sister and jetted off years ago. A real let down for our friendship, at that time in what I thought we had. I almost caught a case myself hunting that bum down. So, I have been there literally since day one. Working long hours and doing side hustles on the weekends, I just haven't had the time for my family like I used to when my nephew was younger. With my wife, with her nursing career, we've just been trying to handle our own responsibilities. We slipped up on our nephew you know Rev." Malcolm, loudly explained as he slowly walked to the curb of the busy street where the Elder was standing. *"However, I thank you and your family for helping me and my family out man with the criminal court. That was a tremendous blessing Reverend"* Malcolm continued to say.

"You said it, a blessing. I praise God greatly every day for blessings. My sister Melonie and I pray together daily at different times of the day for even greater blessings. So, what manifested for your family from God is like you said, a great blessing. Your expression of God's Grace on today has given me another reason to Praise God even harder today than I may have planned to. After I leave from shopping here, I'll go over to my church's noonday prayer service and add a dance to my praise unto God. And Malcolm, don't blame yourself for anyone else's decision. No matter how young they are. We can only set examples Malcolm, and basically earnestly pray to God that our loved one's model what they have seen us display" Elder Jackson loudly and rhythmically responded.

"*Hey, I simply want to thank you today. Now when you are really, ready to play. Then grab your musky gear, sneakers, money and come my way*" Malcolm jokingly replied as the two of them bursting out in laughter, walked towards the busy vegetables and fruits grocery store.

"*They just used you to direct traffic. You don't have to unload the truck?*" Elder Jackson asked as they entered the vegetable and fruits grocery store.

"*Team works around here in these parts' preacher man. Seeing the way that you play basketball, I'm not sure if you know anything about that kind of work*" Malcolm replied as he stopped by the shopping carts.

"*Your mouth still running. The wildest thing is, there is still nothing coming out of it*" Elder Jackson spoke.

"*Hey, Reverend, I'm at work right here almost every day. So, when you want to play, Pastor you see the address on the store door, that means you know where I stay*" Malcolm said as he started backing up into the main aisle. An average height, Asian gentleman wearing a long white apron, quickly came up behind Malcolm and started yelling at him about the broken box of lettuce. As the two gentlemen loudly exchanged words back and forth Elder Jackson pulled out his cell phone to check his incoming messages. Seeing that his sister Melonie sent him an urgent text, Elder Jackson immediately went into his phone's contacts, looking for Jamal's contact information. Knowing Jamal's work schedule, he called asking him to stop by the church during the Noonday prayer service for a brief conversation. Disgusted and upset the average height, Asian man finally stopped arguing with Jamal and went back to the frozen section of the market.

"If you don't mind me asking Malcolm, what was that heated discussion about? He seemed agitated!" Elder Jackson loudly Inquired as he folded his arms.

"Our customer service representative had to leave early due to an emergency. She's more like the manager here. Reverend, that beautiful Mexican woman has been here the longest. She knows this store inside out. You see how large the store is? I think we're the largest vegetable and fruit store in Brooklyn. I may be wrong Elder, but I doubt I am. I sure haven't seen another large fresh produce market in this part of New York City yet. Not only do the customers like yourself, but many of the deliveries that come into this store are because of her connections. The manager upstairs that sits down on his butt all day doing nothing, wasn't prepared for her absence. Something awful happened to her husband downtown in Manhattan. He was in a physical altercation and was arrested not too long ago. She was terribly upset, because she relies on him to pick up her children from school and watch over her family when he comes home from work. Preacher man, I don't know all the details of her personal life, but I've seen the tribe come by this store time from time and that's a lot of mouths to feed.

So, she left the grocery store early crying about possible deportation and the office upstairs marching around the store angry about unorganized administration.

That's why I went outside to enjoy the cool New York City air, because these attitudes are way too hot up inside here. Way too much heated frustration"

Malcolm loudly rhythmically replied as he danced

off towards a stack of boxes in the fruit aisles. Elder Jackson burst out in laughter walking towards the fresh cabbage aisle. Looking for a few firm nice size heads of cabbage he stood next to a senior grey-haired woman that was standing next to her shopping cart looking for cabbage as well as fresh lettuce for her church's pantry.

"Halleluiah, God is worthy to be praised on today. Praise the Lord, Elder Jackson, how are you son?" The senior woman cheerfully asked.

"Good day mother, I'm blessed and highly favored and yourself" Elder Jackson loudly responded.

"Yes, you are. What a lovely family you have. God has sure favored each one of you" the senior woman cheerfully spoke.

"I'm sorry, Mother, I don't mean to be rude, but where do you know me from?" Elder Jackson inquired.

"Mind my manners son, I've been in service since five this morning. Our pastor had us in prayer at the start of the day. Your sister Melonie and her husband are one of our dedicated members." The senior woman apologetically replied.

"Okay, you know my sister. I was wondering how you knew me, mother. That's my heart right their mother" Elder Jackson quickly responded.

"She touches everybody's heart Elder. Everyone loves the Judge! And if you don't, you'd better learn how to. That young, educated man is a saint! You hear me, son? Your brother-in-law is a Saint! That law, abiding citizen Judge, is a blessing in your mother's household. I saw my daughter Melonie shouting and dancing all over the sanctuary in our newly renovated building earlier this morning. Your sister

makes coming to church pleasant. She has a lot to be thankful for Elder Jackson. Not only your promotion to Elder, but her beautiful well-fed children. And your sister has a handful to feed. That's a lot of little girls she got! Now I know! I have a few girls myself. I see her boys too. They look dapper and well nourished. They ought with that handsome thick Judge as their father. I see it all Elder. Now, who I haven't seen in my church lately is your niece, Monica. Can you tell me why that is Mr. Jackson?" The mother of the church softly asked.

"Sure, Mother, I'll be happy to tell you where my niece has been on Sundays lately. She's now a member of my pastor's church. It was her decision. I didn't influence her choice in any way. When Monica called me and alerted me that she would be worshipping with me on Sundays, I was elated." Elder Jackson explained as he slowly weighed the head of cabbage while they stood together in the grocery store aisle.

"MMM. You're elated, you say. Let me ask you sir, is her decision a lonely move or was it a choice to move next to that handsome boyfriend of hers, who drives that expensive new Acura." The Mother of the church softly asked as she stood in the aisle with her hand on her hip.

"Oh, Jamal! Yes, he's a fine young man. He's a very pleasant soul. A blessing to the church, which is what our pastor said" Elder Jackson quickly replied. "If you don't mind me asking mother, how do you know Jamal?" Elder Jackson politely asked.

"Son, I've been following my pastor since he started his church and was conducting worship services in his mother's living room. Lot of people liked his preaching style, because

he's very charismatic, somewhat like your beautiful sister Melonie publicly displays in her form of worship. But she only dances like me. Many people follow what they see. And listen son, I put it down. I might be limping in this aisle now, but that doesn't stop my feet from stepping, in the form of a dance, in our church aisle. I make no apologies for my praise breaks either. I can dance! I will dance and when the Spirit of the Lord is in the room, I will dance even harder. They may have liked his preaching style, but early in his foundational days, many were pessimistic about his pastoral skills. So, when I became a member of my pastors church many years ago in his single mother's apartment along with his two brothers and four sisters, I was dancing all over their living room floor. Honestly, I'm a living witness, it was all eight of us dancing. Including the four other ladies who lived right there inside his housing projects. Now Elder Jackson, I'm elated that on this morning we have a beautiful new building for me to dance in because of the Spirit of the Lord that I believe hovers over our spacious large prayer room. I don't forget. How can I forget. Why should I forget. I can't forget what the Pastor and his family has done for me and my babies. I was pregnant way back then with three mouths to feed and no husband, when I was cutting the floor in his mother's living room. Many days, scared, crying, upset and nervous about how I was going to feed all my babies with no husband to assist. Whether or not their fathers were in my babies' lives, that was my business. When I married my husband and had birthed my last set of children, your sister Melonie's, pastor was still there. When my oldest son shot and killed my husband in my living room because he was not his father, your sister Melonie's pastor remained there. Not only *for me but he stood there for my oldest son as they sentenced him to life in prison. When my precious beautiful baby girl, my youngest daughter who loved her father because she was the "apple of his eye", shot herself in attempt of suicide because she couldn't cope with the pain of losing her dad and is now paralyzed in a vegetable state, because of the bullet's entry into her body, my pastor is still her faithful visitor. But as for Jamal, Mr. Jackson as a seasoned widow mother, I never forget a face. Now all my other children are doing well, and I do have many. That's why I continue to give God much praise even in a dance. But my oldest granddaughter has suffered with drug addiction for years. She's still getting herself, together, but my baby girl is going to be okay. I promise you she will. That's why Mr. Jackson, I don't forget a face. Now my oldest son is not her father but when they locked my boy away, for the rest of his life, his girlfriend at the time remained under me like she was mine own. She loved my son. And my son had a gun because he didn't love himself the way his mother continually loves him. Got caught up in that life that was breaking my heart and my husband along with his girlfriend at the time tried their best to alert him of that fact. He was filled with too much rage to listen to anyone. I say this because those same drug dealers became his girlfriends' friends and protectors when my oldest son was sentenced to prison for the rest of his life. The same ones even introduced their product to her daughter. My only problem was that it wasn't weed she was smoking. I still consider her as my granddaughter, and all my children have assisted me in helping her fight that crack cocaine demon! In my bouts with fighting, I've come across even face to face with some of her, what I call "dope pushers" even though today they're listed as contacts. Jamal's face was one Mr. Jackson. My second oldest son came home from up north at the beginning of this year from completing his sentence in prison. Like my baby daughter who was emotional over the loss of her father, so was my second oldest son. He loved my husband because he witnessed his own father put his hands on me way too many times in my living room and that imagery never left his physic. He never seen my husband put his hands on me violently or aggressively in anyway. Not only tenderly did my husband handle me, but he handled him and his siblings with gentle love and care. That imagery will never leave his psychic. What angered him the most, Mr. Jackson, was that his own brother would violently take that type of love away from him inside of his own living room. After his own mama earnestly prayed and danced hard all over her pastors living room floor which he witnessed, and I pray even today that imagery will never leave his psychic. For such a wonderful handsome blessing from God that my late husband was unto us. We were not starving; we were no longer hungry and with the joint income that had accumulated we moved out of the housing projects that section eight had provided me with and into affordable housing. His anger towards his older brother and the loss of the man he loved as daddy, Mr. Jackson, fueled my second oldest son to commit criminal misconduct. That stuff landed him into the hands of the law and the white female judge gave him a heavy penalty for his criminal behavior. Now Elder Jackson I didn't lie unto you, all my children are doing well, even him because while he was in prison he went to college and graduated with degrees. He was working in prison and now a successful businessman working in corporate America, somewhere located in downtown*

Brooklyn. Halleluiah! My God is great and worthy to be praised! Now I'm going to let you go Elder Jackson, but my son came home earlier this year and was in my window while Jamal, Monica, my neighbor's sons Derrick and Dewayne were talking to one another standing around that new Acura. How do I know, because my son talks to me. Always have. That boy tells his mama everything! That's the reason I know how he was feeling internally during his arraignment. Looking out of my window he showed me Jamal and Dewayne by pointing them out as we both laid our bodies out of my apartment window watching them. My son told me that Dewayne had just come home roughly about six months ago from doing a bid along with him, and Jamal is one of his soldiers. What my son didn't know was that I knew who Monica was. Now she didn't see me and hasn't seen me, even though towards the midnight hours your niece has been hanging in front of my building with her very handsome new boyfriend Jamal. At times I get up throughout the night, pull up a chair to my upper floor window in the high-rise apartment where I live and monitor them. Listen, son, I consider your sister Melonie as a daughter to me. So, your niece is like family to me. And as an ordained Mother and one of the founding members of my church I must look out for our own. Even when your niece can't look out for herself. Now that day my son was going on and on in the apartment building window about one of his former cell mates, Dewayne, Jamal's face was much too familiar to me. Why? Because my granddaughter. I even remember the nasty words he used against me because he felt I blocked his sale. But he could kiss my old black butt. I'll fight for my babies, Elder Jackson! I have lost too much in this life near and dear to cow down to street bums like them. One night I went to my neighbor's house to ask her son Derrick if he could paint my apartment, and I'd pay him well for a good job. That is exactly what he did, a good job. That chubby dreadlock, always wearing navy blue young man is an excellent painter. As he was painting my apartment, I asked him about Jamal and Monica's relationship and why they were always hanging out in front of our apartment building here in Brooklyn. Derrick labeled her a rich girl; new rich booty Jamal was using for his brothers connect. "How do you think he got that new ride" Derrick said unto me. Like my son had done, they are probably about to steal. My slogan has always been, birds of a feather flock together. Elder Jackson if I was you, I'd watch your pockets before them tithes you plan to collect, come up missing" The church Mother clearly outlined unto him as she quickly picked up the fresh head of lettuce and placed it into her shopping cart.

"Mother thank you for the wonderful testimony of what God can do. I appreciate you today. I truly do. You have just confirmed my motive for contacting Jamal for a little discussion" Elder Jackson politely responded.

"Elder Jackson, Motives are an understatement in your case" the church Mother quickly replied as Elder Jackson stopped what he was doing in the narrow aisle and stared directly into her eyes.

111

CHAPTER 9

A SERGEANT REPORT

Arriving at the crowded Lenox Hill hospital emergency entrance, Mike, Freddy and Alonzo stood outside directly in front of the entrance door waiting for Stephanie to arrive. Mike kept his eyes on Alonzo who couldn't stop sending text messages on his cell phone to someone. Suspicious about the attention Alonzo was giving someone the whole taxi ride over to the hospital was skeptical. Alonzo is a young man of many words. That's why he's a candidate for a law degree. This sudden distraction coming from an anonymous person who he has not yet mentioned or shared was leaving an uneasy feeling even in Freddy's eye. Cutting his eyes at Alonzo Freddy leaned into Alonzo placing his arm on his shoulder.

"I can't believe Thanksgiving is here already. That seafood cuisine we had at Stephanie's runway ready penthouse a little

while ago has my taste buds open for my mama's stuffing and candy yams" Freddy loudly said. *"What about you Alonzo? You have plans for the holidays?"* Freddy asked.

"I'll be here for the holidays. Times Square is where I'm going to celebrate my New Year" Alonzo softly replied as he continued sending text messages on his cell phone. Mikes cell phone's ringer sounded, picking up the phone it was Danielle crossing the busy Manhattan, street letting them know they have arrived at the hospital.

"There they go. That wasn't a long wait. We all arrived about the same time. Isn't that right Alonzo?" Freddy asked as he started walking towards the girls. Together as the seven of them entered inside of the emergency room. Stephanie announced to the hospital security guard who she is and gave him the Sergeants' name that she was supposed to meet with, who spoke to her older brother, Gordon, earlier this morning on Ezra's cell phone. As the male heavy-set front desk hospital security guard, read Stephanies drivers license information over his two-way radio, Freddy walked off to the restrooms.

"He Is so dramatic. All in my business. He needs to find another breaking news story and get up out of mines" Alonzo spoke.

"Look who is on the defense! You just as bad as Stephanie when it comes to Aram the handsome doorman" Mike responded.

"You'll need to go somewhere with all that" Alonzo said.

"Oh, its serious like that. Okay I'm with Freddy honey, there's definantly an ally cat purr herself around our luxury high-rise tower at night" Mike said as another Hispanic

male hospital security guard walked over to the front desk, guiding them all through the hospital lobbies metal detectors, across a hallway and towards a locked door from on the outside, that leads into the emergency room unit. As Freddy quickly walked across the lobby towards the door where they were all standing the female Sergeant slowly walked over to them coming from the main entrance lobby. Melonie once again took out her ID wallet and quickly put it in the hands of the Sergeant as she approached them before she inquired about Stephanie.

"Thanks, Ms. Watkins, I see you. Which one of you ladies is Stephanie?" The baritone voice, New York Police Department Sergeant loudly asked as she handed Melonie back her black colored leather Identification wallet.

"I am mam, can you please explain to me in details what has happened to Ezra? I was just on the phone with him, right before he walked up to the post office counter. Now my brother Gordon calls me from his annual ski week located in his hometown in Colorado, some 1850 miles away to inform me that my little brother Ezra is in the ER. Sergeant, I simply don't understand why" Stephanie loudly replied.

"I understand your frustration and desire to get to the root of the matter. However, it may be a little more complicated than you are aware of. Officers did locate his wallet in his pants pocket for identification purposes after he passed out on the floor in the initial interview with my officers on the scene at the post office. According to the trained Emergency Medical Technicians that were present on the scene at the very busy post

office, after they were dispatched, your brother Ezra lost a lot of blood. Most likely he's going to need a blood transfusion. I'm not a doctor, so I can only speculate on that analysis. You can speak to the primary physician on the hospital Emergency Unit floor following this conversation. Due to the amount of blood your brother Ezra loss, He lost consciousness on the floor at the post office. He's in capable hands of the Emergency Unit doctors here at this hospital by my recommendation to the Emergency Medical Technicians earlier this morning, because he was unable to tell them where he wanted to be transported. My officers along with the Emergency Medical Technicians found his cell phone in his pocket when the ring went off. We did not answer it at first until there was a better understanding of what took place in the busy post office. So that last incoming call that your brother Ezra received on his cell phone was from a gentleman named Gordon, in which he informed me that he was Ezra's older brother and after he notified the family of this unfortunate tragic event, that you would be coming here to the Emergency room to meet with me Stephanie. Yes, you are correct. He was in the post office at the counter at the time of the incident that took place with several individuals. One of the arrested individuals that we do have in custody now as we are speaking, launched at certain people with a knife this morning in the post office during a fight between those individuals. It was told to me by many witnesses that your brother was trying to get out of the way when he was caught up amid the fight. Being a good Samaritan, that your brother probably presents himself as was trying to assist the attacker's wife in the middle of the fight as she was being strangled. The attacker, who is the woman's husband, stabbed Ezra severely in rage. Like I said

115

Stephanie, it was a fight between several individuals and the result left several individuals including your brother who were not part of the fight, in the hospital. I have another unconscious victim that is a senior woman of age. I have another woman who suffered a heart attack. There's another and another. It was a horrific event that should never have occurred. It is a tragedy today." The female Sergeant loudly explained.

"Oh, my God" Tiffany frantically shouted out! As she placed her hands over her mouth.

"Like I said Stephanie my officers did speak with him briefly before he lost consciousness. It was reported by one of my deputies on the scene that he kept on calling for you. Asking for your help. "Tell Steph to help me please" "Super Ez. Is in pain". So, I was somewhat relieved that your brother Gordon did clarify who that was and that you are here, granting his wishes" the female Sergeant clearly spoke.

"Oh, Ezra I'm sorry this happened to you" Stephanie shouted out as she burst into tears and cried in Mike's arms, as he stood there by the Emergency unit door embracing his neighbor.

"Officer, Ezra's cell phone can Stephanie have it please. His fiancé needs to be notified of his condition and where he's located. Stephanie doesn't have her contact number. The family figured Stephanie could get it from her brother's phone. And listening to what you have said that was probably her trying to call him before you spoke to his brother, Gordon" Melonie clearly spoke.

"That's not a problem Ms. Watkins, I can arrange for Stephanie to collect his wallet as well" the Sergeant replied. "What I will do is have the Nurse Practitioner come and *talk with you now concerning Ezra. If you don't see me, it's because I've been called to duty. Most likely it will be one of my deputies bringing you the items that you have requested. I will return shortly, to check on things here. Prayerfully it's better news. As I stated earlier, these doctors here at Lenox Hill hospital are efficient and Ezra is in capable hands. And when I return if Ezra is alert and able to talk, I'm going to try and get a statement from him of his recollection of the events that occurred earlier this morning at the post office"* the female Sergeant clearly explained in her baritone voice, as she picked up her two-way radio from off her police utility belt, to speak with her deputies while banging real hard on the solid door with her fist that opened to the emergency unit floor.

CHAPTER 10

WHERE I AM FROM

Jamal pulled his new Acura into the driveway of the recently renovated upper Manhattan Car Wash. A native of Spanish Harlem, Jamal grew up living in this neighborhood and is familiar with all its landmarks. As odd as it may sound this carwash is considered a city landmark. This flourishing business in the Spanish side of Harlem is a documented landmark. Not just the beautiful, designed graffiti painted murals of the musical legends that were born and raised in Harlem who are well renowned around the world, neatly plastered around its exterior walls. The establishment itself is a historical place. It's a Puerto Rican family-owned business who came to the United States and built their legacy in this side of the greater Harlem community. New York City, being the melting pot of immigrants of all nationalities from all over the world.

Different ethnic communities from all over the world are well represented throughout the five boroughs of New York City. The Bronx is not the only heavily dense population of Puerto Ricans but this side of Harlem, known as Spanish Harlem, houses a large population of Puerto Ricans. Why Jamal chose this Car Wash is because the current owner is his mother's cousin. He gets free exterior washes every time he drives his new Acura onto the belts of the car wash. Jamal chose to pay for extra interior detailing, exterior wax, rim and tire shine. Jamal always tips the wash attendants twenty dollars each for their job and service to his new vehicle. Getting out of his vehicle, Jamal played around with the wash attendants speaking Spanish along with them, laughing and joking about their work performance. Even though both of his parents are African American by ethnicity, his mother's stepfather was Puerto Rican and Jamal loved his grandfather though he died four months ago from a heart attack. Walking inside of the car wash store towards the cashier counter, Jamal stopped to grab a bottle Hawaiian scent Febreze.

"Hola, mi amor" the beautiful Spanish woman behind the counter loudly said.

"What up Jessica! What's good my luv?" Jamal loudly replied grabbing the crotch of his jeans adjusting himself, as he read the label on the Febreze bottle.

"You, mi amor. You the one with all the money" Jessica responded.

"Yeah, true that my luv. But money could be problematic!

Sometimes a real pain" Jamal loudly said as he approached the counter.

"What's wrong Papi. Why are you not yourself. I thought you were feeling better. You still think about your Papi Jamal?" Jessica softly asked.

"Every day my luv. I miss my grandfather so much. I wish he was still here with us. That's a pain that won't leave my body Jessica," Jamal loudly replied.

"I thought you and that beautiful Chica you've been driving around Harlem with was making you happy" Jessica softly responded as she exchanged money with another Spanish customer at the busy cash register.

"That's not it! That girl right there is my heart! That's my luv! She excites me in every possible way. Yo, Jess. that right there is nothing but beautiful. Folk just don't know what I'll do for her. She's rocking with the kid too. Now you know Monica's special. She got the right one. I try to tell Monica that too. I don't think I'm as expressive as I'm supposed to, but I try my best to show her how I'm feeling. It's hard Jess. You know I used to be a knucklehead. How I got my car between you and I, isn't a secret. But I'm not moving weight like that anymore. I just did what I had to do at that time. That's why I took the bull crap job in Monica's building. It's good money and it keeps my nose clean. Literally. I'm not with the powder game anymore. I stopped that! Been stopped! It's these cats out in Bushwick Brooklyn that I rock with from time to time on some other small hustle that's becoming my new headache. There connect who lives here in Harlem is becoming annoying. You feel me?" Jamal loudly said as he snatched up the bottle of Febreze from off the cashier register counter

once again grabbing the crotch of his jeans, adjusting himself.

"You need to watch yourself mi amor! Your Papi just die, months ago. You're not well yet for the streets. Your head is still messed up. If she loves you and shows love to you, then Jamal, focus your attention on her love. No more danger, mi amor. Only love you need now Jamal" Jessica spoke.

"What you think I'm out here trying to do Jess. I see her every day. I even take her away with me here to my block! My home! You feel me?" Jamal loudly replied.

"Away from what?" Jessica asked.

"She's money! You feel me? She's from money. Wealthy parents and wealthy neighbors, a building full of big money. Monica lives in that expensive luxury tower that I work in as one of the overnight parking attendants" Jamal quickly replied.

"Oh, mi amor, you're doing so good too. Let me tell you something, "you should never make your money where your make your honey". I know what I'm talking about. Jamal, I'm sure she's a nice young lady but you don't need that money pressure. You know what I say? You feel me? You don't need that girl's family to pressure you because you're not like them. I'm not saying to you not to be the girl's friend. But past friendship becomes trouble if you're not associated with her surroundings. Your Papi just die and you're obviously still not well. You don't need anything that will make you feel bad." Jessica explained as she continued exchanging monies with customers at the busy cash register inside the car wash store.

"My luv, I hear you clearly. I just need to disconnect with

this dude around here. Then I'll feel better. Monica doesn't know anything about the few large quantity crack cocaine, runs I did to Miami and back that got my money up. I stacked my thirty thousand dollars for my new whip" Jamal said.

"If I was you, I would keep it that way. Why are you even here in my workplace talking about it?" Jessica softly mentioned.

"I'm tired. Little to no sleep my luv. That's all. I worked overnight, I was with Monica all morning, now one of the pastors from my new church is texting me that he needs to see me today. I must drive all the way back to Brooklyn to meet with him at the church. I'm tired, Jessica, that's all. I enjoy the church services. A friend of mine invited me shortly after my grandfather passed away. I think the message God is sending to me is working." Jamal loudly spoke as he reached into his pants to pull out his wallet.

"Oh, that's great! I didn't know you were going to church. That's wonderful Jamal. Does she go along with you?" Jessica loudly asked.

"Yes, that's her uncle that was texting me not to long ago. He's one of the Elders of the church. Monica loves her uncle very much" Jamal cheerfully responded. Jessica stopped what she was doing at the cash register and stared directly into Jamals eyes.

CHAPTER 11

A LOVE AFFAIR

As Stephanie and Tiffany walked through the door of the emergency room unit floor with the female Sergeant, Melonie, Danielle, Mike, Freddy and Alonzo went to find a seat in the small waiting area outside of the Emergency unit. Taking a seat Freddy crossed his legs and stared at Alonzo who was still texting someone on his phone.

"That must be some court case you are discussing with someone. Because your eyes been glued to your phone baby girl since we left Aram outside about to fight that delivery worker" Freddy loudly said as he uncrossed his legs and leaned back in the hospital waiting area chair. Melonie got up, turned around and kneeled in front of her seat to pray.

"Mind yours Freddy. Don't you see prayer is in session." Alonzo quickly replied.

"That's beautiful what Melonie is publicly doing right

now. We all need it. That Lady cop just dropped a heavy one on all of us. One thing I always gave the Islamic faith applauds and credit in doing is praying. When it's prayer time for them no matter where they're at. They will roll those mats out, kneel and pray even in public. I was at the airport earlier this year in January on my way to Salt Lake City, Utah and in the lobby at LaGuardia airport this whole family rolled their mats out and started praying. What Melonie is doing right now is beautiful honey." Mike said putting his hand on Danielle's knee.

"You should have never mentioned that stuff about her oldest daughter Monica and Jamal in front of all of us. She's not happy about that. I saw the expression on Melonie's face when you shared it. And I know that's going to be an issue when we leave this hospital." Danielle whispered to Mike.

"How did we go from talking about assuming the posture of prayer to what I discussed earlier in Stephanies penthouse apartment." Mike quickly responded.

"That's why she's on her knees even now Mike" Danielle softly whispered.

"Danielle I was just talking about the beautiful way people pray in public. Like what I saw in the airport on my way to the ski trip in Utah. Not only did the plane land safely. But there were no injuries on the ski slopes, and I had a wonderful birthday week in Salt Lake City." Mike replied.

"Girl, how did you know his name was Jamal?" Freddy asked.

"Zack mentioned his name to me when I ran into him earlier by the elevator" Danielle replied. *"From what I'm hearing Jamal's a sweetheart. Pleasant, polite and always*

wiping down his new car with a rag in our parking garage. Now what Chong told me in my apartment before we left the building to come here to the hospital is some breaking news." Danielle continued to share.

"Girl, you, penthouse divas always got some hot tea flaming! It just doesn't stop with you'll!" Freddy dramatically said as he laid across two chairs in the hospital's small waiting area kicking his feet in the air.

"I asked Chong what I have been missing around the building at night besides Melonie's daughter keeping company with our overnight parking personnel. He shared with me of Aram's wonderings. Not just with the model you mentioned earlier. The model on my floor whose apartment Zack was creeping from when I bumped into him earlier" Danielle quietly shared.

"Oh, the tall handsome hottie who's always traveling overseas to ski. Like he can't ski here upstate New York. We have slopes. And if he wants the feeling of getting out of the USA, Montreal Quebec is right here! Canada is day's drive away; they have plenty of snowy mountains for him glide on" Freddy loudly said as he sat up in the waiting area chair. *"But he's happily married"* Freddy continued to say.

"Well, you thought he was happily married" Mike clearly spoke.

"He's married and he's happy Mike!" Alonzo loudly said as he lifted his head from texting on his cellphone.

"Look who's still on the defensive end. Girl, you are angrily defending everybody today. I don't know what's ruffling your little briefs Mr. future lawyer. But something is on your mind baby boy" Freddy loudly said to Alonzo,

as Melonie Got up from praying on her knees by the waiting area chair.

"Amen! Melonie, thank you for the prayers" Mike loudly said.

"Amen, girl, we sure do need that right about now" Danielle said.

"So, what happens at night Alonzo on Danielles east wing floor" Melonie loudly said as she sat in the chair.

"Oh, mother superior has ears honey, you better share and put it all out in the air" Freddy spoke.

"Brian and I have been seeing each other for quite some time now. I didn't mention it because he's bashful. He keeps his business to himself" Alonzo said.

"Down low, he's on the down low is that what you meant to say" Mike spoke.

"More like low down, from what Chong said to me Alonzo. Zack and Brian are going to the ski resort in Aspen next month." Danielle said.

"Girl bye! He is not low down. They are friends. The model and I are friends. Aram and the model are friends. Zack and I are friends. But Brian and I are lovers. Aram knows that much and like me we both keep that quiet. Since we never enter or exit the building together or have been seen as a couple it's not a discussion" Alonzo spoke.

"Are you'll having an orgy" Freddy loudly asked.

"Something like that" Alonzo quickly replied. *"We all have some things in common. We all like to ski. The attraction is on ten. Every now and then, we all get it in."* Alonzo replied.

"Well, who's getting into who" Danielle asked.

"No Dee Dee. Whose Aram getting it into? You Alonzo? Freddy asked.

"Brian and I are happily getting it into each other" Alonzo replied.

"Haha! Girl, that's a good answer. You go boy!" Melonie loudly said as she burst into laughter. *"Danielle, girl you listening to Chong, he's messy! He's nothing but trouble with them loose lips of his. That's why he stays patrolling the building all day with that two-way radio in his hands, to collect all the tenant's garbage. And spread it!"* Melonie continued to loudly say as she burst into laughter. *"Doesn't that man wife go to one of Stephanie's yoga classes? That's the real reason why Alonzo kept that one on the hush from us. All you must do is ask Steph. They all friends."* Melonie continued to say as she burst out in laughter. *"Yes, Freddy you are correct. Mother Superior hears everything. Danielle why was Chong inside of your apartment today if you don't mind me asking"* Melonie inquired.

"I'm shocked!" Mike said. *"Though I saw the chemistry in the lobby earlier between you and Aram. I'm still at awe"* Mike continued to say to Alonzo.

"I'm not! Listen Melonie, I was so upset with Chong girl, when I saw him in the walkway this morning on my way back over to the east wing, I let him have it! Do you know I waited all day for him to come and no one showed up for the leak in my bathroom. Melonie, the water was all over the place. I was furious. Nobody showed up after I kept calling downstairs to the front desk. On today after he gave me some crappy excuse why but the problem was resolved, he came to inspect and make sure there wasn't anything else." Danielle explained.

"After the incident!" Melonie loudly said

"Days after, girl!" Danielle replied.

"That doesn't make any sense. Child I would have been fused him out. How's the apartment any water damage?" Freddy asked

"No, because I was up all night into the next day moping up water even though it ran out of the bathroom." Danielle replied.

"Child you would have to pry my lips off him. Chong knows he was dead wrong for that one! I would still be fussing his flat butt out" Freddy spoke.

"All that money we pay for rent living in that luxury tower. He has you in your apartment soaking up water like a porter. No girl I'm with Freddy, somebody would have had to answer for that one" Alonzo said.

"That's why I was totally disappointed with him on today. And I told him to his face." Danielle loudly spoke.

"I know this may not be the appropriate time for us to be having this discussion, but what's been going on with the plumbing in the building lately. Why all the leaks. It's not the first time I've had this conversation with a neighbor lately." Melonie said. *"You're absolutely correct, Alonzo as popular in New York City as our apartment building is, we should not be having these issues."* Melonie clearly said.

"This didn't just start. It's been happening for a while. Earlier this year when I returned to New York from my ski trip in Three Valleys, France, in which I had wonderful time, and I will be visiting there again soon. Arriving at my apartment,

I cut on the hallway light close to the bathroom and there was water on my floor. I checked the toilet to see if there was a leak. Mind you I've been gone for a whole week. So, the water had to start leaking for an hour or two before I arrived. After I flushed the toilet, no water. I looked by the walls, no water. After I used the toilet, walked over to the sink and turned on the water to wash my hands, the water just poured onto the floor. Girl, I hollered! I called Chong, he never came. I called the front desk no one came. I went the entire weekend without utilizing my bathroom sink because the pipe under the drain was leaking. On Monday morning around the same time we left today someone knocked on my door. I had such an attitude I don't even remember the boy's name." Freddy explained.

"Girl, it was similar with me last week. The hot water in the bathtub wouldn't cut off. Now I have three little ones. My children are young. So that was a serious problem for me. I don't need to spend extra time in the hospital emergency burn unit because one of my kids accidentally decided to go into the bathroom and stick their hands in the tub full of water. Or stick any of their fingers underneath the running hot water. I called and called no one came. I called out from work, and you'll already know that was a major problem. We had a foreign Ambassador on the premises of the United Nations that I had to meet with that day. Meeting with them from my living room was an insult to my division. My husband telephoned Chong when he arrived home that evening. Around ten thirty at night someone came to change the washer in the bathtub faucet. I didn't have anything to say to anyone because I was upset. My husband handled them" Melonie loudly explained.

"Yeah, if you go to Jimmy about the problem Chong gets

mad with you. If you go to Chong and the problem is still not resolved, then Jimmy gets mad with you. That's been our issue with the maintenance staff at the luxury tower." Alonzo spoke.

"I wonder if that's what's going on in Bradley's penthouse apartment. Before you came, he knocked on Stephanie's door without any shoes on, to ask if she had experienced any washing machine difficulties. I know his neurotic behavior has annoyed her but that might be something there concerning his plumbing." Melonie said

"Perhaps. However, I'm still shocked at you Alonzo laying down pipe with Aram" Mike spoke as the deputy carrying a phone and wallet walked towards the hospital Emergency unit door. As the door opened Tiffany exit the unit along with the female Sergeant. Taking the cell phone and wallet from the deputy's hands, Tiffany quickly ran outside of the hospital to make a phone call to Ezra's fiancé.

"Ms. Watkins, Stephanie would like to see you in the emergency room, mam" the female Sergeant spoke in a baritone voice. Melonie quickly arose from the small waiting area chair and walked to the door. Entering the emergency unit, it was extremely busy with nurses, practitioners, nursing assistants, Emergency Medical Technicians pushing gurneys and medical personnel walking in all different directions. The Sergeant escorted Melonie down the hall pass workstations on the left and right. They walked past sick patients who needed medical attention on the left and the right. Going through another door into a small hallway and

through another door there was a small unit with six glass door rooms. It was the intensive care unit. Stephanie was seated in a chair next to a hospital social worker. Melonie immediately ran over to Stephanie and sat next to her. The female Sergeant left the ladies in the unit and walked back towards the Emergency unit floor.

"I saw Tiffany take a cellphone and another large item from a deputy out in the waiting area before the Sergeant asked me to come here to see you" Melonie softly said.

"I asked her to contact Ezra's fiancé. Also, for her to call my brother Gordon and let him know everything. See if he spoke to my parents. The reception is horrible back here. I have little to no signal. My hands are even shaking Melonie, I feel so bad right now. I feel helpless. I need to do something for Ezra, but I don't know what it is I need to do for him Melonie" Stephanie nervously shared.

"It's okay to have these feelings. They are normal. That's your younger brother and even as adults you still want to protect him. That's an okay feeling to have Stephanie." The African American hospital social worker softly said.

"The reception isn't better in the lobby area either. I checked my phone several times, but I don't have a signal at all. I texted Monica earlier before we left the apartment building for her to pick up the younger ones at their schools since originally it was my day. The nanny has the day off when I'm off from work. However, Ms. Monica wasn't at school today. Thanks to Mike sharing with us earlier at your house, I know who she's with. My husband texted me while we were on our way to the hospital that he spoke with Monica and told her to also make *dinner for everyone tonight. Like I said, my signal has been lost since we entered the hospital building, so I'll deal with her little nasty butt when I see her at home."* Melonie softly spoke.

"Wow, Melonie. How did you know she wasn't in school today?" Stephanie softly asked.

"I'm a United Nations leadership staff member. You know I always have eyes on my child. She chose to attend that particular New York City public high school, her senior year in junior high school. I admit, my husband and I gave her free reign. Everyone in my field of work has their children enrolled in private schools. Because of her parents' professional status, my daughter Monica always has eyes on her" Melonie clearly replied. Stephanie wiped the tears off her cheeks, feeling sadness from the pain her brother Ezra experienced today, crossing her leg and turning her head slightly she stared Monica directly in her eyes.

CHAPTER 12

THE BUILDING WORKERS

As Phillip the senior staff porter wiped down the large marble columns in the towers main entrance lobby, Chong the handyman supervisor stepped off the upper floor elevators along with one of the newer male tenants. He and his wife moved into the luxury tower in April along with their pet dog a large German Shephard. They really didn't socialize much with any of the tenants, they only spoke to the building staff. In the evening sometimes, you would see the wife standing at the front desk speaking Russian with the female Russian concierge. The husband always publicly talked with the Super and his wife for long periods of time. Making their way into the lobby Chong stopped near Philips commercial janitorial cleaning cart to take a call on his cell phone. The male tenant stopped at the front desk to speak with Max and Marisol about his laundry service. Disconnecting from the phone call Chong took his two-way radio out of his vest pocket and commanded another porter to meet him downstairs in the lobby.

"Making new friends Chong. I see you trying to get that extra Christmas money in your stockings this year." Phillip, the senior staff porter loudly spoke.

"I don't have time for your nonsense on today. Busy, very busy. Lot of work lots and lots of work" Chong replied as he checked his cell phone again for recent text messages.

"Nothing I say in nonsense. Lot of sense I have buddy. Been in this world longer than your mumbling butt, has been wearing diapers. I know you trying to get that extra president into your lace stockings this year from the new mutes on the block" Phillip continued to say.

"Wipe my hallway good. That's all you need to be focused on. More work, less talk and maybe then jobs can be completed downstairs instead of me every day having to find someone to finish only what you start" Chong loudly replied.

"The day I don't finish my job buddy is the day I retire. I was a handyman long before you knew how to spell the word English, Mr. butt kisser." Phillip, the senior staff porter loudly spoke.

"That's why Jimmy put me in charge of all the handyman work because your senile self couldn't handle the job. I was asked to come to this building and clean up the mess you started" Chong loudly replied as he walked towards the front desk to speak with the porter he commanded to the lobby.

"You can walk away and perpetrate like you're important. My Christmas card is still going to be filled with important

presidents this year buddy" Phillip loudly shouted as he continued wiping down the large columns in the luxury tower lobby.

"You gentlemen cat fighting over holiday gifts from the tenants this year" The tall muscular African American security guard said in a bass tone as he stood posted directly across from Aram by the huge Brass glass front entrance lobby doors.

"Chong knows what time it is my brother. He isn't a fool. That's why he took off running over to the front desk a second ago. He knows I'm the man in here," Phillip loudly said to the tall muscular African American security guard that was posted in the luxury towers lobby. Since the incident earlier this morning outside directly in front of the luxury apartment tower, the Super along with the building's security supervisor tightened up security on the building's premises. Reinforcing the buildings rules and making sure none of the delivery persons violate the buildings doorman. As a result of the altercation outside of the building this morning, people were arrested and bruised because of the brawl. The Italian Super kept an eye on everything that took place in the luxury tower, being the person who oversaw its twenty-four-hour operation. Acquainted with all the tenants, he and his wife always publicly displayed a high degree of hospitality. The commander of the security guard staff was a retired detective of the New York Police Department. His two assistants in charge were ex-military soldiers in the Army and the other assistant is a Marine. Lot of the security guards were either ex-military or had some affiliation

with the gangs in New York City. The security guards were employees of a contracted agency with the Luxury Tower's management. The third person in command that was basically in charge of the guards while they were on post, was a white man who always wore a trench coat and drove around on the building's grounds in the Luxury tower's owned security vehicle. He had neither military nor police background history on his resume but was good friends with the Super and his wife. Jimmy was the Supers eyes and ears. After the mornings incident in front of the building, everyone witnessed that he's the Supers hands and fist too. Jimmy oversaw all the operations day and night in the building. Jimmy didn't socialize with the tenants as much as his workers liked to do. Many said that the white man with the trench coat who stayed in the security vehicle was hired by Jimmy.

"With the holiday season fast approaching, many of the kids are going to be home from school in the coming days so we must be prepared" the Super said as he entered the lobby walking towards the huge brass doors.

"Yes sir, let me get this door for you" Aram loudly shouted opening the door for the Super as he walked outside to smoke his cigarette. The new tenant quickly followed him out the door joining him in a private conversation. Jimmy entered the lobby walked towards the door but stopped before proceeding to the door then quickly turned around and walked to the Luxury apartment buildings front desk to talk with Chong, Max, Marisol and the other porter.

As Aram closed the lobby huge brass doors, he took off his doorman cap to wipe the sweat from his forehead.

"They have you working a double again on today?" Aram loudly asked the tall muscular African American security guard.

"No, the boss called me soon as you started arguing with that Mexican cat Aram. I know because his words to me were "Shawn what are you doing? I need you here stationed in the lobby right now! Something is going down in my lobby cameras that I don't like. I need you here right now! Take a taxi. There's about to be a major problem in the lobby! I'm watching it in the cameras as I speak." We've already discussed the situation with the disrespect of the building workers with these delivery persons in our meetings, so I already knew the deal. They'll probably pay me from eleven to seven. I wouldn't be surprised if the boss himself stays on the premises after seven this evening" Shawn the tall muscular African American security guard replied in a bass tone.

"That's what's up! My man got my back all day!" Aram loudly replied as he placed his cap back on his head. *"I like that, I like that! We must look out for one another. That was crazy what took place earlier. That fight should never have happened. Why can't you follow simple instructions. We're not bad people. It's the buildings' rules. It's here for everyone's safety. Not just the tenants. The delivery person's safety too is important. If something happens to them in this building it can be a big problem. Now people have scrapes, bruises and are in handcuffs in jail. Why? Because you don't want to listen to*

me. I'm not a bad person. That is why I'm the day doorman. I love everyone" Aram loudly said.

"Lover boy talking about his main event that took place earlier" Phillip said as wiped his rag around the huge brass door frame in the lobby.

"Better conversation than you and Bruce Leeroy who's standing over their talking with Jimmy. Both of you cat fighting in the lobby over tips in Christmas cards the building staff will receive from the tenants in a few weeks." Shawn the tall muscular African American security guard replied in a bass tone.

"I get all the love around here. I'm a good guy. I love everyone" Aram repeatedly said in a loud tone.

"More like makes love to everyone around here" Phillip the senior staff porter quickly replied as Shawn grabbed the crotch of his black slacks holding himself and busted out in laughter.

"Hey, don't hate on me because the female tenants here find me irresistible" Aram loudly replied.

"The male tenants too" Phillip loudly responded as Shawn still grabbing the crotch of his black slack holding himself continued in laughter.

"I wonder what them two outside talking about" Phillip spoke as he continued wiping the frame of the huge brass door.

"No, he doesn't speak to any of us here. That guy is very secretive. He only talks to bossman" Aram loudly spoke.

"I don't care who he speaks with. I'm curious what that conversation is about" Phillip quickly replied as he continued wiping the brass door with the rag.

"Why I'm really posted in the lobby. That's the topic of their discussion. What Aram said was correct. To add to that, we do have a lot of very important people that live on these premises besides Aram's sneaky freaky housemates he plays touch and feel with all night. You have the NBA player that moved in alongside the Judge and his family, also the television host and his quiet cocaine parties. You have the retired Rock and Roll singer and her family" Shawn honestly replied. *"Don't say anything Phil, they're going to terminate one of the evening security guards on today"* Shawn continued to say.

"Don't say anything Shawn I heard there have been a few mystery burglaries in our building" Phillip replied. *"One tenant even reported that not only is their most expensive jewel missing but they could tell someone had slept in their bed while they were out of town. Whoever it was left the hot water faucet in the bathroom turned slightly on. That same tenant said they could remember a cigarette bud in their garbage can they saw one night when they returned home from work before they left for the vacation"* Phillip continued sharing.

"I forgot who I was speaking with! The top man in the building. Forgive me Phil, I slipped up big time" Shawn jokingly said.

"Why are they going to wait until this evening? Why not terminate the jerk now!" Aram inquired as he turned to the huge brass door for the tenant that stepped out of a taxi.

"Your fiasco earlier here on the building premises Aram which drew the New York Police Department. Now we need all, hands-on deck to deescalate the hostile environment. Make the tenants aware that they are safe living here. Because my coworker, whoever they are, is going to jail which will require more police presence." Shawn the tall muscular African American security guard replied in a bass tone as Aram opened the huge brass lobby door for the tenant that stepped out of the taxi.

"Good day gentleman" Bradley loudly said entering the lobby's door.

"Good day sir" Shawn quickly replied as Phillip stared at Shawn with the rag in his hand.

CHAPTER 13

HOSPITAL CARE

As Tiffany entered the small Intensive Care Unit inside Lenox Hill Hospital, holding Ezra's cell phone and wallet, one of the Doctors slowly walked over to Stephanie to give her an update on her younger brother's condition while Melonie remained seated next to her.

"I know you saw that Ezra is heavily sedated. He's resting and probably will be in and out of sleep for the remainder of the day" the young doctor loudly spoke. *"He's going to be admitted"* the young doctor continued to say. *"We will notify the Sergeant when Ezra wakes to speak with her team. As the Sergeant has given instructions for my medical team to do. The subscapular pain he was experiencing upon the arrival of the New York Police Department at the post office as he lay on the floor was due to the penetration of the blade. Now I'm not sure if the Sergeant mentioned this to*

you concerning the blood and the assumptions of her deputies. Their observation of Ezra closing his eyes before the Emergency Medical Technicians arrived to examine and treat him, at the time they felt it was due to the amount of blood they witnessed around the wound as he lay on the post office floor. While the medical staff was moving Ezra from the stretcher onto the examination table here inside of the emergency unit, he woke up. That's a sign he was not comatose, Ezra responded to stimuli and his response to the impact of the initial attack is what blackened him out. His pressure levels are way too high so we're working on that now to get his blood pressure down. Intravenously we're administering him medication along with the pain medication he has already received. Now there was a significant amount of blood lost but he's stable. As for any surgeries, I'm waiting for another specialist to arrive to look at the results of the Magnetic Resonance Imaging that we have already taken. Our biggest concern now is getting his pressure levels down because they are extremely high before we proceed with any other medical treatment. It can be several factors that's causing high blood pressure, stress, anxiety, the fear of not knowing and I'm pretty sure your presence will be helpful in aiding Ezra at this time. I was notified by the New York Police Department deputies that it was your name he was calling on for help. Anything that can help bring his pressure levels down is very much appreciated. Along with the specialist I have another team that will be coming down shortly to review the information that we gathered and together we will find the best treatment for your brother. I'm going now to speak with the trauma unit, so I'll get back with you Stephanie in a little while" the doctor clearly explained.

"Thank you, Doctor, Oh God my brother" Stephanie *nervously shouted out!* *"He just came back home from a beautiful ski trip in Switzerland and now he is in so much pain. My little brother doesn't deserve this torture from anyone"* Stephanie shouted out as the doctor slowly walked away to speak with the registered nurse in the ICU Unit.

"Gordon is on his way to New York Steph. He already has a flight coming from Colorado and is on his way to the airport. He told me "For you to hang on tight we're on our way." He said, "Your parents are on their way here to New York City from Salt Lake City as well" I haven't spoken to either one of them so I'm not sure of their status Steph." Tiffany softly shared.

"That's great, Ezra needs the support from his family today and you need the love of your parents" Melonie spoke.

"Wait there's more you're going to love this one Steph. Gordon also said "your sisters are coming too" Tiffany spoke.

"Oh, are they?" Stephanie quickly replied.

"Nice, I haven't met them yet. This visit will be loving." Melonie responded.

"This visit will be interesting. Like you said Ezra needs his family, that's sweet. All of us together, that's something" Stephanie replied.

"Steph, you said you need a man in your house now you have two, that you're even familiar with" Melonie responded.

"It's the two cowboys that's going to accompany my twin sisters from Wyoming to New York City. That's the something I'm referring to" Stephanie replied as she stared at Melonie directly in her eyes.

"Yeehaw! They are bringing the saddles to the penthouse" Tiffany said.

"I'm going to need flight information, so I can make sure I'm home to let everyone in" Stephanie replied.

"That's different flights, different times most likely different airports Steph. I'll help you gather that information. Maybe Danielle and I can pick someone up, roughly your parents from the airport when they arrive" Tiffany suggested.

"You can always call the building Steph. Have the front desk notify security of their arrival. They have the master key. Security can always let them in with permission. I have little ones, so I know how effectively that system works. Monica has misplaced her keys often and she spoke to the concierge who requested the security guard staff to open my apartment door. Last week my oldest son left his keys on the kitchen table and security let him into my house after school. When Tiffany receives everybody's flight arrival times then you can relay that message to the concierge, and they will get the security guards to allow your family access to your penthouse at the times they arrive. You sign for it at the concierge when you come home" Melonie spoke.

"Yeehaw, the, boys are bringing the saddles to the penthouse. Freddy is going to love this wild wild west ride, high up in the New York City sky. Wait until you tell him who's coming to Ezra's bedside. This might turn out to be one of the wildest Thanksgivings we've had yet" Tiffany said as Stephanie stared into her eyes.

CHAPTER 14

CAUGHT IN THE ACT

As Elder Jackson walked up the busy block in Brooklyn towards the church building, Helen, the arts and craft lady, stopped to speak with him as she exited the famous Brooklyn Caribbean restaurant. Helen, who was a former member of the church that Elder Jackson now holds a leadership position, is internationally known for her decorative clergy robes and designer fabrics. Her art classes have won numerous awards and many celebrities who live in the city attend her classes. Elder Jackson assisted Helen in hosting her first art workshop which was held at the church years ago. The art workshop gave her the notoriety and clientele that she needed.

"Hey Elder, I know God is real. I was talking your name all day" Helen loudly spoke.

"Good afternoon, Helen, it's good to see you out on the block today" Elder Jackson replied.

"I heard your niece Monica, is a member of the church now. That's a blessing. Her father going kick your butt you are being messy Uncle Jackson" Helen said as she burst out in laughter.

"That was her decision not mine.

Welcome back to the Fold, Helen.

Are you ready to get yourself back in line

You are coming inside for prayer today.

I know that your dark closet needs a lot of intercession so let's pray.

Are you coming inside of the church to rejoin the Fold?

Are you coming to pay, your tithes, for all of them items your business have sold"

Elder Jackson rhythmically responded.

"Lord Jackson, the judge doesn't play them games about his family. I told you a long time ago you are messing with fire. Too much loving and kissing going on in that building stairways that you love to call a house of God. Now you have your own family members all caught up in the mix of that staircase sexcapade. When the Judge finds out about that boy in them pews, sexing his little angel. Your sister's big fat husband going to kick your dirty black butt all up and down this street" Helen loudly said as she burst in laughter. "And I'm going to stand right here modeling my latest creation and watch the judge slap you up with his fat hands, you dirty priest" Helen shouted as she slowly walked away.

"Whenever you ready to get yourself right Helen, you know where we are" Elder Jackson shouted as Helen continued walking down the street in laughter, pointing her right index finger high up in the air.

Turning himself around towards the church steps, Elder Jackson noticed a black Audi with light-tinted windows parked close to the church. Familiar with the church membership and their cars, Elder Jackson knew that the car didn't belong to any of the church members. He has seen this Audi parked here in that same spot numerous times. Since the church had experienced a break in two months ago, the pastor wanted to keep a good watch over his church building. Some of the members that live within blocks of the church throughout the day circle the perimeter of the church monitoring the building. Keeping an eye out for any suspicious activity. Two of the founding members who have a law enforcement background have copies of the keys to the church locks and doors within the building. One of the associate pastors has the church security camera system connected inside of his own apartment even though he lives on the other side of Brooklyn. With the Evangelist team and the missionaries getting together every other week to hold noon day prayer services, it helps the leadership of the church like Elder Jackson also keep a good physical eye of all the activity surrounding the church buildings perimeter. Today the choir is also having a noonday rehearsal as well to prepare for their Thanksgiving week concerts. The new choir director purposely called for the rehearsal at this time of the day. Being one of the senior officers on board of the church's security staff as well as being the new choir director, he wanted to keep his eye on things inside the large church building. Observing the Audi's license plate number committing it to his memory, Elder Jackson walked quickly to the steps that led up to the front doors of the church building. Entering through the church doors he could hear the church members praying to his right in the sanctuary. Quickly glancing to his left, Elder Jackson saw the broom and dustpan up against the wall in the corner. The strong scent of bleach and pine sol took over the hairs in his nostrils. Taking out his keys, Elder Jackson immediately walked over to a room directly in front of him that was labeled TRUST on the black painted door. Opening the door, he checked the carpet in the dark room when he hit the light switch to see if it had been vacuumed. Turning the lights off Elder Jackson checked his cell phone to see if Jamal had texted him a message of his status to the church building. Closing the door, Elder Jackson heard squeaking from inside of the room. As Elder Jackson locked the room door he walked towards the staircase.

"Everything O.k. Elder" the tall man said in a baritone voice stepping out of the large glass office near the lobby of the church building.

"Good afternoon, Willy. Yeah, I'm fine" Elder Jackson loudly replied.

"No choir members have arrived as of yet sir" Willy replied. *"As you can hear the saints are all here already in prayer"* Willy continued to report being the hired church daytime security guard.

"When the choir director arrives, I need to see him Willy" Elder Jackson sternly said. *"Let me ask you Willy, have you purchased a new car recently?"* Elder Jackson asked.

"No, my wife drives our car. She brings and picks me up from here when I leave sir" Willy loudly replied as Elder Jackson walked away towards the staircase to head downstairs to the kitchen area. Entering the very large dining room area Elder Jackson didn't turn on the light switch. Quietly he tipped himself around the walls of the very large dining room as he listened for a sound. Quietly walking to the back staircase Elder Jackson slowly moved towards the back staircase door. Gently turning the doorknob to slowly pull the door open, Elder Jackson didn't want the building's old emergency exit door to make any loud sounds. Pulling on the door Elder Jackson suddenly cracked open. Listening carefully, he could hear sounds of female moaning coming from inside of the staircase. Quietly easing himself through the cracked door Elder Jackson tipped himself onto the stairwell to quietly see what was taking place inside his church's building in the early afternoon. Slowly peaking his body around the column, he saw one of the daytime janitors Derrick, having sex with a young Hispanic girl from behind, as she was positioned on her knees, on the church buildings cold back staircase leading upstairs to the main floor. The dining room lights suddenly brightly turned on, catching Elder Jackson's attention as he turned his head back towards the staircase door as it loudly swung open.

"Elder Jackson you back here man" the choir director loudly yelled.

"Oh my God" the Hispanic girl shouted as she

quickly rose her body off the cold steps trying to pull up her pink panties.

"Oh damn" Derrick said as he tried to gather himself, pulling up his pants allowing his extra-large black hoodie sweatshirt to fall over his waist area.

"What's going on back here! What is this" Elder Jackson loudly yelled turning towards Derrick and the young female Hispanic. *"Derrick what are you doing back here? And who is this young lady?"* Elder Jackson yelled as the choir director a tall African American male who was wearing a police uniform.

"Nah, D. Don't tell me man that's what you be doing?" The choir director loudly spoke as the Hispanic girl pulled up her blue jeans over her pink panties.

"Are you insane Derrick? This is not what Pastor had in mind when he hired you! You have totally disrespected our church. You have abused our trust and took advantage of the pastor's kindheartedness" Elder Jackson loudly said.

"Nah, D. This is a violation my dude. I can't believe you did this man! Come on young lady you have to leave before I arrest you for trespassing" The tall male choir director loudly spoke as the girl hurried herself down the stairs in embarrassment.

"Yo, Victoria, I'm so sorry baby. I didn't mean any of this to happen to us my luv. Please don't hate me baby. I love you Vicky" Derrick shouted as he twisted the hair in his locs, leaning his chubby body against the church's back staircase cold wall.

"Victoria, if I ever see you around here, I'm going to report you to the authorities. Now if you want to come to a

place that teaches you how to handle and respect your temple our church doors are always open to you. Inside our clean, vacuumed, dust free sanctuary there is an altar which has licensed and ordained able leaders like me, to help instruct you how to present your temple. I would suggest for you to repent, ask God for forgiveness for the adultery committed in his house. There's a prayer service happening right now upstairs that Officer Daryl, will be gladly to escort you to, so you can discuss with God any further choices you plan to make today" Elder Jackson loudly spoke as Daryl the tall choir director escorted the young Hispanic lady out of the church buildings emergency back staircase back into the dining room area.

"Derrick, I'm beyond disgusted at your behavior today. If it was that serious where you couldn't constrain yourself and had to bust a nut. Then you should have clocked out, left the church building, asked to leave for the day, then left the building, signed yourself out or had an early lunch and made that mess outside of the church building. Out of our sight on your own time. There is absolutely no excuse or reason you could give to me right now. That was disgusting Derrick! I will make sure you do not get paid at all today" Elder Jackson shouted as he opened the loud emergency back door and entered the very large dining room area as Daryl quickly came running back downstairs to join them.

"I'm terribly sorry guys" Derrick softly replied as he continued twisting the hair of his locs letting the buildings emergency back door loudly slam behind them.

Elder Jackson didn't reply as he walked over to the

stove located inside of the kitchen and looked on the floor area around the stove. Staring at the heating pipe that went from the floor to the ceiling, Elder Jackson walked over to the kitchen wall and put his right ear to the wall to listen for a sound.

"Where's your coworker Derrick? He's somewhere smashing too?" Elder Jackson loudly asked.

"He should be upstairs on the third floor, waxing the classroom floors if he's not in the front desk with the old man" Derrick quickly replied. *Where's your radio? I need him downstairs here with us right now!"* Elder Jackson loudly spoke as Derrick walked over to a closet in the dining room area, locating his leather jacket that was hanging up on a hanger inside the closet, Derrick, pulled out the two-way radio from the leather jackets pocket and asked his buddy Kent *"to report to the basement dining Hall immediately to speak with Elder Jackson".* Going into one of the large pantry cabinets, Elder Jackson pulled out the heavy-duty flashlight to search the area behind the stove. Shining the bright light in the dark areas behind the stove Elder Jackson searched for holes.

"I need you fellas to help me pull this stove out from the kitchen wall when Kent arrives. I'm waiting for Jamal; he can help us." Elder Jackson loudly spoke.

"The old man said we can use this pastor" Kent loudly said, as he quickly entered the dining room area with a large shovel in his right hand. Watching the video cameras from the front desk inside the church lobby main office, Willy, the hired tall church security guard, knew what Elder Jackson was attempting to do.

"Jamal arrived, sir but he went to the bathroom. I told him you were downstairs here" Kent said as he handed Elder Jackson the large heavy shovel.

"Great when he comes downstairs to join us, I'm going to need us to move this stove so we can hit the rats that is lodging on the stoves heating system. As winter is approaching critters find possible nesting grounds to shelter in place. I heard them squeaking from upstairs inside of the trustee's room wall, whose carpet hadn't been vacuumed by Derrick. Let me ask you Kent. What have you been doing all morning since you arrived here at the church?" Elder Jackson loudly asked.

"My normal day janitorial task sir before I go to lunch" Kent asked as he stared at Derrick.

"Oh, is that true Derrick?' Elder Jackson inquired.

"As far as I know Elder. Look guys, I'm terribly sorry. That was my back. I take full responsibility for everything wrong that you saw" Derrick replied as he continued twisting the hair of his locs.

"Yeah, I know what he was doing Elder. She has been inside the church before. I don't think we should all get in trouble because Victoria and Derrick like to kiss in the staircase." Kent replied.

"Kiss, that was more than lips touching what Daryl and I walked in on some minutes ago down here" Elder Jackson replied. As Jamal entered the basement dining room.

"Listen Jamal hold this shovel and when we slide that stove away from the wall, I want you to hit whatever runs out" Elder Jackson said as the four gentlemen, Daryl, Kent, Derrick and Elder Jackson slowly slid the stove away from the wall. Kent quickly grabbed the flashlight

Elder Jackson had laid on top of kitchen counter and shined the light on the wall. Looking at the hole where the gas line had been connected, Derrick immediately went into one the side cabinets and pulled out the box of tools that were stored inside of the cabinet. Pulling a hammer out of the box, Derrick quickly walked to the hole in the wall and started banging on it, chipping off some of the plastered fragments around hole. *"I see movement"* Kent yelled as Jamal moved towards the hole with the large heavy shovel. Banging the hammer harder, Derrick tried to enlarge the hole by breaking the cemented wall. Elder Jackson grabbed the kitchen cooking mittens that were hanging over the sink. Daryl grabbed a broom that was up against the wall on the side of the refrigerator. As the squeaking got louder, Elder Jackson and Daryl reached their hands inside the wall to grab the large critter. *"I see it"* Daryl yelled trying to grab the tail. *"Watch yourself man don't let it bite you"* Jamal yelled as he assisted Derrick in trying to enlarge the size of the hole by banging the shovel around the edges. As Elder Jackson grabbed the tail, he quickly thrusted back. The fellas jumped back out of Elder Jackson's way as he pulled the large possum out of the hole. Walking fast to the church building's emergency back staircase, Elder Jackson went through the door and out the emergency back door that led to the empty lot behind the church. Tossing the large possum outside onto the empty lot, he quickly shut the door. Daryl entered the staircase holding another possum by the tail as the critter swung from his hands. Elder Jackson opened the emergency exit door once again as Daryl tossed the possum outside. As they entered back inside of the large dining room, Elder Jackson started clapping his hands together as a symbol of joy for accomplishing a task that had been pressed upon him for a while. As the gentlemen pushed the stove back towards the wall, Elder Barbara Simmons came downstairs to investigate the situation.

"Praise the Lord, Praise the Lord" Elder Barbara Simmons loudly spoke.

"Hi, Elder Simmons, it's always good to see you" Kent said as he took the broom back upstairs to the main floor Janitorial closet where it belonged.

"Alright, Alright I came to give a word of encouragement from the Lord on today at the prayer service, but Willy suggested to me that I come to see you all downstairs here" Elder Barbara Simmons said.

"We're getting rid of trespassers Elder. That's all." Daryl said as he looked at Derrick.

"Oh, I see, well we definitely don't need them in our church building isn't that right Derrick?" Elder Barbara Simmons loudly replied.

"No, mam, that's why I'm here to help Elder Jackson get to the root of the problem" Derrick responded as he put the flashlight and the hammer back into the kitchen's pantry cabinet.

"Don't play yourself Derrick. I'm not the one guy! Don't be funny around me. Listen, Elder Simmons we just tossed some possums out into the back lot that we discovered trying to nest behind the stove. How are you feeling today?" Elder Jackson asked.

"*Blessed and well favored Elder*" Elder Barbara Simmons quickly replied.

"*That was a beautiful robe you were wearing, when you preached on Sunday*" Daryl loudly complimented Elder Simmons.

"*Thanks Daryl, it's one of Helen's creations. She's great and her work speaks for itself. I saw some of your choir member upstairs in the lobby, are you'll going to rehearse on the second-floor chapel room?*" Elder Barabara Simmons politely asked as Elder Jackson stood and stared at her.

"*Yes, that is what I had planned to do. Well, I'm going to get back upstairs "before the natives get restless" since I am the one who called this nonscheduled rehearsal. Willy told me you wanted to see me Elder Jackson*" Daryl the tall African American choir director/ church security senior officer said, still wearing his New York Police Department uniform.

"*I did Daryl, but the choir members that are patiently waiting upstairs need you. I don't need to hold you up any longer. I might have solved another suspicious mystery that was on my mind. With you being an active police officer and a member of this church, man, it is a tremendous blessing. Even what you just did for me downstairs here was good work, my brother. I'm thankful for all that you do Daryl*" Elder Jackson said.

"*I appreciate that Elder Jackson. And listen you might need to speak to your niece Monica. Bowman told me she didn't come to school today until it was time for his chorus class*" Daryl shared as he walked away heading upstairs to conduct his church concert choir rehearsal.

"I just need to know Derrick; how did you get Veronica passed Willie? Or do I need to speak to our Bishop and terminate his services as well" Elder Jackson spoke as Elder Barbara Simmons stared at Jamal.

"Elder I'm truly sorry. Listen I'm taking the total blame. You can put it all on me. I'm a mess up! I'm a screw up! I've been like this my whole life man. I'm totally sorry for violating everyone's trust. If anyone should be punished, it's me. I've committed adultery right below the sanctuary. I boldly disrespected God. I was caught during the act! I'm dirty, I'm a sinner! However Elder Jackson I beg of you don't stone Veronica or anyone else that works alongside me" Derrick sorrowfully pleaded while twisting the hair in his locs as Jamal stood quietly still and stared at Derrick.

"Oh, you are smashing Shawns wife!" Jamal shouted out as Elder Barbara Simmons remained staring at Jamal.

"Inside the church!" Elder Jackson loudly replied as he turned himself towards one of the round tables in the very large dining room area.

"Fellas have a seat" Elder Jackson loudly requested as he took a seat on one of the folding chairs at the table. *"Listen I need some honesty from both of you. I need as much clarity at this moment as I can get"* Elder Jackson continued to speak as both Derrick and Jamal sat in chairs around the table. Elder Barbara Simmons quickly walked inside of the kitchen to look around the stove area. *"I need some honesty from both of you. I'm a priest for God's sake or haven't you'll noticed. Derrick, I know where you live at in Spanish Harlem. Jamal, I know you have had my niece up there at*

night around his building seated in your new car. I know both of you are affiliated with Dewayne. My question today to both of you, is what your true intentions with our membership are here in this church building" Elder Jackson asked.

"Man, I'm sorry Elder Jackson. I really am for what you walked on today with Veronica and me. I know you're really upset with me but don't drag Jamal into the middle of anything" Derrick apologetically replied.

"Drag me into what man? I had no idea you were smashing Shawn's wife! And if he finds out, then Derrick, where's that going to leave me?" Jamal shouted out.

"He's not going to find out Jamal. She and I have got nothing to do with you. What happened today was a real slip up. Come on now. You'll see Veronica's body. I couldn't help myself" Derrick loudly responded.

"Like I said, in your slip ups when he finds out, and perhaps comes for me. What? I'm going to have to body that big dude. I didn't come to this building on a Sunday to seek the Lord because someone envying another man's woman. I love Monica! That's a fact Elder Jackson! Your niece and I are good. I joined this church because when Derrick invited me, I was in a dark place. I felt God. I was feeling better about myself. I lost my grandfather and that hurt me. Elder Jackson, your niece is helping me cope with such a great loss in my life every day." Jamal shared.

"Elder Jackson let me ask you an honest question? How did you know I had Veronica back their man?" Derrick inquired.

"I ran into Helen outside of the Caribbean Restaurant earlier, Elder Simmons! Once she started running her mouth,

I knew you were up to something in here. And you still haven't answered my main concern yet Derrick" Elder Jackson responded as Elder Barbara Simmons remained in the kitchen softly humming a gospel song to herself pretending not to be listening to their conversation.

"I'm not up to anything but doing what the church asks for me to do Elder Jackson. How you know my brother Dewayne anyway?" Derrick asked.

"I know a lot of things young man. Don't let the bible knowledge and collar fool you. My brother-in-law is a judge. And speaking of my sister's family, what's up with Monica skipping out on high school Jamal?" Elder Jackson loudly asked.

"You sure Elder? When I spoke with her earlier this morning on the cell phone, she was in class" Jamal replied.

"Oh really? I'll find out. My sister has been texting me all morning and I know it has to do with you. Brother Daryl doesn't lie, and she doesn't normally text me, so I'll find out" Elder Jackson responded.

"Yeah, I heard the cop Daryl talking a minute ago about Monica and chorus, but how does he know about her high school classes" Jamal asked.

"Bowman is his lover. That's Monica's school choir director. He comes here to church every now and then with brother Daryl, but rarely" Derrick replied.

"I need you guys come with me. I must pick up some things from the hardware store for the church. We are taking your car Jamal" Elder Jackson sternly demanded. The three gentlemen arose up out of their seats at the round table, in the very large dining room area, to

head upstairs towards the church lobby entrance. Elder Barbara Simmons quickly walked over to Elder Jackson, pulling him aside, to speak to him privately.

"I know I must go upstairs and preach this word; I believe that God gave unto me this week. However, you need to go see your sister Melonie today. Don't delay Jackson. You owe her a serious apology. That's her child. I suggest you go to your sister before you discuss anything with Monica" Elder Barbara Simmons spoke as Elder Jackson turned his head and stared at Derrick.

CHAPTER 15

THE HOSPITAL CONVERSATION

As Tiffany made her way through the emergency unit door, entering the small waiting area, carrying Stephanies cell phone, she quickly walked over to Danielle and sat down.

"The good thing is Ezra is alert and not in a coma. They took MRI's and Xray's of him before we arrived. They are currently waiting for the specialist to come to look over everything before they proceed with any more treatment. Now he is heavily sedated. The bad news is that his blood pressure is too high at the point of concern of the physician inside the Intensive Care Unit" Tiffany shared as Freddy dropped his head into his hands while Alonzo put his hand on Freddy's shoulder.

"How's Steph." Danielle softly inquired.

"Should you have to ask Dee Dee? That's her baby brother. The only reason Ezra is living here in New York City is because

161

of their close relationship. I know she feels somewhat responsible, but we know that what happened to Ezra this morning in that post office, is not because of Stephanie. Hopefully Melonie can pray to her out of that mode of thinking. Like I said that's her brother, so her feelings are emotionally sadden at this time. Which is the reason I'm going outside where I can get a good reception, to speak with her family on Stephanies cell phone. Get all their exact arrival information, so we can contact the tower's concierge and make proper arrangements for her family to get inside of Stephanie's penthouse apartment without any problems" Tiffany quietly shared.

"When you say they all, who's all that is coming so close to Thanksgiving" Mike asked.

"All of Stephanie's siblings and her parents. But you know they all live in different Mountain states. Gordon has his flight already and is probably at the airport now as we're speaking. Stephanie has given me specific instructions for each of them, so I'm going outside to carry out my girlfriends wishes" Tiffany explained.

"This is truly sad. So, unfortunate to happen to such a goodly young man" Danielle responded.

"Mike, you should have never shared that intel to Melonie about Monica. I saw her face; she wasn't the bit amused. It's going to be problems later in you'll building" Tiffany said as she bounced up and quickly walked through the lobby towards the street exit of the hospital.

"Everyone is making me feel bad now. I thought I was doing the right thing" Mike replied.

"Obviously you weren't" Freddy said as he lifted his head from his hands. *"You see the whole family is on their*

way. Mormons don't understand City life. Now they have a family tragedy with one of the boys. I know Stephanies mother is devastated!" Freddy responded.

"How do you know their Mormons? Have you ever met her mother?" Mike replied.

"No, but it sounded good to say. And if she's on her way, catching a flight just like that, then Stephanies entire family is in a state of panic." Freddy replied.

"Exactly the same as I did earlier to Melonie about her daughter Monica in the apartment. I was going with the flow. Just like you Freddy, it sounded as if it was something good to say at that moment. I didn't mean any harm to anyone." Mike explained.

"Mike, let it go. Now is not the time. We'll deal with that at another time if it presents itself." Alonzo softly replied as he leaned back in his chair.

"I have a question, Mike; how do you know so much about Monica, anyway?" Danielle inquired as she crossed her legs.

"Alright, Ms. Barbara Walters! Prime time interview special. She's in her Oprah Winfrey role now girl. Go ahead Dee Dee! Ask the trending questions because inquiring minds like me, girl, want to know" Freddy dramatically said crossing his leg as he burst in laughter.

"Shut up Freddy" Alonzo responded as he burst in laughter.

"Jimmy told me all her little business. Poor child can't hide anything around there" Mike replied.

"How could you with all of them cameras" Freddy quickly responded as he continued laughing.

"Like whom would want to, with all of them eyes watching them monitors" Alonzo replied.

"Specifically, Jimmy isn't he running the whole show? I know the Super is supposed to be the boss. But everyone knows that his faithful assistant Jimmy is the show" Danielle quickly responded.

"That's one big mean guy. He surely doesn't speak to anyone. Well, I don't speak to him. Holding a conversation with Jimmy that is. He looks like a troublemaker" Freddy replied.

"Would you'll let me finish please. Jimmy had an argument with Monica's young parking attendant boo. Something over Jimmy's car was supposed to remain parked in the front of the garage because he leaves the premises and comes back throughout the day. Also because of what you just highlighted, Danielle, he runs the operations throughout the building. My guess feeling of entitlement. However, Monica's little boyfriend keeps his new Acura parked in the front of the garage by the attendant's small office, when he's on duty at the Towers lower levels parking garage. He's in charge of everything downstairs. That's a tremendous responsibility to watch over all that money in our parking garage. From Porsche, Lincoln's, the talk show host, his Bentley to Benz and Ferrari's. He takes his attendant job seriously. Jimmy felt disrespected when he asked, the young man to move his car, and he told Jimmy no! So, while I was in the gym on the second floor, Jimmy was walking around fussing about the guy and how he messed himself up when he put his hands in Jimmy's face. Then while I was doing free weights on the third floor, Jimmy was pacing himself back and forth with *the water vac talking about how Monica's boo doesn't know who he's messing with"* Mike explained.

"Our overnight attendant's name is Jamal, like I mentioned earlier. If Jimmy comes into the building for work around seven in the morning during the weekdays, they should have little interaction with one another, Mike. Now I might not know as much of the building news as you do. But in our building, the hours between six in the morning and ten in the morning have always been considered rush hour. Many of the tenants are leaving the building, many in their cars from the parking garage. Building staff and guests are constantly coming into the garage to park their cars. So, I can't see much interaction with all that busyness in the parking garage, if Jamal leaves at eight in the morning. That might be why Jamal's car is parked by the exit ramp so he can get into his own car and leave for home. Sounds more like Jimmy has something else on his mind. Might just be Jamal and the Supers wife playful interaction which I have witnessed on occasions. Jimmy could be jealous their friendship" Danielle replied.

"I've seen them talking to each other in the parking garage. Matter of fact I've seen them talking early this morning when I went to the deli to get my coffee, however I didn't see our girl Monica with them. I did see his shinny Acura parked on the top of the ramp at the entrance of the garage" Alonzo responded.

"Girl, wait a minute. You'll queens don't stop serving hot tea! I mean in one breath honey you took me out again. The Supers wife and the skinny black boy? Girl bye" Freddy dramatically replied as he slid down in his waiting area seat covering his face.

"You never know what that's about Fred?" Alonzo quickly replied.

"You would say that" Freddy quickly responded to Alonzo as he sat up in the waiting area chair.

"I'm still shocked about that one Feddie. Alonzo hit me hard with his building wanderings too" Mike spoke.

"That maybe the reason why everyone likes Stanley, the white weekend attendant over Jamal the Caribbean style week attendant. What I'm saying guys is that it might be more reasons why Jimmy is publicly fussing and snitching on Jamal" Danielle said.

"Now That's true. That staff is always having some drama. They are always fighting about something in the building. The security guards are always arguing with one another. One night I came into the building through the security entrance and that tall security guard, Shawn was physically fighting one of the Spanish night porters. Chong doesn't like Phillip and Phillip always gossiping about Max. It's always some kind of drama like what we witnessed in front of the building this morning" Freddy replied.

"While I was in the gym that day, Jimmy was telling me about Jamal's work performance and how he's getting himself in trouble with the Judge by having sex with his daughter" Mike continued to share.

"Melonie isn't the one to be messed with either. Personally, I always knew the New York Police Department had their eyes on our building because Melonie is a United Nations leadership staff member. You'll see how she whipped the badge out on the Sergeant earlier. Even how the Sergeant respectfully addressed her. Which is also why I'm saying that it might not have been

a good move, Mike. That leak out your mouth in Stephanies apartment can lead to disaster. Her status may cause our friend Melonie to handle the matter with her daughter differently than you may have expected" Danielle responded. *"Look at what Freddy, Mike have witnessed with Jimmy and the African Americans. I say that because isn't the commander of the security guards who is always wearing a trench coat and drives the security car around our building good friends with Jimmy?"* Danielle spoke.

"I always see them talking together, just about every day" Mike replied

"He may have instigated the fight that Freddy witnessed with Shawn" Danielle said.

"Yeah, Dee Dee. That battle rumbles this morning with the delivery guys and Aram in front of the building had me thinking earlier. When Jimmy stepped outside it was like the fight escalated. The delivery guys looked angrier with Jimmy and the Super than with Aram. One of the reasons I suggested for us to leave" Alonzo replied.

"With the delivery guys I really don't understand why they get so hostile with the doorman and security. I know a lot of buildings that don't even let them inside of the building. They must call the tenants to come downstairs to the lobby door and collect their deliveries. At least our building the security guards escort them upstairs to the tenant's apartment. I see our building's delivery system as a bonus compared to other New York City residential skyscrapers. So, this morning I feel they were dead wrong with all that hostility" Freddy responded.

"I agree, just obey the buildings rules and you'll get a tip" Mike spoke.

"I got a tip for Aram alright, honey. But I see he's been getting it daily from Alonzo" Freddy said as he busted out in laughter.

"I'm shocked!" Mike said as he leaned back into the waiting room chair and stared at Danielle.

"You'll have given me too much on today! Here I think I'm living with the grand. And everybody in the building playing with one another in the sheets including my own buddy. Too many secrets!" Freddy dramatically shouted out.

"You mean playing in the car. The new Acura at that" Mike quickly replied.

"Lord, Mike not the new whip! Mother Superior is going to crack the ruler over everyone with her ten commandments preaching self. Not her baby girl" Freddy shouted.

"Girl, Monica knows she hot" Danielle replied as she leaned back in the waiting room chair, fanning herself with her right hand.

"Not as heated as Melonie is" Alonzo responded.

"Oh God! You'll have served too much hot tea. My tongue can't take any more of this tea. I'm already overheated" Freddy shouted putting his hands over his face again as Mike stared at him.

CHAPTER 16

MY SONS FATHER

As Tiffany returned to the Intensive Care Unit, Melonie was seated alone rocking in the chair with her eyes closed and her arms folded.

"You didn't want to go inside of the room with Stephanie and speak with our younger brother, Ezra?" Tiffany softly inquired as she comfortably sat in the chair next to Melonie.

"He's still heavily sedated so I'll let Steph have this moment inside the isolated room with Ezra. I know this is terrifying for our girl. Everyone's worse nightmare. I thank God that his life wasn't taken, and Ezra's condition is not as bad as it could have been. It's still tragic though. Girl, this city is full of craziness. An unstable mentally insane couple walking the streets terrorizing civilians in a post office. Just sick! That's why I remain, prayed up and I continually praise dance extra hard unto the Lord for my babies. Even for Monica's spoiled

butt! And there will be no baby! No extra baby I'm going to have to labor in prayer for" Melonie replied.

"How do you know it was a mental insane couple that did this to Ezra" Tiffany asked.

"Stephanie was just sitting here telling me. She told me what the Sergeant said to her, when the two of you, first came inside the Intensive Care Unit" Melonie softly replied.

"Oh, I'm sorry girl, I didn't remember. May not have heard that discussion because of all the busyness here in the Emergency Unit. Now this Intensive Care Unit isn't as active as the other emergency unit but there's still a lot of medical personnel constantly moving around. When we first walked through that door and entered the emergency unit, I must honestly admit that I was distracted by all the fast pace medical attention patients were receiving all around the unit. So many patients laid on gurneys, family members positioned around them, talking and medical physicians moving around with medical equipment, while we were walking to see Ezra that I was simply distracted. I think I do remember Stephanie asking the Sergeant a question about Ezra's attackers. However, the constant beeping noises on all those machines along with the constant moving of medical personnel deferred my attention from their conversation of Ezra's attackers. Which was also my reason for volunteering to speak with her family to somewhat ease their primary concern about Stephanie not being alone here at the hospital. I know Hearing the sound of my voice lessens the stress tensions of worry. Like you just said girl, this is horrific for Ezra's entire family, so our Steph right now is in shock. Another one of my reasons for making sure her family's arrival is better organized as they may expect."

Tiffany quietly shared as she crossed her legs in the narrow hard chair, inside of the Intensive Care Unit.

"You are absolutely correct Tiffany, girl that's why I'm not even going to share with Steph, the information of Aram in the bed with Alonzo who sitting out there in the waiting area" Melonie softly responded.

"What? Melonie, are you serious?" Tiffany replied.

"That's what they're all talking about, out there in the hospital waiting area Aram's butt Robic's with Alonzo and one of Steph's students who is our neighbor's husband" Melonie softly replied.

"What! Eesh! Unlock the tight ends for me" Tiffany responded, as she burst out in laughter.

"Aram is far from Steph's mind now anyway. Earlier she was bothered by Bradley's recent behavior on her penthouse floor. With Ezra in this condition, I don't think Bradley or Aram is in any of Steph's dating plans into the new year. If anything, she's going to make her brother Ezra stay with her inside of the penthouse for a good while or at least until he fully recovers," Melonie explained as Stephanie calmly exited the glass isolated room. Slowly walking over to the empty seat on the other side of Melonie, Stephanie dropped herself down. Taking a deep breath and then slowly exhaling, blowing her breath into the air inside of the Intensive Care Unit Stephanie closed her tear-filled eyes.

"How's our brother Steph?" Tiffany quietly asked.

"He's stable, it's just hard for me seeing my little brother like this. Knowing that he was in so much pain that publicly he was calling out for me to defend him, and I wasn't there. I'm in pain for my brother. You know how much Ezra loves

skiing. He Just arrived back to New York, from Switzerland for God's sake. This is heartbreaking. Thank you, ladies, for being here at the hospital with me. Especially you Melonie, I know you have a diplomatic career, and you're here for my family. I very much appreciate it, girl" Stephanie softly said as she wiped the tears from her eyes.

"We'll do anything for you girl. You know it! We're all just glad that Ezra is alive and getting the best medical treatment possible" Melonie softly replied.

"I spoke to everyone, of your family members and I have the flight arrangements. I also took the liberty to alert the front desk of their arrival times. I told Marisol that you will contact the Tower, when you come out of the emergency room with your loved one to confirm the family's stay inside of your, penthouse apartment" Tiffany softly explained.

"Brownie will sure be happy that there's plenty of company coming to his penthouse playground. Plenty of people to rub his belly and feed him treats" Melonie replied.

"Wow Tiff. Thank you. I appreciate you so much right now. This is quite overwhelming. I just didn't expect this. Now I do have things in place in case of an emergency, but I didn't foresee an incident of this magnitude involving my little brother. I didn't even have his girlfriend's cell number. Yeah, he's my stinky butt. However, Ezra is my superman" Stephanie softly replied.

"His girlfriend said she was on her way when I spoke with her, Steph. I'm not sure how far his girlfriend has to travel. Ezra is a good guy. He's going to bounce back and be even stronger on them ski slopes than he's ever been" Tiffany responded.

"Yeah Steph, Ezra will always be your superman, girl. You're going to receive his defending muscular strength again soon, which Ezra displays weekly as well as publicly over you. That's not going to change. Especially living in our building girl. Because our doorman Aram who portrays to be a superhero along with his new centerfold model playmate has been tossing the sheets with Alonzo, his boyfriend Brian and our neighbor Zack" Melonie shared.

"Oh, so they are swingers" Stephanie quickly replied.

"Wait, you knew Steph?" Tiffany quickly responded.

"Who swinging what girl? Wait! I'm now like Freddy, you'll be serving it heavy today. Lord Heavens Mercy" Melonie replied crossing her legs as she slouched down in her narrow hard seat.

"Zacks wife is in my Yoga gym class. Her twin sister recently started coming to my gym class only, but that was only because his wife and Ronald my Hispanic assistant have been intimate the last two months. Not only does the twin sister know about their steamy love affair, so does the whole Yoga class know. They make it obvious not just in my sweaty steamy yoga gym class, but out on the gym floor, they're always grabbing each other, bending over each other and holding each other. At first, I was thinking the sister came to back Ronald off her because his personality is so aggressive. After a while I realized the twin sister was the decoy for any of our neighbors who are members at the gym not to speculate on them as a official couple. Now the three of them come and leave the gym together. I guess they're swingers" Stephanie replied.

"Orgies, swingers, girl, I don't know who's swinging on whosevers body parts, but Freddy and Mike did not know.

Girl, so you know they're not going to let that hidden intel go" Melonie rhythmically responded.

"If the relationship is that serious and he's aggressive isn't that dangerous for your neighbor Zack?" Tiffany softly inquired.

"Yeah, but they are two consenting adults and its really not any of our business. I just happened to peep it" Stephanie replied.

"Girl, you clocked it repeatedly. Over, over, and over again" Melonie quickly responded as she burst into laughter.

"Melonie, you hear me clearly girl. He's young and fine too. Muscle down! In my Freddy voice. His aggression works in my class because he can push the men as well as the women who attend the Yoga gym class to hold difficult positions. Ronald is a good authoritative pusher. He works at the post office during the day, somewhere in Manhattan" Stephanie shared.

"A muscular postal worker, now that's hot! That's exactly what Ezra needed today in his situation. However, I believe the angels of the Lord were there to help defend your brother Steph. It could have been far worse. I know it pains you to see him in any type of discomfort but he's alive" Melonie replied.

"Amen, I agree with Melonie Steph. Yes, this situation is really messed up, but I believe God is still here at the hospital helping Ezra. Your Hispanic gym assistant does sound hot though. Sounds like Zacks wife has herself a trophy" Tiffany responded as she crossed legs.

"Yeah, I must call Ronald to inform him of my emergency

here. I'm going to need him to fill in for me tonight and probably remain the official Yoga instructor until I feel comfortable returning. I pray it's not too much of an inconvenience for him. Like I said, I know he works at the post office during the day and he's also a message therapist. He's always at our gym looking for potential customers. He's a sweetheart though underneath all that male testosterone. I talk to him about Ezra all the time. I hope he understands how much I need his leadership abilities now" Stephanie continued to share.

"I'll call him girl. Let me hear what this tough Spanish speaking Ronald sounds like. I'll ask him to take over for you Steph." Tiffany volunteered.

"I know you will call Ronald now girl, after hearing about his body skills. But he's our neighbors side piece, he's already on someone's plate and not on the buffet table looking to be served" Melonie responded as she continued to laugh.

"My reason for questioning your neighbor, Zacks safety. I know your apartment building is heavily secured but matters of the heart can get dangerous" Tiffany replied.

"That's why Steph. Said they are swinging! Lord Jesus, please keep me closer to thine altar, because my neighbors are swinging all over the place. The only person I want to swing on is my Teddy Bear. And girl, my husband has enough for me to swing all over our bedroom on all night long" Melonie replied.

"The images of you griping the judge at any time are not what I want to be thinking about in my head at this time girl" Stephanie sarcastically responded.

"You need to be worrying about why your daughter Monica trying to grip that boy working in your apartment building" Tiffany spoke.

"Tiff, girl, I know. I'm going to kick Monica's butt when I get home. Skipping school and sneaking around my basement with a damn fool" Melonie rhythmically replied.

"I'm surprised no one in the building has brought their love affair to your attention. Nosey as your neighbors are. You and your husband are respected in the community. Both of you are active on the community boards and active on all your children's school boards. I always loved the fact with both of you'll busy careers that the two of you still find time to be visible in your children's lives. Myself I was raised twenty-four seven by our nanny. I'm not sure about my older sister but there were many times I desired just to be with my mom. That's why I took her death so hard. Honestly, I felt like I really didn't know the woman. It's a burden I carried for years Melonie. I'm still going to therapy once a week because of this fact. In a way I envy your relationship with your children Melonie. With my son I vowed to be active in his life. He's my only child. And girl I'm telling you today I'm not having any more" Tiffany confessed.

"You say that now, but you probably will" Melonie quickly replied, as she placed her hand on tiffany's knee.

"Now and later! I'm not having another baby. Nothing else is coming out of my coochie! That was enough. Girl, I still can remember throwing the cup of ice at Steph. While she in my ear breathing heavy, calling herself coaching me by continually saying "you are doing fine Tiff. You are almost there! Breathe girl, just breathe and push a little harder." I really wanted to slap her harder with her no children having self" Tiffany said as she burst out in laughter.

"That was funny Tiff. Your doctor didn't help me at all

while you were in labor. She in your other ear, talking about "you haven't dilated yet." I was like doctor, whose team are you on" Stephanie said as she burst out in laughter.

"It's so good to hear you laughing Steph. Ezra is going to be alright! He's a fighter. He is strong like you girl." Melonie spoke.

"I hope so Melonie. I really love my brother. I agree with Tiffany. As active with your children you are in the building. No one telling you what they have seen concerning Monica is alarming. Long as you'll been living in our luxury tower and are always at the park publicly interacting with your little ones. I'm surprised none of the other mothers didn't bring Monica's sneaky relationship to your attention. Speaking of being sneaky. Tiffany, what happened earlier this morning with your creepy baby father George?" Stephanie softly inquired.

"George is being a real butthole! We had the discussion of him not staying at my house under any circumstances time and time again. I'm happy I don't have to fight with him to see his son. From the expressions on his face, he loves his boy and that's fine with me. My sister told me not to be hard on him because I'm going to need George to be present in my child's life. I have always taken my sister's advice not just because she has three children and one on the way but because of the fact that's my big sister. However, this African creeps me out Steph. I admit he sparked a flame the two and a half years we dated. When we met at John F. Kenedy airport in the winter my flight had been delayed and then canceled on my way to the annual ski trip in Mammoth Mountain, California. I was attracted to him. That was then this creep now is not the same

man I had loved. I have even said to him that he was much happier working as a Transportation Security Administration agent at the airport than now as a full-time conductor for Amtrak. There are both good jobs in my eyes but maybe the change of careers has altered his personality. Even before my son was born and we had split up, he was constantly trying to sleep with me and my neighbor at the same time. I think he was successful with her. As a matter of fact, I know he slept with her repeatedly. I've seen her with several African men over the years. I was not giving into him because I didn't want to be bothered with his altar ego. He was almost abusive. Mentally I couldn't deal with the drama back and forth anymore. I didn't need stress at the time with my pregnancy. I don't need stress currently either. Flys off the handle at any given time. Shows up unannounced questioning me about my personal intimate business. Explaining to me that he has a right to know what naked white man is around his son. His boy is a black prince and someday he'll be a king like his black African father. So, he must know who I am exposing my child to. He's a creep! A real butthole" Tiffany loudly explained.

"Oh Lord Heavens Mercy. Let me ask you girl. What country is your child's father George, from again?" Melonie softly asked.

"George is from Guinea. He became a United States Citizen through the naturalization process long before we met, and I conceived my son" Tiffany quickly replied.

"You and your neighbor love yourselves some black men. Girl, you went to the motherland and got yourself real black royalty" Melonie sarcastically responded as she burst out in laughter.

"Shut up Melonie" Stephanie said as she burst out in laughter leaning her head on Melonie's shoulder.

"Royalty my white butt! He's a jerk!" Tiffany quickly responded.

"Listen Your sister was absolutely, right. Girl, I have five children and by tomorrow I may have only four after I go home and kick Monica's spoiled butt. As a proud parent of African American children in America, your son is going to need his African father in his life. It would be different if the two of you weren't speaking, he was never there during the pregnancy or denied your son then it would be understandable. The fact that he is displaying an effort to be in his boy's life is beneficial in his development. Now the other stuff he's talking about is you'll stuff. But you were dealing with that Niger, way before you got pregnant by his mean self. However, he is playing an intricate part in the development of your child's growth and that is beneficial" Melonie replied.

"He's a jerk! Now George is trying to stay with me because he feels someone has a personal vendetta against him. They are trying to blow him up! George's paranoia is just as narcotic now as it was before I got pregnant. You're right Melonie! He's creepy. I told him to go to the Federal Bureau of Investigation and let them deal with his apartment situation. Maybe they'll put his creepy butt in a witness protection community." Tiffany loudly replied.

"Girl, you don't mean that. You know you want that African man close to his son" Melonie replied as she burst in laughter.

"Boy come closer, stay closer, I want you to be closer, boy come closer and give me that wood, let me swing on that wood,

I want that African good" Stephanie Rhythmically spoke as she burst out in laughter while stomping her feet.

"Shut up Steph. If he only could, then you know she would, get that African good" Melonie quickly replied as she burst out in laughter as she joined in on Stephanie's stomping while shaking her head back and forth.

"He's too creepy for me ladies. His apartment building has been under renovation for some time now. First it was the bedbug's infestation he had inside of his apartment. I definantly wouldn't allow him to stay in my house. I didn't need any fleas in my clean crib. I even told him to hire a maid to clean his apartment. At least with his horny flirting self, George could sleep with his cleaning woman as well. That would give him a new project to be involved with. Then it was the power outage problems George was experiencing. It ended up killing his pet lizard. The reptile depended on the heating lamp to maintain a certain temperature in the terrarium that he had set up and built inside of his apartment for survival. Every day, all day no power in the apartment, which meant no heating lamp. George needed to stay with me because he was grieving. He had no heat last winter. It was making him sick. George needed to stay with me. He has no hot water every other week, George needs to come to my house to shower. Then last month they had to break into the kitchen walls inside of George's apartment to do some pipe work. George is convinced somehow; they messed with the stove's gas line. Every time George turns on the stove, the entire hallway smells like gas. The neighbors reported him to the building management. George is frantically upset, and he feels the west Indian construction workers that are part of the building's renovation crew did it on purpose in attempt to

blow George up. He said, one of the guys came at him the wrong way one day, so George stepped up to him and they fought. Now he feels there's a personal vendetta against him in the construction staff. His safety is important, and all morning George was trying to convince me why I should allow him to stay in my apartment with his son." Tiffany explained.

"Wow tiff" Stephanie quickly replied.

"I hear what you are saying Tiff. Girl, that's a lot. The concern is that he is still your son's father. You don't want anything to happen to him. And you don't want to sleep with him either. Let me say this, as an international career woman who spends a great part of her day interacting with foreign constituents, I don't know how long George a legal American citizen has been but from what I'm hearing from you in his tone there is a sound of fear. I'm not just talking about the incident today with the gas line. Yes, there are plenty of wonderful opportunities afforded by everyone here in America but to survive in America you must be productive. He is a father now and that is a tremendous responsibility. It's a wonderful one, but a responsibility. Girl, I have five children and even my teddy bear at times looks stressed when it comes to paying the bills. Though we have a team system, he and I governing our monthly expenses. And tomorrow, if Monica survives my wrath on her spoiled butt, it will now be Monica, my husband and I handling the monthly expenses. I think it's time for her to start working and carrying some of the weight around my house since she wants to act grown and hang out with street boys who I don't know in my apartment building's basement. I'm not sure what George's monthly expenses are after the arrival of your child or his monthly income. But Tiff.

Girl, somewhere amid his taking on new responsibilities even with the transit system, he has become fearful. What you'll together have created is a bundle of joy and at the same time is an expense" Melonie responded.

"Melonie, you are going to make Monica work" Stephanie quickly replied.

"Heavens yeah! It's about that time Steph. You skip out on my church service, to lay and play with some boy, then it's time for you to help me raise my boys if you desire to stay under my roof. Which is probably the lesson that my husband is implementing with her today. I'll be the judge when I get home to see how well she follows her father's instructions. But you'll have one child, Tiff. I have five children, and I'm telling you the birth of your son is what changed his tone inside of your home. Now as for my neighbors' tones with my husband and I have always been a little flaky. Not everyone is as hospitable, friendly, outgoing, as Steph and Dee Dee. They're sure, not Freddy, but girl I'm going to get on Marisol for not telling me. Our tower's concierge Marisol has four daughters of her own, so I'm sure Marisol knows why I'm going to kick Monica's spoiled butt when I get home. My husband and I have always modeled ourselves in our residence respectfully for various reasons. Yes, we worked hard to achieve the status as well as the income that we do have today but girl, we are aware of our stiff neck surroundings. That's why I'm also going to talk to Jimmy. That boy will not be working in my building come next week" Melonie explained.

"Oh, you are putting an end to it all" Tiffany replied.

"Why are you contacting Jimmy Melonie?" Stephanie inquired.

"I have been living inside our apartment longer than you Steph. I'm aware of who really runs things daily under our roof. If anything took place that was suspicious inside our apartment building, then the assistant Super, Jimmy would know about it. He watches those surveillance cameras inside of the tower like a hawk. I'm not concerned about him not making me aware of my daughter's new love interest. However, that Italian man from Howard Beach Brooklyn, is not too fond of blacks. That is also why there are no black people working in the building during the day. Only two black porters work overnight and weekends. My husband and I were talking about that one night when his nephew spent the week with us. That new couple who's always smoking outside doesn't speak to my husband or I at all, but they speak to Jimmy. My Teddy Bear came home one night and told me that another one of his colleagues had a case in their courtroom. It was the employment address of the defendant Stanley, our weekend parking attendant, which prompted them to my husband's chambers. Being aware of my husband's address, the judge discussed the case with him because of the nature of the crime. He abducted the brother of his neighbor, who kept sitting on his car along with his Hispanic friends. The battle was originally over a parking space in front of the building. Stanley and his neighbor had been exchanging racial derogatory words with each other for a few weeks over the parking space. Stanley told his neighbor that if he or his brother continued to disrespect him, they were going to pay by blood. Stanley beat and tortured that Hispanic boy, leaving him tied up in an abandoned garage near Howard Beach, Brooklyn the entire weekend until the New York Police Department found him. What really concerned the judge was Stanley's racist criminal history. My husband's response was that he wouldn't be surprised if Stanley was a candidate for a white supremist group or already part of one. The other judge agreed and wanted to make my family aware of the employees in our apartment building. That is why I know the caliber of the young men my oldest child is dangerously interacting with and not letting her loving parents know." Melonie responded.

"Melonie, you're going to sick a possible bigot on the boy" Stephanie replied.

"Girl, he's going to keep his hands off my baby one way or another. I'm going to have a heart to heart with my brother as well. I know the good reverend didn't withhold intel to his loving sister as dangerous as this seriously is" Melonie responded as she folded her arms sitting in the narrow hard chair, while Stephanie's best friend Tiffany stared at her.

CHAPTER 17

THE SCHOOL FIGHT

Throwing away her half-eating tray of food into the crowded sixth floor cafeteria garbage can, Cindy slowly walked over towards her boyfriend Carlos as he rolled diced on the high school cafeteria floor with his close friends in the corner behind two long tables. Being high school students, they were expected to conduct a level of behavioral responsibility while inside the school building, unfortunately this school period was the most watched period during the day by the school safety agents because of the large attendance of students in a single large room from all four grades at the same time. According to the school deans and principle something was bound to happen during the lunch period. Security made sure all eyes were on deck inside of the cafeteria. Two-way radios in hands, there was constant patrol by the safety agents the entire lunch period. Approaching

Carlos to stand next to her tall handsome basketball jock boyfriend, Cindy took out her earbuds to listen to some of the newest hit track songs she downloaded onto the app. in her cellphone. Turning up the volume on her cellphone so she could feel the sound of the bass pulsating through her eardrums, Cindy started to shake her hips back and forth. One of Carlos basketball teammates noticed the wiggling of Cindy's hips and jumped up out of his seat from one of the long cafeteria tables and slip behind Cindy, so her butt was up against the front crotch area of his jeans. Moving his body along with Cindy's the two of them danced together. Some of the other students who witnessed the two of them dancing, grinding together started cheering them on loudly. Carlos, in jealous anger, shoved his teammate hard off away from his girlfriend Cindy, knocking him back into the wall behind the two long tables. One of the teammates, friends, saw the shoving, immediately jumped up and ran over to Carlos, to punch him in the face but Carlos ducked, as the boy's fist missed his face. Quickly swinging back, Carlos hit the boy with his fist into the boy's bottom chin area as they started fighting each other inside the large busy cafeteria.

"Carlos, stop! Please, I don't want you to get in trouble! Oh, my God! Carlos, stop! I don't want you to get suspended and kicked off the team for this idiot" Cindy frantically screamed while the two boys continued to swing at one another with their fist. The school safety agents aggressively pushed their way through the crowd of students making their way towards the two fighting

teenagers. Grabbing each of them with force, the safety agents pulled the two teenagers apart as Cindy began to cry frantically, pleading with the school safety agents, that it was her fault the altercation happened. One of the school Deans came angrily running through the crowd to help escort the two teenagers out of the crowded cafeteria with the school safety agents. Following the agents and the school Dean, Cindy quickly walked behind them in tears. Kaneesha spotting Cindy ran back into the bathroom in a panic, yelling for Monica to hurry, that something awful has happened to their friends Cindy and Carlos. As the school safety agents closed the school cafeteria floor doors, blocking the high school stairwells to separate the fighting teenagers and the crowd of high school students that followed, Kaneesha and Monica were not allowed to leave the floor to follow their girlfriend Cindy to the administration office. Monica continued texting Jamal to see if he was home or perhaps awake. He wasn't responding to any of her texts. Knowing that the day is getting late, and her youngest brother elementary school was soon to let out Monica, called Stephanie's cell phone to see if her mom was with her.

"Monica don't worry about the call backs, as soon as the period bell rings, we out of here. Straight to the administration office to check on Cindy. They're straight wilding now. Let me find out if someone put their hands on my girl. I'll get locked up for real. That's for sure! Not today, they aren't ready for the smoke. When we go downstairs, I'm going to call my brothers. They are messing with the wrong ones now. Watch. You don't

want none of this! None of it! Let me hear, my girl Cindy said someone even tapped her. Bodied! You are dropping today! That's my word!" Kaneesha angrily yelled.

"Who did you see go downstairs with Cindy" Monica nervously inquired.

"I saw them officers surrounding Carlos and Cindy crying to the Dean who was pushing the officers. There was another group of officers in front of Carlos, but I didn't see who they had" Kaneesha honestly replied.

"This whole day is messed up. I just want Jamal! I want my boyfriend's lips on my body. I miss him, girl. Now he's not picking up. I'm worried. Why doesn't Jamal want to speak to me when I want his lips on my lips so bad. I want to feel the exhales of his warm breath all over me" Monica honestly loudly confessed.

"Who was that you were just trying to call" Kaneesha inquired.

"Moms good friend Stephanie. She's one of our cool neighbors that lives in our building's penthouse. If something happened to my mother earlier, then she would be with her. I would have called my uncle, but the sound of his voice is going to make me think about Jamal. Kaneesha, girl, I miss my babe! I want his hands on me now. I want to feel Jamal so bad girl" Monica continued to confess.

"I hear you girl. He got you open! My boo, she does that to me too. I'm not going to lie; I want to see her right now too. She's been on my mind all day. I miss her lips and tongue all over my tongue ring. Yearning the sweet smell of her perfume on her hoodie even has my couchie a little bit moist. Knowing that she'll be downstairs in front of the school building when

I exit the school entrance door is what's keeping my anxiety calm. Now my anger is a whole different story. This rage I'm feeling is because of my girl Cindy. Not knowing what went down with my girl Cindy, it upsets me. It is pissing me off" Kaneesha honestly confessed.

"I hear you girl. These guards in this school are nasty. They been riding my nerves all day" Monica loudly replied as the school period bell rang. Moving with the crowd of students through the cafeteria floor stairwell doors, the two girls hit the stairs, pushing and hurrying their way down to the first floor so they can immediately link back up with their good friends Cindy and Carlos. Reaching the crowded second floor staircase, Monica saw Mr. Bowman slowly walking up the stairs. Trying not to make eye contact with him Monica kept turning her head so her hair could cover her eyes.

"I hope you're not cutting anymore classes young lady" Mr. Bowman yelled out on the staircase putting her attendance out into the open.

"OK, Mr. Bowman, you are doing too much now. We already sang soprano for your Christmas Choir earlier. Now you need to go ride somebody else and stop playing us so close" Kaneesha aggressively responded.

"I need to do what?" Mr. Bowman said as he stopped on the steps delaying any movement in the crowded staircase of high school students from either direction, as he placed his hand on his hip while staring at Kaneesha directly into her eyes.

"Mr. Bowman, we don't have time to play around and talk with you. Something has happened with my mom at home

so I must leave the school building early to pick up my siblings and something just happened to Cindy's boyfriend upstairs inside of the lunchroom cafeteria" Monica quickly replied as she pushed Kaneesha out of his face, down the stairs so together they could quickly get to the first floor. Cindy was standing outside of the high school administration office crying and talking to one of the office personnel about what occurred inside of the cafeteria. Seeing the girls coming towards them, the short stocky office personnel turned herself, cutting their conversation and quickly walked back into the office shutting the office door.

"What was all that about Kaneesha" loudly shouted out as they slowly walked toward Cindy.

"Hey, you'll found me. That idiot pushed up on me while I was dancing to my favorite song by Carlos, and he tried to take the idiot's head off. Carlos doesn't need to be suspended" Cindy loudly shouted out in tears. As Monica embraced her in a tight hug.

"This whole day is ending up lousy. I still must get to my sisters and my brother school to take them home" Monica softly spoke.

"No, I was talking about her running off and slamming the office door when she saw us walking down the school hallway a second ago" Kaneesha inquired.

"Yeah, that was suspicious" Monica replied.

"Like you said girl, this day is horrible. I didn't know it was going to happen like that. Over a simple dance. The idiot threw the first punch! My love whipped his butt for trying to hit him. However, that idiot missed while attempting to throw

the first punch. Carlos finished him up like a champion boxer practicing on a gym speed bag" Cindy loudly responded.

"What, Cindy, are you serious, girl? Carlos, floored that boy? Wait, who's the other boy he was fighting?" Kaneesha asked.

"His own damn teammate girl!" Cindy loudly replied. *"This is so messed up. I don't want Carlos to lose out on his basketball privileges. Everything was going good between us"* Cindy spoke.

"Don't blame yourself girl. It's not your fault. Boys are going to do what boys are going to do. You can't control a good guy like Carlos. Times like this you must step back and let your man do what he does girl. You must honestly admit Cindy, he did that! That fight is not going to mess with your relationship. Sounds like he was defending you as well as not tolerating any kind of disrespect. The whole school just witnessed your boyfriend, put it down for your honor. Now I'm not going to enter into any classroom until I know Carlos is not mad at you" Monica said.

"You're not going to class because you have sisters and a brother to pick up" Kaneesha quickly replied.

"Shut up Kaneesha! I'm here to make sure our friend and her man are good" Monica spoke.

"Her man is a beast! Our Cindy has a good man" Kaneesha replied as she hugged Cindy in a tight hug. The high school administration office door reopened, as two teachers who were having a loud conversation quickly came walking up the hallway towards the girls from the other end of the hallway.

"Monica, your volleyball coach was walking around

upstairs by the classroom you are supposed to be inside right now, not huddled out here in the hallway with your friends, is looking for you. She is upstairs saying that "your mother has given permission for you to leave and go home" One of the teachers that was walking up the school hallway loudly said. The Dean slowly stepped out of the office along with the office personnel. The Dean reached out and handed Monica a red slip of paper as the two slowly walked proceeding past the girls to conversate with the other two teachers. As the four of them loudly conversated, Carlos slowly walked out of the administration office with a similar red slip of paper in his hand. Sadly, looking at his girlfriend Cindy, he stopped and embraced her as she wept in his arms.

"Carlos, I heard you was trying to knock your teammate out while Monica had me in the girl's bathroom taking her sweet time." Kaneesha said as she stepped close to Carlos giving him a high five with her right hand.

"Shut up Kaneesha! Are you good Carlos?" Monica loudly asked Cindy's boyfriend as they stood in front of the administration office holding hands.

"Yeah, I'm good. We've been beefing with one another for a minute now. I thought it was just on the court but today when I saw him trying to put his penis on my girl's butt directly in front of me, I knew what his real problem has been" Carlos loudly said as he put his knapsack around his arms onto his back.

"You got the hottest girl in the school Carlos. That's his problem" Kaneesha quickly replied.

"That's right and he's jealously wishing he could ball like

you in our high school building Carlos" Melonie responded as Carlos stared at her. Slowly walking out of the administration office with his two-way radio gripped tightly in his hands, was the six foot seven inches tall, white male school safety guard, Paul, who stopped stood and looked directly into Monica's eyes. He then slowly turned around to shut the administration office door.

"Isn't it time for class? I know the lunch period ended a long time ago" Paul sternly spoke as he turned back around to them standing in the high school hallway directly in front of the administration office.

"We have red slips, and we are out of here! You'll need to stop playing so close!" Kaneesha loudly replied as the four teens proceeded to walk down the school hallway on route to the high school building's lobby's front entrance doors. The Dean turned and stared at Paul, as the four teenagers quickly walked past with plans to leave the high school building early.

CHAPTER 18

TRUE FEELINGS

As Jamal pulled his new Acura in front of the Brooklyn hardware store, there was a short senior West Indian descent, bald gentleman standing in front of the store with a shopping cart full of bags. Elder Jackson quickly hoped out of the front seat to greet the senior gentleman while Jamal shut off the new car's engine.

"This new whip rides like a beauty my G. You got it! You are doing it big out here in these streets my G." Derrick loudly spoke, as he leaned himself back comfortably into the butter soft leather, resting his head gently onto the Acura's head rest, seated in the back seat, on the passenger side of the new car.

"I'll be honest with you man; I was doing it big inside of my car early this morning out in Coney Island with my girl Monica" Jamal loudly replied. "We blessed my backseat today" Jamal continued to say.

"Ah, man I'm comfortably sitting in your wet spot" Derrick loudly responded as he quickly sat up looking down at the back brown butter soft leather seat.

"I know you're not complaining, soaking up our church's stairwells with Victoria's body fluids. Come on man! During prayer service? How are you going to let the devil use you like that in front of all those religious leaders. You work in the building every day. You couldn't have chosen a quieter time? Like when the church members are not in the building having church" Jamal loudly said as he checked his cell phone for text messages.

"I know man, I messed this one for real" Derrick quickly replied.

"Elder Jackson, my future Uncle in law is not going to let this one go. Did you see the look on his face. His whole attitude towards both of us has changed today. You don't know how angry that's making me man. I've done all that I possibly could to make Monica comfortable around me. That's my heart every day. I don't need anything or anyone to savor what we've put together. I even brought Monica to the block. Introduced her to all of you'll. Respect was shown and respect was given. This is how you do me Derrick! I'm not feeling respected man. My pops Man! I honestly told you how my grandfather's death was tearing me up inside. I confided in you with my feelings. I trusted you with this church stuff. I was telling one of my gang sisters earlier at the wash, I'm feeling better about everything now and the church family was helping me get through my pain. Now look at how I'm feeling. Elder Jackson summoned me to your smash party. I know what you and Kent are doing with them project garden tools inside the church building.

From what Elder Jackson said earlier about that woman's conversation with him outside in front of the church building, while we were downstairs in the church dining hall, it's looking as if everyone knows about, you'll smash parties. That must be the talk of the community. The whole block is buzzing about your smashes. Now I got to look over my shoulder with my man Shawn. This is crazy" Jamal loudly explained as Elder Jackson slowly walked back to the car.

"I'm sorry Jamal. You hear me man. I'm truly sorry" Derrick sincerely apologized.

"Nephew, pop open the trunk!" Elder Jackson yelled through the closed tinted passenger door window as he walked to the back of Jamal's new car by the trunk area. *"That's my future nephew who drove me over here to see you, Deacon Wayne. He joined our church and now is an active member of the congregation. He even has Melonie's eldest daughter praising God in our church"* Elder Jackson continued to loudly say.

"Is that right Elder Jackson. That's God man. He's answering our prayers daily like I just told you man" Wayne the senior bald gentleman loudly replied as he pulled the loaded warehouse cart towards Jamal's new Acura. Taking the bags out of the cart and putting them neatly into the car's trunk the two-gentleman continued to loudly converse about their beliefs in God.

"Honestly, I knew about the prayer service, but I didn't know about the choir rehearsal. I'm like man, don't them people have jobs. What everybody works at night like you" Derrick loudly spoke as he leaned his body back comfortably in the leather back seat.

"*Everybody has a job as far as I know, but you Derrick. Keep bringing your pieces to your work place and you will never hold a job*" Jamal responded.

"*What's really bothering you man? I know my penis action is not on your mind man. What's really, good Jamal*" Derrick loudly inquired.

"*My Job man. It's a good job. It pays my bills. Well, it's okay. I'm the senior man on the night shift. I like how that goes for real. I don't trust my coworker Stanley at all. His relationship with them suits, on the luxury tower's security staff has always concerned me. There's this Hindu dude, his nickname is "Buddha" or that's what the security guard staff call him, he and Aram, the loudmouth annoying morning doorman, they be working the models inside the apartment building. They have their own operation going on in there. The problem I'm having is Budha don't rock with Stanley. At All. They can't stand one another. That messes me up on the days I don't work because your brother Dewayne's Connect does more of their transactions on my days off. So, like this morning, she kept calling me while I'm trying to get into Monica's panties. I saw the look on her face in front of her back high school doors before she sneaked inside. Her whole mood switched up on me in the car when she saw the caller identification number on the display panel here. Now Monica's blowing up my phone, which she doesn't usually do. Her Uncle wanted to talk to me, which he doesn't usually do, knowing I should be home sleep, about whatever is up. I'm guessing Monica's worry of your brother Dewayne's connect. Monica sees me with her in the morning before the lady goes to work inside one of the other luxury rental buildings management offices, two blocks*" *away. My luv Monica never asks me any questions about the woman's friendly conversations with me, even though I know it's bothering her young tender heart. I'm trying to stay clear of my workplace on the days when I'm not supposed to be in the luxury building high-rise tower because the assistant super and I are about to come to blows. I'm dead, serious about to catch a case with that Italian cat because his mouth is wreck less."* Jamal honestly shared as Elder Jackson closed the Acura's trunk and proceeded to the front passenger side of the car. *"That's why I need to stop with your brother man"* Jamal continually said.

"Elder Jackson just confirmed it while we were in the church's basement" Derrick loudly replied as Jamal stared at him through his new Acura's rearview mirror.

CHAPTER 19

THE DETECTIVES ENTRY

As Tiffany quickly entered the small hospital waiting area Freddy was leaning up against a hospital wall, talking on his cell phone discussing color patterns with his colleagues while Mike was standing up conversating with two nurses that he knew from the neighborhood. Walking over to Danielle Tiffany took a seat directly next to her placing her hand on Danielles knee.

"How's Steph and Ezra Tiff?" Alonzo softly asked.

"She's still waiting for the doctor's full assessment of Ezra's open wounds condition. They still have him heavily sedated. Is that a good thing or a bad thing, girl I really don't know. Steph. Is feeling sad about the whole thing. Hopefully her family coming into town will assist in lifting the load that her broken heart is carrying. You'll know how protective she normally is of her younger brother. This is heavy on my bestie Stephanie's heart. Ezra's blood pressure has to go down and

like I said before that is still their main concern. He doesn't need any stroke symptoms. We need our superhero to be strong and fast on those ski slopes. Steph is sad, very sad so I'm going now to talk to her gym assistant and see if he can fill in for her during her absences. I'm now a fulltime assistant today" Tiffany clearly explained.

"Maybe we should go get some flower, get well balloons, card or something" Alonzo softly replied.

"That would be nice. That's a good idea Alonzo. Let me ask you Tiffany, is her gym assistant a team player?" Danielle softly asked.

"That's an understatement from how Stephanie describes him" Tiffany responded as she stared at Alonzo directly in his eyes.

Entering the Emergency section of the hospital building were a deputy, and two gentlemen dressed in suits. Freddy, noticing how they were staring at Danielle, Tiffany and his close friend Alonzo, ended his cell phone job related meeting and walked back to the small seating area. As the three individuals stood in front of the Emergency Unit door, Freddy quickly sat down. Mike, observing the deputy and the two gentlemen in suits continued his conversation with the Lenox Hill hospital nurses. As the hospital security guard slowly opened the emergency unit door, amid speaking to the New York Police Department deputy, she pointed in the direction of Tiffany, Danielle, Alonzo and Freddy as the deputy along with the two gentlemen in suits proceeded to walk in their direction. Mike immediately ended his conversation with his neighbor friends and rejoined them in the small waiting area.

"Good afternoon, Tiffany" The male gentleman in the suit spoke.

"Yes, that is me how can I help you gentlemen" Tiffany *nervously replied raising her right hand.*

"Tiffany my name is Detective Patterson, and this is my partner Homicide Detective Haley, and we are here at the hospital to speak with Ezra and Stephanie. Do you know where we can find the two of them" Detective Patterson inquired.

"They are both in the Intensive Care Unit, inside of the Emergency unit on the other side of those doors you were just standing in front of" Tiffany quickly replied. *"She is back there with her good friend Melonie and neighbor, a United Nations leadership staff member"* Tiffany continued to share as the two Homicide Detectives looked at each other.

"May I ask you Tiffany, what is your association with Ezra and Stephanie" Detective Haley loudly asked as Mike quickly sat down in the waiting area chair.

"Ezra and Stephanie are my closest and dearest friend's sir. These are Stephanie's neighbors as well as good friends. We were all together in Stephanies penthouse apartment when Gordon, Ezra's older brother called her from his ski trip in Colorado" Tiffany honestly replied.

"Homicide, the female Sergeant that spoke to us earlier didn't mention anything about a homicide today at the post office" Alonzo loudly spoke.

"And you are sir?" Homicide Detective Patterson loudly inquired.

"My name is Alonzo I'm another close and dear friend to the family who is an active law student" Alonzo quickly replied.

"The fight that took place in the post office on this morning, that I know you are all aware of, there were several individuals who were injured and in need of serious medical attention besides Ezra. Who were all transported to different hospitals throughout Manhattan. One of the other victims have died. We need to speak to Ezra and his sister Stephanie" Homicide Detective Haley shared.

"Oh no, Ezra, oh God! Let me take you to them. I was just about to use Ezra's cell phone to contact his fiancé to see where she is presently located. His fiancé is supposed to be on her way here to the hospital. I was also going to call Stephanies gym assistant to have him fill in for her yoga class" Tiffany sadly responded, slowly raising up out of the chair to escort the officers into the Emergency Unit to speak with Stephanie as the two Homicide detectives looked at each other.

"Tiffany, you mentioned that you have Ezra's cell phone; I may need to confiscate that cell from you" Detective Patterson said as Tiffany turned and stared at Alonzo.

CHAPTER 20

DAYCARE PICKUP

Approaching the crosswalk a block away from the high school Melonie, Kaneesha, Cindy and her boyfriend Carlos stopped to figure out what direction they were heading now that they had all left the school building together.

"What's the deal with Jamal Melonie? Why the silent treatment suddenly?" Cindy asked.

"Leave her alone tend to your own champion boxer that's standing here?" Kaneesha quickly replied.

"Maybe he's sleeping, since he worked overnight." Melonie softly responded.

"My girl wore that fine boy Jamal out" Cindy replied as she wrapped her arm around her boyfriend Carlos.

"It's still early I'm texting my boo now, telling her that I'm traveling with you Melonie to pick up your brother and sisters

and for her to meet us at the elementary school" Kaneesha spoke.

"Yeah, we'll walk along with you as well Mel. I'm not used to being out of school so early. Plus you can use the company until Jamal hits you back on the cell" Carlos said.

"I can't believe they let Kaneesha, and I walk out the building without challenging us on why were leaving school so early in the day" Cindy spoke.

"They all a bunch of butt holes. They can all kiss my huge black butt" Kaneesha replied.

"Girl, you need to stop messing with them school safety guards, the last thing you need is a problem with our high schools law enforcers" Melonie replied. "Thank you guys for walking with me, I'm going to pick up my baby sister first and then we'll go over to the elementary school to get the two pains in my black butt" Melonie said as the teenagers crossed the huge New York City street on their way to the subway station to travel uptown.

"How long is your suspension Carlos" Melonie loudly asked as they entered busy New York City Subway station.

"Nah, I didn't get suspended. The Dean that was in the office was waiting for the principle I thought, until that very tall, ugly White security guard entered inside the administrative office and asked the Dean why Cindy was standing outside of the office crying. That's when the office worker stepped outside the office. When she came back inside, the three of them huddled like there was a play about to executed on the

game court" Carlos said as he pulled out his train pass to show the transit clerk inside of the New York City Subway station.

"His name is Paul. He's creepy I'll admit" Melonie replied.

"Paul went inside of a desk drawer, inside of the administration office while never taking his eyes off of me and pulled out the red slips, handing them to the Dean. The Dean filled them out and handed my red slip back to Paul. When he handed me the red slip, he told me to go home and there will be no basketball practice for me today. That was it" Carlos shared as the teenagers stood on the Subway platform waiting for the uptown local Subway train.

"I told you'll that dude is fake! They know it. Phony Wack no shot having, skill less, waist of my time and energy. That's what he is. A waste. Even Paul knew it. What could he say? I put a serious hurt on the cat. He wasn't ready for my fist and tall Paul knew it" Carlos continued to loudly say.

"Tall Paul, Champ you crazy" Kaneesha shouted out as she burst out in laughter.

"I feel bad that I missed it" Melonie replied as the Subway train Fastly approached the crowded city train station.

"Girl, my baby got skills not only shooting hoops but throwing jabs at a real idiot" Cindy responded as the teenagers boarded the uptown local Subway train.

"I heard the roar in the cafeteria. Carlos your quick jabs and upper cuts drew a cheering crowd in the cafeteria today" Kaneesha replied as they all sat together on the Subway train.

"*Like I said before, he and I have been at each other throats for a while. So, my teammate had it coming. I'm not worried about any retaliation. His whole side crew is Wack! None of them can rock with me on the basketball court. I'll wash all of them. You are going to boldly step towards my girl in my face. You warranted a butt whipping*" Carlos loudly responded as Cindy rested her head onto his chest. *Now the coach is probably upset. I'm sure he's going hit me up on my cellphone tonight and fuss me out for fighting my teammate. He'll probably punish the whole team for what happened. I'm prepared for it. One thing you're not going to do is disrespect me*" Carlos loudly explained.

"I had your back. Ask Melonie, I was going to call my brothers and really get it lit in the school building. I said it too. If I heard someone even touched my girl Cindy, I was coming with some heat" Kaneesha loudly replied.

"*Yeah, she was getting upset in the cafeteria girl. I'm glad we were out though. I needed fresh air. I wasn't feeling school today.*" Melonie loudly responded.

"*That's because you've been feeling on Jamal all morning in his new car*" Cindy quickly replied.

"*He'll hit you up later today. If you were with him this morning Melonie, then let him breathe a little. Don't smother the dude. He's into you. You know it. Its when you don't see the dude, or he never calls you is when you must worry about being ghosted*" Carlos replied.

"*Or replaced*" Kaneesha shouted out as she crossed her legs.

"*Where he be at anyway when he's not sleeping at the crib*" Carlos loudly inquired.

"*Further uptown than we are headed now. He hangs out in the low hundred streets. On the East side. I met some of his friends*" Melonie replied.

"*That's where that dude lives at, I fought earlier. His gang is trash though. I saw that today. All mouth no skills. They from Spanish Harlem. I don't care what uptown projects he's from you will not disrespect me at any time. I hope my teammate understands the message I threw him today*" Carlos responded.

"*If he doesn't, you'll be waxing that butt again Carlos*" Kaneesha shouted out as the train pulled into the station where they would be getting off the Subway train.

"*Today is really a wicked day. Our Jamaican economics teachers' husband is locked up in jail because someone probably disrespected him you know how serious the Rasta Farian's are about being respected. I missed her teaching our class today*" Cindy spoke as they all exited the Subway train.

"*Girl bye! You don't pay attention in class who are you talking too*" Kaneesha sarcastically replied.

"*What if she can't come back to class because her husband must go to trial for seriously hurting someone that didn't respect him. Like assault or attempted murder. You'll didn't see the way she ran out of the building. That problem with her Rasta Fari, husband and the police are serious*" Cindy explained as they all slowly walked up the staircase to exit the subway station.

"*She has talked about her husband in the class lessons before. I remember her using him as an example in scenarios when we were problem solving governmental incomes and resources. She did mention him as a Rasta Fari who she's still madly in love with. That substitute teacher who replaced her this morning in our Economics class, him knowing me is also what's upsetting to me. He must have told his wife the excuse I gave him for coming in late and almost missing his lesson for the day. That's why my father called me while we were in Mr. Bowman's class"* Melonie shared as they walked down the crowded city block towards the building that facilitated the daycare program for Monica's baby sister.

"What did the judge say?" Carlos loudly asked

"We are doing what my dad asked for me to do right now, Carlos" Melonie loudly replied as they continued walking down the busy New York City midtown block. *"He was extremely upset that I missed Economics class, and my father hung up on me"* Melonie continued to say.

"He was pissed! You might catch it when you get home Chica. Don't worry we'll both be catching it" Carlos replied.

"How do you know for sure; it was our Economics substitute. I said to you earlier that attendance sheet Mr. Buendia turned into the administration office is what's entered the school's computer system." Cindy loudly responded as they walked down the street while she held her boyfriend Carlos's hand.

"Yeah, ma, you right because the board of Education monitors everything. For example, your parents are going to receive a card in the mail in two business days. Whether the school's administration called your parents today or not. Don't ask me how I know" Carlos loudly replied as he burst out in laughter.

"You think it was the computer entry that ignited my dad's fury about me missing Economics class less than a half hour after the class had ended on my cell phone" Melonie replied.

"We see your point" Kaneesha quickly responded as she answered the incoming call on her ringing cell phone.

"I didn't get a chance to see any of my volleyball teammates today the little bit of time I was inside of the high school building. Maybe my teammates Korean boyfriend will let her know I snuck into the school and was having some issues" Melonie said as they entered the daycare building to pick up her little sister.

"Text them. Send a text to one of your teammates and let them know about your emergency. Precisely, the team leader. That's what I do. I'm sure the coach is going to find out from the Dean anyway. Coming from your team makes it look good, as a team player" Carlos softly suggested as they all stood in the building's lobby while Melonie looked at the directory to see what floor her youngest sister's daycare program was on.

"I'll do that Carlos. You are correct Thanks" Melonie quickly replied as she walked to the stairwell on route to the second floor to pick up her sister. As the three teenagers remained in the buildings lobby Kaneesha ended her phone call with her girlfriend.

"She's almost at the elementary school. My boo doesn't play when it comes to me. Even though I told her that we had to come here first. I think mentioning the fight got her shook" Kaneesha shared as she placed her cell phone into her pocketbook.

"I think you walking the streets of New York City without her, is what prompted her to expeditiously make her way to Monica's brother and sisters' school" Carlos replied.

"My baby loves me. What more can I say. Monica isn't the only one with lips all over her body" Kaneesha responded.

"Ma, pause! That's too much graphic detail" Carlos loudly replied as he burst out in laughter.

"That's way too much tongue activity! Lots of lip action, that's what it is" Cindy quickly replied, as she stepped up towards Kaneesha to give her a high five.

"You'll straight wilding in this lobby" Carlos responded putting his hands into his pockets. As Kaneesha turned and looked outside through the glass windowed doors in the building's lobby.

"Why that man sitting inside the parked car directly in front of this building looks like the school safety agent Paul" Kaneesha shared as she stared at the parked vehicle through the glass doors. Carlos and Cindy quickly moved next to her to catch a glimpse of the car.

"Yes, he does without the uniform though" Carlos quickly replied as he continued staring at the model of the car.

"It doesn't surprise me. Who's the parents of the children we are here with. She can walk around blinded to the judicial watch if she wants. Their mama does work at the United Nations" Cindy said as she slowly walked away from the glass doors to stand by the marble column inside the lobby.

"Carlos, when did you have boxing lessons? How did you learn to fight like you did earlier in the cafeteria during our

lunch period?" Kaneesha inquired as she slowly moved herself away from the glass doors.

"I always knew how to fight. As far back as I can remember. I've fought in our school before. Freshman year, I had a fight in the school auditorium, with those same bums" Carlos replied as he walked over to his girlfriend Cindy and wrapped his arms around her waist.

"I don't remember that one baby" Cindy softly responded as she slowly turned around and wrapped her arm around Carlos's neck.

"Yeah, babe, it wasn't with him though. One of them other Wack dudes from his Spanish Harlem project crew. I'm still not thinking about them bums. I'm not even sure what projects they're from. It's so many of them project buildings uptown there. One of my aunts and cousins live in one of the Spanish Harlem projects. My favorite cousin Victoria, when she brought that Audi not too long ago, had a birthday dinner party for her baby daddy Shawn and the whole family was there celebrating both. My brothers, cousins and my boys were uptown there partying in her project building with no problems. I didn't see none of them Wack high school bums outside or around those projects building anywhere. So, I'm not sure which ones they are from. That move today on you my love, had me tight. Directly in front of me. You going to put your penis area on my girl. Now you are just asking me to put hands on you. Period!" Carlos shouted as he grabbed Cindy holding her tight.

"Audis are nice. One of my older brother's best friends that lives in our building drives an Audi. I know your cousin loves her car" Kaneesha replied.

"That's my favorite cousin even without the car. And that Audi is straight fire! She always looked out for my brothers and me. Her baby father, Shawn, is a cool dude. Little mean though. My Aunts don't care for him too much. I'm thinking that's why Victoria combined his Birthday celebration with her new car celebration. So, we would all attend the party. Mom said he's gang affiliated and is probably involved with the dope hustle. But he has a good job at that popular expensive luxury Tower they built years ago on the west side. He's been working there ever since the building opened. He's legit, however the car belongs to my cousin Victoria" Carlos responded as Cindy started kissing on his cheek.

"Oh, so that's who taught you how to fight. Your favorite cousin, Victoria's boyfriend Shawn?" Kaneesha asked.

"Not even, my mom taught all of us how to fight. It's four of us, all boys too. I don't know my pops, and my youngest brother, his father is still my mom's boyfriend. They have been together since. He finally moved in with us recently. Don't ask me what that's all about. My aunts always held us all down. My family is tight. My grandmother only had girls, and my family used to constantly tease my grandfather at the family get togethers, when I was younger, that his stamina is weak because he couldn't make one boy" Carlos shared as he burst out in laughter. "My mom and aunts they not only raised us four but gave us skills too. My one aunt is like you Kaneesha, her lady friend is nice with the hands though. I'm not even going to lie; she has got skills. Her girlfriend's fist, punching game, is no joke. My oldest brother talks about her all the time. She can also cook too. She makes a mean Bacala

Ito" Carlos shared as Cindy continued kissing on his cheeks and neck area.

"We are going to aunties house for Thanksgiving baby because Kaneesha cannot cook. No kitchen skills. No pot game" Cindy said as she burst out in laughter as Carlos started kissing on her neck area.

'You know what's crazy? As wild as my brother's behaviors are, they are both nice with the meat in our house. I don't know where they picked up the seasoning skill, but both will have you licking your lips as you taste their meats" Kaneesha quickly replied as Monica stepped out the elevator with her little sister, bundled in her pink coat.

"Hi Melody, looking pretty, as always. That's God mommy's favorite. How was class today?" Kaneesha softly asked as she quickly ran over to her and gave her a big hug.

"We got company watching us outside Monica they are parked in an unmarked vehicle directly in front of the building" Cindy said. As Monica quickly walked over to the glass doors.

"Where are they parked, I don't see anyone" Monica loudly replied as Cindy and Carlos walked over to the glass doors.

"Oh, they left. Whoever it was, left from in front of the building. The guy seated inside of the unmarked parked car resembled our school safety agent Paul" Cindy responded as Monica slowly turned herself around and stared at Melody while Kaneesha grabbed her hand.

CHAPTER 21

GLAD YOU CALLED

"Jamal, this is my first time in your new ride. It drives smoothly. You don't even have to dodge the potholes in the streets because the suspension in this car is durable" Elder Jackson loudly said as he scrolled the display screen on his cell phone.

"Thanks sir, the car has impressed me thus far. No complaints. It's not bad on gas either" Jamal responded.

"I'm glad you mentioned gas because we have one more stop to make. This stop may require a little gas. I'm going to need you to take us to my sister's house asap in Manhattan. She's been texting me all morning and I'm worried about her and the family. I very much appreciate it" Elder Jackson spoke as Jamal looked through his rearview mirror directly at Derrick.

I take it I have no choice sir" Jamal honestly replied.

"Derrick has no choice, but you will always have choices.

My suggestion to you Jamal in life, is for you to allow God to help you in your decision making when it comes to which is the better choice. What may be the right choice for me now. Even if your decision somewhere along the line ends up not being the best choice. As a man of God, I admonish you not to give up. Not to think that life has ended. Don't throw in the towel with a mindset that it's over and there's nothing else to do. Because if God is in your life than there will always be time afforded to you, to make another decision. This time when you make your choice allow more of God into the choosing process. Have you spoke to my niece recently since this morning?" Elder Jackson inquired as Jamal headed for the Brooklyn highway

"No, man, not since this morning" Jamal softly replied.

"Give her a call right now. I know she would love to hear from you, and I need to speak to her" Elder Jackson said as Jamal lifted the cellphone and handed it to Elder Jackson to call his niece Monica.

"See you're making better choices already Jamal" Elder Jackson continued to say as he took the phone from Jamal and dialed Monica's cell phone.

Walking up the block heading towards the crosswalk intersection, Monica stopped walking to reach into her purse to pull out her cell phone, as Kaneesha, Melody, Cindy and Carlos stopped walking and stood with her. Monica, seeing the incoming call on her cellphone was her boyfriend Jamal, she quickly answered the phone call.

"Hi, my love, what you up to now?" Jamal inquired as Elder Jackson turned up the volume on the cars stereo system to hear clearly the wireless Bluetooth connection.

"I needed you, Jamal. I kept on texting you because School was crazy today. My Economics teacher left early before class started. Her Rasta Fari husband was arrested due to an incident in a post office. Paul, the school safety guard and his wolf pack were on me all morning. I couldn't breathe baby; they stayed on my heels. Kept on hounding me, as if I was the prey, all day. Carlos beat up one of his teammates during our lunch period. The Dean sent us all home early. So, I did make it to Melody's daycare. I have her now. We're on our way to pick up my brother and sister. Dad called me because he knows about the Economics class. Jamal, I'm scared. I miss you" Melonie spoke as Cindy and Kaneesha played around with Melody.

"My luv, I miss you too. I miss you so much and you already know that. I want you to pause. Take a deep breath and exhale slowly for me. Can you do that right now, while I patiently wait for your lovely self to perform that for me." Jamal softly replied. *"Now, I want you to think about me holding you and resting my lips on your heart as you take another deep breath and slowly exhale. Listen, my luv, I'm here and I'm not going anywhere. Like I said unto you this morning you got me, and no other female can compare. I want this to be made clear my heart only beats for you that's the truth I only declare"* Jamal softly rhythmically responded as he swerved in and out of the lanes on the Brooklyn highway due to heavy traffic.

"I just want to see you. My body wants to see you. My mind can't stop showing me everything that I've seen on you. You secure me in stressful times like this. You please me all the time and it's your pleasure that I truly miss" Monica

softly rhythmically replied as she pointed towards the building across the street in the other block. The teenagers slowly began to walk in that direction while Monica continued to conversate with her boyfriend Jamal.

"It's you I enjoy my luv, on days like this. Today and beyond I'll give you more love, with every kiss" Jamal softly rhythmically replied as he continued to swerve his new Acura in and out of the lanes.

"You know how make me wet baby. I yearn for your pleasure Jamal" Melonie softly responded as the teenagers crossed the street.

"No doubt, you know I got that ready for you my luv, but listen, who's all that is with you right now" Jamal inquired as he aggressively beeped his horn signaling for another driver to either speed up or move to another lane.

"My girls, Cindy, Kaneesha and the all-star cafeteria boxing champ Carlos. It was he and I that received the early passes to leave school from the administration office. His girlfriend Cindy and my homegirl Kaneesha just followed us right out the school. I'm not even sure if I'm marked present on today because of you and I earlier" Monica cheerfully replied, as Elder Jackson slowly turned his head to look at Jamal. *"Carlos gave me an idea that I'm going to do when I finish speaking with you and that is to call my teammates and let them know about the family emergency on today. When I spoke with my dad he wouldn't give me much detail."* Monica continued to say.

"Have you spoken to your mom?" Jamal softly asked.

"She hasn't text me back since I was with you in the

217

car earlier before I snuck through the back doors of my school building. I'm really getting nervous. Dad mentioned the hospital. I even tried calling her close friend Stephanie but I'm not getting an answer. For me to have to leave school early, pick up all the kids and go home to cook dinner for my other brother without a clear explanation frightens me Jamal" Melonie explained as she pointed out her index finger again, towards the buildings down the block. The teenagers continued to walk down the busy city street.

"Hang up the phone" Elder Jackson quietly whispered to Jamal as he scrolled through his contact list on his cellphone, in search for his sister's contact information.

"I'm here for you my luv. I'm super tired though. I just want to close my eyes" Jamal honestly shared.

"Why are you tired baby? You didn't go home and go to sleep after you left me this morning?" Monica asked.

"I had to go back to Brooklyn to the church and talk with your uncle" Jamal honestly confessed.

"Hopefully it wasn't about me?" Monica quickly replied.

"Hopefully you will hang the phone up" Elder Jackson quietly whispered.

"I'm just tired. I was very sleepy, but I had to make a couple of runs before I headed back to Brooklyn. One of them was to wash the car you know I can't stand a dirty whip. But Monica, let me finish this last errand and I'll call you back when I arrive at my destination. I love you Monica" Jamal softly said.

"I love you too Jamal" Monica softly replied as she disconnected the phone call.

"You feel better girl now that you finally heard from you boyfriend" Kaneesha loudly asked as the teenagers continued walking down the street with Melody by the hand.

"I can't explain it. I feel so much better now that I heard his voice than I did earlier" Monica replied as the teenagers continued walking down the street heading to the elementary school to pick up her brother and sister while Carlos cut his eyes towards Monica to stare at her.

"Jamal, I just don't understand why you didn't mention to me anything about my sister. Not only did you lie to me when I asked if you were aware of my niece attendance at her high school, but you didn't have the courage to share something vital as the emergency news concerning her mother." Elder Jackson spoke as he dialed Danielle's cell phone number. *"I appreciate you driving us to Manhattan Jamal"* Elder Jackson continued to say.

"I apologize Elder. I love your niece. I honestly do" Jamal confessed.

"You are sounding like me now my G." Derrick loudly responded sitting comfortably in the back butter soft leather seat as he slightly tilted his head to the left staring at Jamal through the Acura's rear-view mirror.

CHAPTER 22

THE FIANCE HAS ARRIVED

As Danielle reached inside her jacket pocket to answer the incoming call on her cell phone, Ezra's fiancé arrived at the Emergency unit door. Nervously and anxiously waiting to see her boyfriend, the hospital security guard was not moving fast enough on the other side of the door to open it and give her access to see what had happened to the love of her life. Freddy knew who she was immediately from the sadness of her countenance. Wanting to walk over there to comfort her at this horrific time, he felt it would be best for him to remain seated while the Homicide Detectives were in the Intensive Care Unit with Ezra. As the Emergency Unit door swung open, Melonie walked out being escorted by the Lenox Hill hospital security guard. Walking pass Ezra's fiancé Melonie headed towards the chairs located in the small waiting area, to sit with Tiffany, Mike, Alonzo, Freddy and Danielle as they patiently waited for their dear friend Stephanie.

"Hello" Danielle loudly spoke on the cell phone because of the bad reception, as Melonie sat down next to Tiffany.

"Good afternoon, Dee Dee, its Elder Jackson. How are you?" Elder Jackson inquired.

"Yes, I knew who it was, your name went across my phone's caller identification" Danielle loudly replied.

"I'm terribly sorry to bother you currently. But my niece is having some challenges trying to get in contact with her mother. She is very worried having received word from the judge that my sister Melonie is in the emergency room. And he has given her specific instructions to leave her high school early and pick up the other children from their school. Would you happen to know if that's true?" Elder Jackson inquired

"Elder Jackson, you have called me at the right time. God is truly with you and watches over your entire family" Danielle loudly replied as Tiffany and Melonie quickly turned their heads towards her with looks of surprise displayed on their faces. *"Monica just walked out of the Intensive Care Unit from being with Stephanie and her younger brother Ezra who was attacked in a post office this morning. However, I know you would love to speak to her so I'm going to hand Melonie my cell phone"* Danielle continued speaking as she passed her cell phone over to her good friend Melonie.

"This is bad guys. I feel sorry for Stephanie right now. Like we talked about, she loves her younger brother tremendously. Now you have detectives questioning Ezra in his condition

when he's supposed to be getting the proper medical treatment to make him feel better" Mike softly said expressing his feelings as Melonie quietly discussed the situation with her brother Elder Jackson on Danielle's cell phone.

"Not just any New York City precinct Detectives. Two Homicide Detectives now at Ezra's hospital bedside" Alonzo quickly responded as Melonie stopped talking on Danielle's cellphone turning her head towards Alonzo.

"Yes, this unfortunate day went from a oh no, to an oh my God in an instant. Look at that timing. You see who just entered the emergency unit. Imagine how she's going to take this, walking in on her boyfriend Ezra and the Homicide Detectives standing there at her man's bedside. They are questioning Ezra about the entire post office event this morning. To see her man in a vulnerable wounded state, girl she is going to break down in that Emergency Intensive Care Unit honey" Freddy responded.

"Wait Freddy, how do you know its Ezra's girlfriend. I didn't see her" Tiffany quickly replied.

"I did Fred. I think that it was his girlfriend that had just walked in the Emergency Unit while Melonie walked towards us. I never seen Ezra's girlfriend but it sure fitted the description" Mike replied as Melonie disconnected the cell phone call from her brother Elder Jackson. Handing Danielle back her cell phone, Melonie rested her hand on Tiffany's knee.

"Did I overhear Homicide? Those two detectives that entered the Intensive Care Unit were from the Homicide Division" Melonie Inquired.

"Mother Superior of God you heard right. They didn't identify themselves as Homicide Detectives to you when they came inside the Intensive Care Unit?" Freddy replied, leaning forward in his chair.

"No because Stephanie was inside the room at Ezra's bedside talking with the medical team concerning Ezra's diagnosis" Melonie quickly replied.

"Homicide Detectives, who died?" Melonie quietly asked.

"We don't know Melonie. They didn't say. They also confiscated Ezra's cell phone from me because of its evidence in the post office crime scene. I was going to escort the two detectives inside, but they made me wait outside here. Maybe I should not have mentioned that I had Ezra's cellphone. I was going to call his girlfriend to find out her estimate time of arrival" Tiffany responded.

"Well, Tiff. Ezra's girlfriend is here now. That is one task down Ms. Personal Assistant. You can still make the telephone call to the gym for Stephanie" Alonzo said as Melonie quickly turned her head and stared at Alonzo.

CHAPTER 23

NOT IN MY HOUSE

As Jamal's new Acura slowly approached the Brooklyn bridge, Elder Jackson dialed his brother-in-law, Judge Watkins cellphone to alert him of the events that have taken place on this day. Hearing the sad tone in his sister Melonie's voice, the result of being in Intensive Care Unit with her friend Stephanie, Elder Jackson knew that she hadn't had time to inform her husband of the details concerning Ezra. Derrick quickly text Kent on his mobile device to inform him that they were not coming back to the church in Brooklyn today.

"Good day judge how are you" Elder Jackson clearly said as Judge Watkins answered his cell phone.

"I've had better days preacher" Judge Watkins sternly replied.

"Judge, I just hung up the phone from speaking with Melonie, who is still at Lenox Hill Hospital as you already

have been made aware of. The reception inside of the Intensive Care Unit is poor so she has limited use of her own cell phone. Ezra is not in a coma which is a good sign for recovery. He did lose a significant amount of blood, and the open wound is deep. The doctors are discussing all the results and findings of the medical exams they have been conducting on Ezra all morning with his sister Stephanie as we speak. Melonie said she was distraught. Do you blame her? That type of vicious attack in a public setting as the post office is upsetting. Now while Melonie was sharing with me, I overheard one of their friends in the background mentioned Homicide Detectives being around Ezra's bedside. That was when your wife politely rushed me off the phone. Now she did have a chance to express her concern of Monica's behavior to me. I figured something was up surrounding your daughter Monica, because all day my sister was texting me that we needed to talk. When I finally tried reaching out to her, she didn't pick up her cell phone. So, Judge, I took the initiative to call your neighbor Danielle since I know they all hang out with one another and that's how I spoke with Melonie" Elder Jackson spoke as Jamal continued to drive his new car across the Brooklyn bridge in New York City traffic.

"Did Melonie say to you what caused the sharp force trauma to Sephanie's younger brother Ezra?" Judge Watkins Inquired.

"A mentally unstable couple ignited a riot type situation in the post office service area" Elder Jackson responded.

"Preacher that is one of the reasons why I love your sister very much. She is constantly praying over our family. She'll dance and praise wholeheartedly every chance Melonie

can get. There have been times amid our worship services when Melonie is giving her extra expression of praise to God, while I'll just remain seated in the church pew looking at her as like some of the other members of our church do, viewing as if my wife Melonie is out of her natural mind. On the spiritual side of her devotion unto God, she believes in the power of prayer, the joyous results of praise and reverence unto God. I honestly admit my wife shuffling through the streets in the early morning hours today I felt was excessive. In my profession, throughout the day in my courtroom, I'm face to face with criminally insane or some of New York City's criminal psychopaths with the intent to do bodily harm. Individuals who mentally plan, scheme, plot to carry out hideous crimes and commit murder. Throughout my years as a New York State Judge, I've witnessed plenty of them. As a husband I should be concerned about my wife roaming the streets alone in the dark. My feeling this early morning was that she could, pray, praise, scream, holler and dance unto God in who she wholeheartedly believes in at home, in our bedroom. That attack today, which involves Ezra, has taken place in a public setting, in broad daylight. That is how serious the issues of criminal minds are. In my professional career some of these individuals who are animalistic carry out their perverted madness in the most inconvenient times. I don't know all the detailed circumstances surrounding Ezra's conditions as a victim of a crime in New York City today. I'm sure my wife, when she has a chance, will get in touch with me and fill me in the specifics of the matter. I'm thankful that Ezra's life was not taken in the vicious attack on him today inside of the post office. I pray to God that the perpetrators have been caught, arrested, booked *and charged with the extent of the crimes that he or she have fully committed against young Ezra of the laws of the court of law here in New York City. It is a tragedy. A horrific event that has taken place involving Stephanies loved one today. I'm glad to hear, in my judicial ear, that my loving wife is staying right there, serving love and providing spiritual care"* Judge Watkins rhythmically replied.

"As for my oldest baby Monica, her recent behavior has upset me. It's of the devil. Her missing out on classes as important as Economics before, not my wife Preacher, before I had my contacts in the school release her early to pick up my babies. You are correct I spoke to my daughter and have given her sneaky devilish self, specific instructions to carry out for my family. Preacher, your niece Monica is of age now where she feels independent and grown. Those two feelings don't mix well in my home. Not when I'm daily keeping attempted killers from terrorizing people's homes. Her biggest reason for making your place of worship her new church home. Monica is not that grown" Judge Watkins continued to share.

"Brother, I'm glad you brought my niece up today. I love her dearly, so you know that I only want the best for her. What has happened in that post office to Stephanies brother Ezra, is a tragedy. I know if that had been me your wife, strong as her faith is, powerful as her prayer life that she demonstrates to others, we can both honestly say that it is, your wife would be in the same frame of mind as Stephanie." Elder Jackson said as Jamal who remained silent, driving his new car exited off the Brooklyn bridge veered off into the right lane as they entered lower Manhattan.

"No doubt. My wife would be hysterical! You are correct" Judge Watkins quickly replied.

"My point exactly brother. That is because every day my sister and I speak. And she has a loving husband. Not a day goes by that my sister doesn't contact me in one form or another. Even if it is to say good night and I'm praying for you. So, there is no doubt, like you just said Judge Watkins that my sister loves me. She has no fear in expressing her love or demonstrating her love even if it is publicly. That is Melonie. That's just my sister. In the same token her oldest daughter has adapted her mother's ways. Because if that had been me laying on the gurney inside of Lenox Hill hospital, then your biggest worry would not have been my sister but your daughter Monica." Elder Jackson explained.

"You are probably correct preacher. However, the recent blatant dishonor of our rules and not handling your responsibilities as a student is upsetting as a parent" Judge Watkins honestly confessed. *"I have high hopes for my children. Monica has great potential to be productive in whatever field she chooses to pursue in life. I regard all my babies with high esteem. Her choosing that high school was already disappointing to me. Your loving sister backed me off. It was not my choice. Her choosing your church to worship and not for all of us to be together as a family unit in our church on my day off, is disappointing to me and your loving sister backed me off. It was not my choice. Nobody is going to back me off my child disrespecting me in not going to school to receive an education. I didn't raise any criminals. I will not tolerate any pre-mature rule breakers living inside of my home that I pay for. I will stop the devil's intent with my baby girl right now"* Judge Watkins responded.

"Brother, I love you and I respect you. Just wanted you to know the current situation concerning Stephanie's brother Ezra" Elder Jackson quickly replied as Jamal drove the new Acura up the freeway that surrounded Manhattan.

"I appreciate that what you did Elder Jackson. Continue to have a blessed day brother" Judge Watkins said as he disconnected the cell phone call. Elder Jackson quickly dropped his cell phone into his lap. As Derrick stared at Jamal.

"Where to now Uncle" Jamal asked as he continued to swerve in and out of lanes on the traffic filled freeway.

"To locate my nieces and nephews Jamal like Monica wanted you to do along with her all day" Elder Jackson replied as Derrick shifted his staring eyes off of Jamal and on onto Elder Jackson.

CHAPTER 24

THE WIDE TURN

"What's wrong Tiffany why the disappointed look on your face" Danielle asked as she crossed her legs seated on the narrow chair inside of the small Emergency unit waiting area.

"Girl, I can't get a hold of Ronald. I've repeatedly dialed the cell phone number Steph. has listed for him in her contact list and he's not picking up his phone. I did leave a detailed voicemail message but as time is steady moving, the Yoga classes are Fastly approaching. I can't take the risk of him not checking his voicemail messages in time and no one is there at the gym to instruct the Yoga class. Now Steph. Had mentioned that he is also a massage therapist so he may be with a client and can't speak on the phone. I'm thinking that I may need to run to the gym and talk with the gym administrator. I don't want to leave the hospital, but you guys will be here with Steph in case she's in need of anything" Tiffany spoke as

she slowly took a seat in one of the small waiting area narrow chairs.

"If you think that is best and will help her situation then I admonish you to act on it, girl. Matter of fact I need to call my teddy bear and let him know that I'm still here with Steph in the Emergency unit. He told me earlier that Monica is going to get my babies from school since it's the babysitter's day off, so I'm not worried as much about my children. He may have to leave the courthouse at an appropriate time to make sure everything and everyone in the house is doing okay. This is technically one of my days off anyway, so my teddy bear may need to fill in where my children are accustomed to me being. Girl I'm going to call my teddy bear now" Melonie said as she quickly arose out of the narrow waiting area chair to go outside and stand in front of the hospital for a better reception as she made the call to her husband on her cellphone.

"Gordon's flight should be arriving here to New York soon in a few hours. At least Steph will have family here in the hospital with her. I don't know how comfortable she is with Ezra's girlfriend if that is her inside of the Intensive Care Unit with them. Speaking of them, the Homicide Detectives have been with her for quite a while" Tiffany said.

"Tiff, I was sitting here thinking the same thing. That's why I kept looking at my watch and checking the time" Freddy quickly replied.

"Sounds like a big investigation. I don't know how responsive Ezra is, in his condition" Danielle responded.

"That's why I said I was going to buy some flowers and a card for Ezra from all of us to sign. That would sweeten up

the atmosphere inside of his Intensive Care Unit. The items will make them both feel loved in such a cold and hostile city. With Homicide Detectives now arriving at the hospital, doing an intense investigation, in my perspective this is not looking that well" Alonzo softly replied.

"With her brother Gordon sitting here at the hospital along with her, whenever he arrives, I personally feel that will be comforting for Steph." Mike loudly responded.

"When the cowboys arrive, she will absolutely be surrounded by familiarity" Tiffany spoke.

"Cowboys, girl who saddling through the penthouse" Freddy inquired.

"Her twin sister's boyfriends later on tonight" Tiffany replied.

"The wild, wild west is coming to the Tower. That's the protection my girl Steph needed against annoying Bradley" Danielle responded.

"Dee, Dee that's the testosterone she needed against Aram" Freddy replied as he stared at Alonzo.

"You guys, Stephanie is not thinking about those men currently" Tiffany quickly responded.

"Alonzo is girl" Freddy shouted, turning his entire body towards Alonzo while staring at him, as he burst out in laughter.

"I'm still shocked!" Mike shouted, turning his whole body towards Alonzo, also staring at him as he and Danielle burst out in laughter.

"That is those tower secrets you'll keep brewing inside your luxury building, with a tight lid on top" Tiffany quickly replied as she uncrossed her legs. *"I must get to Ronald for*

my girl Steph. Here you'll hold her cell phone while I take a cab over to the gym to inform them of Stephanies emergency" Tiffany spoke as she arose out of the narrow chair, handing Danielle the cellphone as she quickly headed towards the hospital exit door. Walking outside of the busy emergency room lobby door and into the congested Manhattan Streets, Tiffany stretched her hand out to flag a green taxicab to take her to the gym. Melonie disconnecting her cell phone call with her husband the judge, ran over to Tiffany giving her a hug before going inside of the hospital emergency room. Looking down the block towards the corner to the left, Tiffany spotted a taxicab with its right turn signal blinking approaching the intersection before it came to a complete stop, waiting for the red–light signal to turn green so the taxicab could turn into the block. Tiffany also saw a large box truck with its right turn signal blinking as well that was ahead of the taxicab, already at the red stop light but positioned in the center lane. Hoping the taxicab had seen her, Tiffany stuck her hand out further, waving it up and down as the light signal turned green. Both vehicles simultaneously approached the intersection to make the right turn into the narrow block. As the Box truck made the right turn, the taxicab immediately came to a complete stop, honking its horn as the box truck proceeded in making the right turn, the box truck then veered into the green taxicab, smashing into the taxicab, pinning it between the box truck and the parked SUV. As the sounds of the medal loudly scraping sounded at the intersection, the green taxicab driver continued to honk its horn as the box truck smashed into the green taxicab. What Tiffany didn't see was the passenger inside of the green taxicab seated in the backseat. Jumping out of the driver seat of the box truck, upset and angry, the truck driver begins to yell and scream at the taxicab driver. The taxicab driver couldn't open his door to verbally respond, because of the extensive damage that the box truck did to his vehicle. He continued to bang on his horn letting the truck driver know that he did alert him before the accident. As the two men continued to exchange harsh words back and forth Tiffany slowly walked down the block towards the congested corner, seeing that now the street was blocked from oncoming traffic due to the sudden accident. Observing the truck drivers growing hostility, Tiffany walked faster to the corner so she wouldn't get caught in the middle of another heated argument on today. As the green taxicab backseat passenger door slid open, a tall heavy-set gentleman stepped out of the vehicle and started fussing at the truck driver.

"Hey Tiff? Tiff, you see this madness! He knows he was wrong about that! Hey Tiff. Where are you going" The heavy-set gentleman loudly spoke, carrying a bag in his hand and two get-well balloons.

"Oh my God, Bobby, are you alright?" Tiffany shockingly replied as she immediately ran over to the green taxicab to see Bobby.

"Did you see that, Tiff? Did you happen to witness

this mess?" Bobby yelled as he backed away from the taxicab.

"That was insane Bobby, I'm glad you are not hurt. Call Mike, they are sitting right there not far from the lobby doors. Let him know you were just in a taxi accident" Tiffany replied as Bobby quickly pulled out his cellphone and dialed his lover Mike as she suggested.

"Mike I'm outside of the Emergency room at the corner. A big truck just smashed into the cab I was riding in. I'm standing outside of the taxi with Tiffany. This guy should not be driving period! He was so wrong Mike. The taxicab driver kept honking his horn and the truckdriver completely ignored him" Bobby loudly shared as Mike, Freddy, Alonzo and Danielle came running outside of the hospital to see what happened to Bobby. As the truck driver swung open the front passenger side door of the green taxicab and started aggressively yelling at the taxicab driver who was still nervously seated inside of his vehicle.

"No don't yell at him. You were wrong. You couldn't see a car as big as this one sitting in the correct lane making the right turn into the block. You were in the wrong lane buddy to make that turn. You could have stopped your vehicle at any time, but your stupid self-chose not too!" Bobby angrily replied, as Mike, Freddy, Alonzo and Danielle exited out of the hospital Emergency room running towards the accident scene located on the streets corner. Tiffany stared at the two Asian delivery truck drivers who remained inside of the delivery box truck while the Asian truck driver continued to aggressively yell at the Arab taxicab driver.

"*Call the police*" Mike loudly yelled as they approached the accident scene.

"*Is the taxi driver badly injured?*" Alonzo loudly inquired as he walked over to the passenger side of the truck that crashed into the green taxicab.

"*Call the police! Call the police! Let them see that this guy didn't respect a truck's right*" the Asian truck driver loudly said

"*Does the taxi driver need medical attention*" Danielle loudly asked as she held on to Freddy's arm

"Sir, are you okay? Sir, do you feel pain anywhere? We need to know if you are in any type of pain sir, so we can get medical attention to you right away" Freddy spoke as he leaned himself into the green taxicab passenger side.

"*Call for help please! Look at what this idiot has done to me! Please call for help. Look, my hand was here on the horn, and he didn't care. Look what he has done to my car*" the Arab taxicab driver upsetting replied.

"*Has someone called the police yet*" a pedestrian walking her dogs inquired as she stopped to view the accident scene.

"*Don't yell at him! You were wrong! He honked his horn*" Bobby shouted as Mike stood closer to Bobby to calm him down as Tiffany remained staring at the two Asian delivery truck drivers who remained seated on the passenger side inside of the box truck.

CHAPTER 25

THE DETECTIVES REPORT

"I'm not Gay Steph. I'm super Ez. At least I was invincible before this incident happened to me. I'm not feeling heroic at all right now Steph. I didn't like that at all. I didn't like how that made me feel Officers, honestly speaking. Why would you say that to me. If you are employed to work, then do your job. I don't even know you. Honestly, I really didn't care what his name was. He continued to share that information with me, and I wasn't interested the least bit. You are a post office worker. I just wanted my mail to be delivered by the postal service. He kept pushing the issue. He kept pushing himself to me. He continued flirting with me. At least that's how I saw it and it was in a public place. It started to upset me, Officers. Why would you come at me, like that? That's not me Steph. And I told the postal worker he had me mistaken for someone else." Ezra softly shared as he laid medicated on the gurney in the Intensive Care Unit.

"*Do you remember the name that the post office worker gave to you?*" Homicide Detective Patterson inquired.

"*No sir I don't. I can only remember the pain that I felt. Like nothing else I have ever felt Steph.*" Ezra softly replied as Stephanie grabbed his right hand with her right hand as the tears fell slowly from her eyes.

"*Oh God Ez.*" Stephanie softly whispered.

"*You verbally communicated to the post office worker that you were feeling uncomfortable by his conversation to you*" Homicide Detective Haley inquired as he continued taking notes on his mini notepad.

"*Like I said Detective, I told the post office worker that I was not into the kinds of stuff that he was offering. That I'm not into making any new friends and I only wanted to mail my large envelope through the postal service*" Ezra softly replied as Stephanie shook her head in disbelief.

"*If you don't mind Ezra, can you elaborate on the stuff. What exactly were the things this post-office worker offered you?*" Homicide Detective Haley inquired as he continued taking notes on his note pad.

"*Something about him being a massage therapist, running a business and doing full body massages on his leisure time. Why would you ask another guy that in a public setting? I don't care about your free time. I don't know you! And I didn't want to know him. I understand, this is New York City, but when I did give you the inclination that I wanted a male masseuse. I'm in a happy committed relationship with a beautiful girl from Montana. I don't cheat on my girlfriend. The money I just spent on our ski vacation to Switzerland was for us to celebrate her birthday together as a happy couple. I did all of that to prove to her my true feelings for our relationship. The big muscular Hispanic kept swerving in his chair, that was annoying me as well and making small talk which I uncomfortably felt was flirtatious. I didn't care about the fliers he wanted to give me to promote his business. The whole conversation of him oiling down my body is not why I entered the post office"* Ezra softly, emotionally shared as Stephanie who continued holding her brother's right hand stared at him.

"What kind of fliers did he offer you? Do you know?" Homicide Detective Haley quickly asked.

"I didn't see, I tried my best to ignore the guy. He was annoying me" Ezra quickly replied.

"You just said Hispanic. So, you do remember the ethnicity of the post office worker?" Homicide Detective Patterson inquired.

"Yes, he was Hispanic, and he had muscles. He was a big muscle guy that kept swerving side to side in his chair. Like he had some restless pinned up energy. But I wasn't the one he needed to release his frustrated desires too. Like I said Officers I'm not into that lifestyle. He beat the husband up bad as if he was doing it for my honor" Ezra softly shared as Stephanie let go of her brother's hand as she standing by his bedside. *"Before I heard the sounds of the police officers shoes and radios enter the post office building commanding everyone to stop"* Ezra continued to share.

"So, when did the Hispanic post office worker come from behind the workstation? Can you recall?" Homicide Detective Haley inquired.

"When the husband stabbed me, and I screamed because

the other woman bit me on the hand. She only bit me because I attempted to stop her. I didn't want her to strangle the man's wife to death Officers. I really thought I was doing the right thing. And now look at me. I've been stabbed, I'm in the hospital and I'm in severe pain" Ezra softly replied.

"Yes, Ezra, we see you have been brutally attacked. Its not fair what happened to you" Homicide Detective Patterson replied.

"So, you didn't see when this Hispanic post office worker came from his workstation?" Homicide Detective Haley asked

"No because as I tried to get out of the way as the man's wife attacked the black woman and everyone suddenly started fighting each other right there inside of the post office like a elimination battle wrestling match, I got knocked into the fight by other male post office workers who ran towards the fight trying their best to stop everyone from killing each other" Ezra softly replied.

"Oh God, Ezra" Stephanie whispered as she wiped the tears that fell from her eyes.

"As the post office workers who left their assigned workstations, entered the busy service area, colliding into you, which knocked you into the fight between the five, six, seven, or eight customers, as you put it Ezra, can you remember if anyone attempted to come to your rescue?" Homicide Detective Haley inquired.

"No one physically helped me. I stumbled into the black woman and the stanchion ropes. She literally had one of the stanchion ropes around the man's wife's neck trying to strangle her to death from what I could see. I knew the wife

started the whole fiasco. Her wild pacing back and forth. Yelling, screaming, ranting and using profanity was basically unnecessary so I understood why the black lady warned her that she was going to hurt her" Ezra responded as Stephanie stepped closer to the Intensive Care Units gurney and grabbed his right hand.

"When did the African American woman have the opportunity to grab a stanchion rope?" Homicide Detective Patterson inquired.

"I was facing the Hispanic postal worker when I could hear the argument behind me. The African American woman continued to warn her that the wife's threats were making her upset. The filthy language, name calling was going get her a butt whipping. And that's what she did in my opinion. The wife started it. People were laughing, calling on the postal workers to intercept and stop them but no one came out. The arguing intensified between four individual detectives. I heard a crash sound of medal, immediately I turned around hoping to God it wasn't a bullet, and the wife was acting narcotic. The Jamaican guy was trying to stop her. The husband started yelling at the Jamaican guy and the African American woman, I'm not quite sure if they were together but together, they fought back. The wife was directly behind me yelling and screaming at them. Out of nowhere she just ran and attacked that black woman, but the black woman beat her up in my opinion. The two men started fighting each other and then the crowd surrounding them went crazy. Some people fell all over the stanchion ropes.

I'm not sure officers, but people hit the ground quickly. That's when immediately I started moving to the left and the post office workers rushed into the area pushing me back to the right, into the two women as they fought each other hard. Like I said I tried to stop her from strangling the woman, but she bit me on my hand. And then the husband stabs me trying to kill me. The pain took all my strength away. It was the Hispanic postal worker like I said before, who came to my aid, and beat that husband down until the police entered inside of the post office" Ezra shared as Stephanie stared at her younger brother.

"Okay Ezra. We're not going to trouble you anymore. We have no more questions during this time. Perhaps if you think of anything Ezra, or remember any other important details of the incident, here's my card. Our number is there" Homicide Detective Patterson said as he handed Ezra the card.

"Detectives let me ask you something. Why didn't the police come to the post office sooner? All that arguing and yelling before the man's wife started attacking the customers?" Ezra softly inquired as the team of doctors stepped up to the Intensive Care Units glass window.

"That's a question that will need to be addressed. Ezra it is still an ongoing investigation on what took place at the post office this morning which led to several individuals like yourself in multiple hospitals and a woman dead. The more information that we can get from witnesses like yourself that was present during the violent altercation will help expedite the investigation but until we have enough evidence and facts,

we don't know any specifics. Now this is your cellphone, and I suggest that you keep it on you, we will not have to confiscate it because you have cooperated with us in the Homicide investigation. We do appreciate your cooperation in this investigation and yes, it is a tragedy. I suggest you contact an attorney because you will more likely need one. There is news media camping outside of the hospital. I'm sure they will be trying to get in here to speak with you about what took place today inside of the post office. The hospital security is alert of the situation and is in full cooperation with the New York Police Department that will do their best to keep you isolated as possible. I'm sure the Sergeant and her deputies will be here to speak with you again about what took place on this morning inside of the post office. If you have any questions, concerns or need to talk Ezra don't hesitate to reach out. Most likely we'll be contacting you again with follow up questions as the investigation continues" Homicide Detective Haley explained as Homicide Detective Patterson signaled for the medical team to come back into the Intensive Care room along with Ezra's fiancé who was seated outside of the room waiting patiently to see him.

"By the way officers what happened to the large envelope I was mailing?" Ezra politely asked as his girlfriend slowly walked into the Intensive Care room.

"Not sure Ezra? Was the service transaction completed between you and Ronald at the post office counter? I know you did say he made you feel uncomfortable" Homicide Detective Patterson replied as Stephanie stared at him.

"Yes, that's the Hispanic guy's name Ronald. Like I said officers I was trying to ignore the guy. He kept smiling

at me and swinging left to right in his chair, offering me body massages. It was annoying, Officers. I simply wanted my important envelope delivered. I have someone anticipating receiving the delivery. The fight happened when Ronald questioned me about how I wanted it delivered. Next thing I know I'm down on the floor bitten, stabbed, bleeding and the postal guy, Ronald is beating the man who stabbed up badly. As if he was the hero. Maybe I owe him a thanks, but I felt awkward by him before the attack" Ezra quickly responded as his girlfriend slowly walked in front of Stephanie, grabbing his right hand in shock from what she just overheard.

"I can imagine. We'll investigate what happened to your envelope. Meantime you rest up. It has been an incredibly long morning for everyone. I know the medical staff here have some concerns about your condition and the wound they want to discuss with you. We'll be in touch Ezra" Homicide Detective Haley responded as the two detectives exited the Intensive Care room and the medical team entered the room.

"Officers, can I speak to you for a minute about something" Stephanie politely asked as she exited the room along with the Homicide Detectives.

"Yes, Stephanie what seems to be the issue?" Homicide Detective Patterson inquired as they shut the glass, Intensive Care Unit door.

"I might know something about the postal worker. Is his last name Chavez?" Stephanie softly inquired as Homicide Detective Patterson looked down at his mini notepad.

244

"*Yes, it is Stephanie*" Homicide Detective Patterson quickly replied.

"Ronald Chevez the post office worker is my personal gym assistant and my personal masseur. Yes, he is aggressive and great with his hands. I can assure you he is not Gay. Ezra does not know this, but Ronald knows Ezra and has seen him not only in pics but in person. My best friend Tiffany went outside little while ago to contact Ronald for me, to see if he could fill in for me with the Yoga classes today as well as for the remainder of the week and the weekend" Stephanie nervously responded.

"*He's not teaching any Yoga classes today and I'm not sure about his schedule for the rest of the week. If this is the same person. There is a whole booking process that Ronald is going through as we speak. He still must see the judge. As from what I'm hearing from your brother Ezra, if this is the same person, then the Ronald that's in police custody, is facing several charges. We are only here to investigate the case because of the murder*" Homicide Detective Haley immediately replied.

"*Them charges which the post office Ronald is facing then gets technical and legal counsel is advised. So, if it is the same person then my suggestion to you is, to notify the gym that they will have to find a replacement for your classes.*" Homicide Detective Patterson shared.

"*You mentioned that you know Ronald is not Gay. How do you know that fact*" Homicide Detective Haley inquired.

"*My friend and neighbor that lives inside of my luxury*

building, who you may have met that's seated in the waiting area is in a love triangle with the husband of one of our neighbors. Now he is gay. Ronald Chevez is in an open relationship with that neighbor's wife. She is not only my neighbor but our Yoga student. Ronald has been trying to get business in our luxury tower for a good while. I personally felt that he designed those fliers thinking it will attract the right customers from inside our luxury tower. I'm the one that designed his massage business fliers. I'm a video designer. Part time health and fitness instructor. Yoga is my specialty. That is why Ronald was aggressively and sarcastically messing with my brother. In his own playful and aggressive manner. That is also why he physically defended my baby brother who labels himself super Ez." Stephanie softly shared as both detectives stared at her.

CHAPTER 26

REVERENDS WATCHFUL EYE

As heavy traffic continued to move slowly on the freeway that surrounded Manhattan, approaching the forty second street exit, Jamal turned his head towards Elder Jackson who was sending text messages to his constituents on his cell phone. While Derrick remained comfortably seated in the back butter soft leather seat of the new Acura, nodding his head to the Reggae tunes loudly coming from the new, Acura's stereo system and twisting the locks in his hair.

"Yes, Jamal I see the exit. My sister is not at the United Nations today. As you clearly know she's with her neighbors in the emergency room. My original plan was for us to go to her house inside of the luxury tower and speak with Melonie. I know her schedule and today is her day at home with her family. That set schedule for some reason doesn't include you. As a family there are some things that I would like all of us to

talk about. I personally feel that it's time. That was my original plan but now I feel we need to locate my nieces and nephew who are wandering through the New York City streets" Elder Jackson spoke as he stared out the front window looking over the array of cars stuck in Manhattan's traffic, at the view of the United Nations complex whose flags stood tall, towering over the forty second street freeway exit.

"Why is that Elder" Derrick boldly inquired.

"Why is what Derrick?" Elder Jackson quickly replied.

"Why the sudden change of direction. I do think you owe us some kind of explanation since you have us riding around in my mans, new ride, burning his gas from borough to borough" Derrick replied.

"I don't owe you nothing. You owe me more than a lousy apology because you got caught with your pants down in my sacred building of reverence. If we're on the topic of debt and who owe what. Then you still owe me a solid explanation of why you would use my sacred building to sex your girl. I have not received a clear explanation of why you would choose your building of employment to commit adultery. The place where I sacrifice my hard earnings to pay, tithes and sacrificial offerings every chance I get is the same place you chose to release your sexual desire on a Spanish female who is not a member of the congregation. You owe me an explanation of why you disgustingly disrespected my pastors building. You owe my future nephew Jamal a huge apology of why you would violate his trust in committing adultery in his sacred place" Elder Jackson loudly replied as Derrick stopped twisting the locks in his hair and slowly leaned forward in the back seat.

"*Elder Jackson, I'm sorry man. I honestly made a bad judgement call. Honestly, I thought I could get away with it, because I have before. I have a problem and it's not sexing in your church building. My problem is Victoria. Maybe I'm addicted to her. I honestly don't know. I have fetish for beautiful Spanish woman, check my porn collection if you don't believe me. I have so many downloads, it's not even funny. My computer hard drive storage is loaded with sexy Spanish porn. Bikini wearing, no clothes wearing, array of colored lingerie wearing beautiful Latinas who know how to move their hips rhythmically off the dance floor. The beauty of it Elder is that Victoria is not on my computer monitor or visual on my flat screen television. Those hips and Spanish thighs are mines looking scrumptious in my lustful eyes. I admit Elder I'm addicted to her scent, it's all up inside my nostrils. I can taste her when she's not with me. Even now as I roll my tongue around the inside of my mouth, like a fluid swab test, the lingering taste of Victorias fluids remains on my tongue. I have a weakness for Spanish woman always have. Victoria is more than a trophy Elder, she's someone that I constantly want to have. I'm sorry you caught me Elder. I know you glad you had. I want you to understand Victoria is not a figment of my imagination, she's the best I ever had. Elder Jackson, when I saw her today, I couldn't just let her walk away. Going casually about her day, no way Elder Jackson, knowing that Victoria couldn't stay, I had to leave her with something big today. So, I put it in her mouth that she could think about me for the rest of the day. I was already erected when she entered the door. That's how bad I have it for her Elder, but I didn't mean* to make her look like a dirty whore. I'm an addict to Victoria, I couldn't help myself with my penis erected I wanted to give her more. That's why you caught us having meaningful sex on the staircase floor. Like I said Elder I thought I could get away with it because I have before" Derrick openly rhythmically confesses as Jamal stared at him through his rearview mirror. Leaning himself back gently in the back butter soft leather seat of Jamals new car.

"So, what you think that justifiably excuses your actions. You are far past termination my man. My first reaction inside the staircase was to take some type of criminal action. Press some charges. That's not a store front building my pastor has given you responsibility to maintenance over. How many floors are in our church building? The pastoral staff has trusted you with a tremendous amount of responsibility. One of the main reasons you were given the job was because of your faithful membership of our congregation for several years. You aren't new to us. Your actions today are new to me. You aren't foreign to the people in our congregation. Your visible record showed that Derrick is a good candidate to have the maintenance position in our church building. You and I know that our church building doesn't remain empty throughout the day all week long. So, my first reaction is justifiable! In a sacred place at that. With a young lady I don't even know. That is trespassing! That is a crime!" Elder Jackson shouted, as Jamal turned his eyes towards him again.

"I apologize Elder Jackson. I'm a sex addict. I admit it man. The answer to your question Elder is no, and I want you to hear my reason. I want you to ease up on me man. As a man can you understand that it wasn't a plan. I did it and I'm sorry for it man. Empathize with me brother, like you are presently doing with your soon to be nephew who is madly in love with your niece." Derrick responded.

"I'm mad man! As a man I'll honestly admit I'm way past upset. Niger I'm straight pissed. Totally disgusted! Until I figure out how to handle the situation, I'll advise you not to say anything to me" Elder Jackson quickly replied.

"You're doing fine Elder. I feel you're handling it right now sir" Jamal said as he turned up the volume on his car stereo blasting the reggae music.

"Why don't you turn on some gospel music, Christian music, or a religious podcast. Turn to a Christian broadcast that will probably calm my nerves. I am a licensed ordained Reverend you know" Elder Jackson said as Jamal burst out in laughter. *"On Sunday do the two of you listen to anything that I say. I know that there are several of us on the pastoral staff. Besides our Bishop, when I preach on a Sunday, do you'll listen? Do you listen to any of my sermons? I know I sing a lot, but when I speak do you receive anything that is spoken?"* Elder Jackson inquired as he turned his eyes towards Jamal.

"Reggae keeps me calm Elder Jackson" Jamal quickly replied.

"Reggae is not doing much for my nerves right now" Elder Jackson responded as he picked up his cell phone to continue texting his constituents.

"By the time we reach Monica and her siblings, they will be at their house at the rate we're moving in this traffic" Derrick spoke as Jamal immediately turned the car stereo to a Christian broadcast while Elder Jackson lifted his head and cut his eyes at Jamal staring at him.

CHAPTER 27

A COWORKER'S CONFESSION

Standing in the elementary school building lobby, Carlos and Cindy kept their eyes focused on the vehicles parked directly outside on the city street in front of the elementary school building. The sudden disappearance of the parked unmarked vehicle in front of Melody's daycare building, the teenagers identified the driver as Paul, the school safety officer, was suspicious. As school buses slowly pulled up within the elementary school's city block, double parking next to the school's administration permitted parked vehicles, Keisha and her girlfriend hugged each other tightly in front of the school building. Happy to see each other after a long eventful school day, the two boldly stood together as they kissed on the lips in front of the elementary school building.

Monica and her baby sister Melody were on the

second floor of the school building, speaking with the elementary school's Assistant Principal Ms. Silva, about the early release of their brother and sister. Ms. Silva sent her administrative assistant, Ms. Almeida, upstairs to the fifth floor to get their brother Malek from his fifth-grade class. Makaila, their sister's second grade class, was in the auditorium for a class presentation. As the Brazilian Assistant Principal casually conversed with Monica, she kept her eye fixated on Monica's chest area. Knowing the large hickey that Jamal placed on her beautiful brown skin was there, Monica zippered her jacket all the way up to the neck area, flipping the jackets collar up so the zipper could almost reach the bottom of her chin. Ms. Silva, seeing the sudden move played with the identification badge that was hanging from around her own neck as she continued talking about the school's holiday plans for their students. Ms. Silva quickly buttoned up her top collar button of her own blouse that she normally left open as she continued discussing the elementary school's holiday agenda. Malek happily entered the administration office with a surprise look on his face as his baby sister Melody ran and leaped into her brother's arms. Monica told her younger brother that something had happened at home and their dad wanted them immediately to return home. Malek, who was a young science major started showing off his hip hop dance moves in the administration office, along with his little side kick Melody who imitated her brother as they expressed their excitement of the early schools' releases. Malek also didn't care for the regular four-day babysitter too much and was happier that his older sister Monica picked him up over his religious mother because together they would have more fun on their trip home across town. Walking downstairs to the general floor of the school building, Ms. Silva asked Malek if he wanted to present one of his science projects to the entire school at one of the holiday events. Malek jumped down the last three steps, challenging himself in a stair jump contest with his classmates, ignoring Ms. Silva's holiday general assembly invitation.

"Malek, are you going to answer Ms. Silva? She asked you a question. We haven't left the building yet" Monica spoke as she slowly helped her sister Melody Walk down the stairs.

"I don't know Monica. I don't want to but if you mention it to dad, then I'm going to have to do it" Malek honestly replied as he adjusted the bookbag on his shoulders. The female Brazilian administrative assistant Ms. Almeida entered the stairwell from the ground floor level with their sister Makaila. As little Melody reached the ground floor off the last step with her little pink boots she jumped up and down excitedly to see her older sister Makaila wearing the same pink outfit but in a bigger size. As the two younger sisters embraced in a warm welcome, Monica quickly pulled out her cell phone and dialed Jamal to find out if he was near the elementary school in his new car. Ms. Silva started playing around with the identification badge that was hanging around her neck again, turning to her administration assistant while cutting her eyes at Monica's chest area.

"That's a lovely jacket Monica, from what store did you pick that up" Ms. Almeida the administration assistant inquired as she buttoned up her top collar on her blouse under her long burgundy sweater.

"Thank you, but I'm not sure what store it's from. My mom may have brought it for me, when her and Ms. Stephanie went shopping" Monica replied as she begins to text her boyfriend Jamal, because he wouldn't answer her call.

"It has a gift look so that's understandable Monica. I thought you were going to say my boyfriend brought it for me as a present" Ms. Almeida quickly responded.

"No, one of my mom's gifts. Okay, you guys ready we have a little bit of traveling to do across town. Zipper up your coat Makaila its cold outside, Thanksgiving is next week, spring is over boo boo" Monica said as she reached down to grab her sister Melody's hand.

"You children have a ride coming to pick you up. Do your parents have a car coming for you?" Ms. Almeida inquired as the Brazilian Assistant Principal Ms. Silva opened the ground floor stairwell door, to head to the auditorium for the remainder of the class presentation.

"I have someone from my uncle's church coming to pick us up, that's who I was calling but I'm not getting an answer. He may still be in traffic. As you may know my uncle and I are very close. I'm an member of his church now. The driver should be enroute. If not, my school friends are waiting for me in the front lobby, so we'll be fine. Thanks, have a good weekend" Monica said as she turned pulling her sister Melody by the hand walking to the lower steps that led to the elementary school buildings lobby entrance.

Heading down the lower steps the lobby exit stairwell door flung open as a delivery man carrying restaurant bags entered the staircase.

"Monica! Hey, what a surprise. I see you here with the troops" the tall African American male restaurant delivery worker loudly said.

"Hi Jay" Malek shouted as he slowly walked down the lower steps behind his big sister Monica towards the lobby exit.

"Hi Jason, you're surprised, this is different for me as well. I'm used to seeing you dressed in a security uniform" Monica replied as she stood in the lobby staircase doorway.

"Why I look different outside of my uniform?" Jason the tall restaurant delivery man asked.

"No, you look good Mr. Jay" Melody shouted, as Jason burst out in laughter.

"Young man how can I help you" Ms. Almeida loudly inquired as she stepped forward toward the lower steps.

"I have a delivery for a Joan" Jason quickly replied, as the children followed Monica through the open door entering the lobby where Carlos and Cindy were patiently waiting.

"I'll take it for her she's in the general administration office" Ms. Almeida loudly responded as Jason moved away from the stairwell door allowing it too loudly close.

"Did you'll see Paul again" Monica loudly asked as they approached Carlos and Cindy.

"No just a bunch of school buses" Cindy replied as she embraced Makaila in a tight squeeze bear hug.

"I tried calling Jamal back but I'm not getting any answer. With my love not getting any sleep he might be cranky as well as tired. I would be" Monica shared as she reached for the lobby door to exit the elementary school building.

"More like stank! With your nasty attitude having self" Cindy sarcastically replied as she put her arm around Makaila.

"That would be my girl Kaneesha outside here in front of the school doing God knows what with her better half" Monica loudly shouted as she walked through the door stepping outside.

"Excuse me hoe! I know you're not talking, with your Coney Island back seat self" Kaneesha loudly replied as she rushed over to the door with her hand on her hip.

"Watch your mouth in front of my sister slut" Monica quickly responded as they both burst out in laughter. While Monica slowly walked over to Kaneesha's girlfriend and gave her a hug.

"Monica, I want pizza" Malek yelled out as he stood outside putting his hoodie over his head.

"Hey, Monica I'm glad you didn't leave. There's something I want to talk to you about" Jason loudly spoke as he exited the school building and Kaneesha quickly grabbed Melody's hand pulling her away towards her, so they could talk outside in private.

"What's up Jason" Monica softly asked.

"You and Jamal that's what's up! All in the cameras like you're trying to get us overnight security guys fired. You see I'm out here busting my butt no sleep working second job just so I can eat. New York City cost of living is high baby girl. Your

luxury tower pays but even that salary can't cover my bills. I have another little one on the way and they're not trying to give us overtime pay. Every now and then I can work a double shift but those racist cops at your building isn't trying to hook a brother up with good pocket money. Speaking of your man and my boss are not the best of friends. Jimmy and Jamal are enemies. I try to watch myself around that fat want to be fake pretending like he's a detective riding around all day in the luxury towers building security car lazy self. We've had our words or two as well but that was over a year ago. So, I know he is a jerk. Now your man and that crew is some serious heat between them. The only thing that is keeping him from the unemployment line is the Supers wife. Their cool relationship nobody can touch. As for me she sniffles too much. Even in the summer months when there's no wind or cool air the Supers wife has the sniffles. There aren't that many allergies in the world for your nose to be so red twenty-four seven. You feel me, Monica. You need to watch yourself around Rudolph and the rest of the reindeer. Specifically, Jimmy, because I know he has been watching you in those building cameras with Jamal. Why he hasn't said anything yet, you and I both don't want to know. Watch it, Monica! This Christmas season won't be Jolly for you, what heat Jimmy got coming for the both of you. It's tip season too. You have no idea the battles that take place over the tenants' envelopes to the luxury tower building staff. That's when the entire building staff get real Grimmie with each other. Your parents have always been generous to me, and I know that's only because I'm black. I'm not saying they're not generous in giving to everyone else that is employed in your apartment building, but my Christmas card from them *is what helped fund my car that I do deliveries in. I don't know who funded Jamals car. It's because of your parents' generosity, I've been looking out for you, Monica. Your mom's friend Stephanie's penthouse neighbor has been looking out for your mother as well. Jimmy isn't the only one that have been watching the cameras and what I see in those screens Monica is that we are now entering cutthroat season"* Jason softly shared as he picked up his cell phone to check if received any delivery messages.

"Thanks for looking out for me Jason. I love Jamal. We have something very special" Monica replied as her cell phone rang. Taking the cell phone out of her jacket pocket seeing that it was Jamal on the caller identification, Monica quickly answered.

"Hi Jamal, we're finished where are you?" Monica loudly inquired.

"My love, we're approaching the street exit now. Still a little way to you" Jamal responded.

"Great, I'm taking the kids to the pizza restaurant. You can meet us there if you would like" Monica replied.

"Which pizza shop my love, there are dozens in the city" Jamal replied as he burst out in laughter.

"Three blocks away from the school it's called "Louie's crust", when we get there, I'll text you the exact building address. I don't know it by heart Jamal. I love you Jamal thanks for calling me back" Monica replied as she quickly disconnected the call. *"Jason, I must go feed my family. Thanks for the lookout. We good Jason"* Monica said as she walked back over to the children and her school friends while Jason stood staring at her.

CHAPTER 28

THE ELECTRICIANS ENTRY

Walking back to his door post in the luxury tower lobby, Aram took off his doorman uniform cap to wipe the sweat from his forehead. Slowly proceeding to the huge brass door, Jimmy the Assistant Super, came from the East Wing section of the tower yelling and screaming in search for Chong about the electricians not being notified of the basement electrical problem.

"Marisol, get Cornel on the phone for me right now! Tell him I need him down here immediately! I don't want to hear any damn excuses either. This doesn't make any sense at all! Where the hell is Chong? I paged him five minutes ago. If I don't see him, everyone is getting fired!" Jimmy loudly demanded, as he turned to walk away from the concierge front desk. *"Aram, why don't you have on a cap. Put the damn cap on or go home!"* Jimmy loudly yelled, as Aram quickly placed his cap back on his head, pushed

opened the huge brass doors and stepped outside of the building towards the curb where the taxicabs daily stand waiting for tenants.

"Jimmy, Chong is on twentieth floor inspecting a leak in a tenant's bathroom. Also, Stephanie's entire family is arriving this evening from the Midwest. They will be staying in her penthouse until further notice" Max loudly responded.

"Okay, why are you telling me this? Does it look like I care about that right now" Jimmy loudly and angrily replied.

"Stephanie is not on the premises but has granted her entire family access to her penthouse apartment" Max quickly responded.

"Oh, well it's Thanksgiving time. So that's expected in a residential building. You do have the apartment entry request form filled out completely with names and tenant signature for the security staff, am I correct?" Jimmy loudly inquired.

"It wasn't Ms. Stephanie that made the arrangements" Max replied.

"I beg your pardon. What are you saying to me? "That there is no entry request form signed by the tenant" Jimmy loudly asked.

"That's what we're saying sir" Max answered.

"Stephanie knows the rules. And why am I just hearing about this dilemma?" Jimmy angrily inquired as Aram entered the building lobby again.

"We just received the phone call from her assistant that there is a family emergency" Marisol replied as Jimmy silently walked away to the upper-level elevators enroute to see Chong without responding to Marisol.

"He didn't like what you said at all" Aram spoke as he slowly walked to the front desk.

"You'll are my witnesses. He's been informed and I told him" Max said.

"I'm glad you said something because I didn't want to be the one to relay that message" Marisol spoke as she stood up out of the swivel chair behind the marbled desk.

"You'll know how he is; you see he was ready to fire everybody a few minutes ago. Let him go upstairs and take that frustration out on Chong" Aram loudly replied.

"That's going to be a problem. I can tell you guys now. That's going to be a big issue with my supervisors" Shawn the tall muscular African American security guard spoke in a bass tone as he remained posted in the lobby by the front door.

"The guy Jimmy is still mad from what happened earlier outside in front of the building with those stupid delivery guys. He's probably going to be angry like that till Monday. That's why they have you standing up here with us" Aram replied.

"No, the fight was one thing Aram. Yes, he probably still aroused from that whole building staff verse delivery workers and police officers with guns drawn fiasco. But that entering a tenant's home without written consent is sketchy." Shawn the security guard loudly responded in a bass tone.

"Yeah, but what were we supposed to do?" Marisol asked as she walked over to the coffee maker to refill her favorite mug.

"That's why I brought it up in front of you'll as witnesses that the concierge informed him. Aram isn't the only one that knows Jimmy around here" Max replied as he took his seat

in the swivel chair behind the large marble concierge front desk.

"The guy Jimmy stays with an attitude. He probably needs to get laid. I never see him with a woman. He says he has a girlfriend. But I've never seen her. Listen, I know guys like him that's all they do is fuss. Mr. tough guy. Now he's beefing, with Jamal. What's that? The parking guy. For what? A parking space? He yells at me over a hat. It's almost time for me to leave anyway. The guy needs some sex. He's sexually frustrated" Aram spoke as he casually walked back over to the buildings huge brass lobby doors.

"That's your answer to life Aram? What's your favorite sexual position? That might be your problem now" Max loudly replied as Shawn grabbed the crotch area of his black pants holding himself while he burst out in laughter.

"Shawn you're correct. It's a problem. When the tenant's family member arrive hopefully the Supers wife will be around on the building's premises, because whoever is at the front desk can notify her of the situation and allow her to assist in the serious matter" Marisol loudly said as she took a seat in the swivel chair.

"The penthouse apartment at that, man that's a serious problem. The security office is not going to take an unfilled apartment entry request form lightly." Shawn quickly replied in a bass tone.

"Penthouse apartment? Wait I missed that conversation I was outside. Who are we talking about because if it's Stephanie's apartment, then you're going to have to worry about Bradley. He's a freaking weirdo! The guy was standing

at the penthouse apartment door, with no shoes on his feet when I left her penthouse apartment this morning after helping Ms. Watkins and Stephanie with a heavy box. The man is a pest" Aram loudly shared as he took off his doorman cap again to wipe the sweat from his forehead. *"Bradley is a pest, and Jimmy needs some sex"* Aram continued to say as the new couple entered the lobby with their large German Shephard from the upper floor elevators headed outside to stand in front of the building and smoke their cigarettes. Aram quickly rushed to huge brass doors, pushing it open to let them out of the building.

"You just mad Aram that Bradley's not letting you sex Stephanie" Marisol loudly responded as Aram the Armenian doorman slowly walked backed to the front desk.

"Ms. Watkins not going to let you have Stephanie either. Melonie will pour some holy water on your hot butt if you try and sleep with her friend and cool your freaky self-off" Max sarcastically replied.

"She looks good too. A well-dressed educated Moca skin woman, I'll take both. Stephanie is a gymnast too. Positions unimaginable. We will all together create heavenly positions. The way she exhales, Stephanie could blow on me all day as I meditate to heaven. An aerobics instructor is all I need to freak off in my bed with a church sister that can twerk. Now that threesome will be one for the books" Aram jokingly replied as he burst out in laughter.

"You know that big fat judge will body slam you hard, right on this lobby floor if you even look at his wife in the wrong way.

That's one sick fantasy that will never happen for you buddy" Shawn quickly replied in a bass tone as he grabbed the crotch area of his black pants holding himself.

"Jamal is crazy! He needs to stop playing around with that man's daughter. She is always sneaking around, entering the different stairwells throughout the building. Monica isn't experienced in building management. That young girl doesn't know the security camera system. Neither does her dumb boyfriend. This luxury high rise apartment building is Camera loaded. Dropping her off around the corner so they won't be seen on the building's surveillance camera's system coming into the building together. Or seen getting out of his car inside of the garage cameras. In the morning Monica is seen getting inside of his car at times in the garage cameras. Jamal is crazy" Max softly spoke as Shawn moved toward the front desk.

"That's why Jimmy going off. He's beefing with Jamal over a parking space. The man has race issues too, everyone knows that" Aram the Armenian doorman replied.

"That young vagina doesn't have my boy Jamal thinking straight. He is deep in that young wet stuff now. That's probably part of the problem" Shawn replied as he stoically stood by the front concierge desk. *"You know he don't want to let that young wet stuff alone. I didn't know about the staircase though"* Shawn replied in a bass tone.

"Well, that's what I'm hearing from the overnight guys" Max answered.

"Who my security guard colleague Jason? That's what he told you, they be in the stairwell together" Shawn the tall muscular African American security guard inquired in a bass tone.

"I have seen Monica myself in the camera's using the stairwell when I'm here in the morning" Max quickly replied.

"Yeah, she uses different staircases and exits. She'll use the emergency exit by the lounge room, and no one uses that exit at all" Marisol said as she chuckled in laughter while sipping her cup of coffee.

"But then you'll see Jamal's Acura going flying past the front lobby doors to pick her up" Aram spoke.

"So, we asked Jason one morning about Jamal and Monica. He said she knows the building staircases layout better than the building's fire guard and the towers fire safety director. She sneaks in and out throughout the night like we can't see her" Marisol quietly shared as Aram quickly ran back to the lobby doors to let the new couple back inside the building along with their large German Shephard from their smoke break together. Entering the lobby the new couple hurried upstairs to their apartment in the upper floor elevators.

"But that's what gets me about this place. And I've been here now for a few years. They go off on the wrong crap like a little while ago. Him sounding off at Aram about his uniform cap. Threating everyone about the possibility of losing their job over an Oriental guy who cannot see. The Chinaman probably lost his way. Long as I've been here, he's always playing hide and seek games. Soon as something goes down the Chinaman like a ghost. Gone, nobody has seen him, and we can't find him. Then his excuse is always oh, I didn't see that, or I didn't see you called. I'm very busy, I was on another problem, you should have called me. How he's lasted this long I will never know. Today he and Phil going back and forth in front of me

is hilarious. That old cat owes every tenant in the building money. That is one sneaky old cat. I know he owes Jimmy money because I have seen Jimmy go into his pants pocket and hand Phillip money but it's usually when he's rushing to do something important inside the building. Phil got a sob story for every tenant inside of the luxury tower. A true hustler. That's how he knows everyone's business. Sneaky mother sucker. To me he's a funny old dude, with a real hustle. That one time he borrowed that money from one of his outside friends and he dodged him like the plague. Phillip dodged him like Chong dodges handyman work on a regular day. That friend waited for Phil by the bus stop in his car, followed Phillip here to work. When Phil was by the security area cleaning, the man came inside the building and told Phil to pay him his money or he was going to kill him. It was hilarious. Phillip's old butt was so startled he couldn't even yell for us to come help him. I guess he paid the dude the owed money. A perfect stranger did what most of the building has probably thought about doing to him one time or another. Yet no one is aggressively confronting the stuff that might need to be addressed. The wrong crap! When other things should be addressed. Like that entry request form not filled out. Definantly not signed by the tenant is a serious issue. Yet Jimmy walks away, saying nothing" Shawn shared in a bass tone, as the husband of the new couple came downstairs again with his large German Shephard to the lobby to go smoke another cigarette while Aram rushed to the lobby Brass door to open it for him again.

"I hear what you're saying, that's why we don't pay the two of them any mind. Where's Phillip now" Max loudly responded as he sipped on his bottle of water.

"Somewhere with his phone, through the buildings halls the old man tends to roam, collecting his bus fare home" Shawn the tall muscular African American security guard rhythmically replied in a bass tone as he grabbed the crotch area of his black pants, holding himself while he burst out in laughter.

"My point exactly" Max quickly replied as Bradley Stephanies penthouse floor neighbor entered the lobby from the upper floor's elevator.

"Ladies and gentlemen" Bradley loudly said as headed towards the lobby exit brass door.

"Okay Mr. Bradley have a good day" Max loudly responded as Bradley exited the huge brass door that remained open by Aram who stood outside holding the door turning his head looking away from Bradley.

"I had to get on Phillip one morning. I mean the day hadn't even started and already you're asking me for money. Five dollars here, seven dollars there, ten dollars here, thirty dollars and I'll pay you back on Friday. "Aren't we both working with the same intentions. Aren't our weekly goals the same? My weekly plan Is not included a disappointing feeling on Friday because someone can't pay me back the money I lent them. I did not get up out of my bed to come to work to be let down. I told him, aren't we both employed by the same employer. What does it look like me giving away my earnings for your habit. Taking away my kid's milk money for your pockets to blow it on your habits. You may need to quit whatever it is you're doing if you can't make it to payday. You begged the wrong Chica this morning Papi. I don't have anything for you. I have for me and my kids" I had to stop

him. Please take that begging broke hand and go wipe down some building furniture. Get it out of my face because I don't want to see it" Marisol loudly shared as she continued sipping on her cup of coffee.

"That's why he hangs over on that side of the lobby. He'll hang over there by the doors and mess with Aram, but he doesn't come over here to us" Max loudly replied as he sipped on his bottle of water.

"Mess with me about what. Who want to mess with me now?" Aram loudly inquired as he walked back over to the front desk.

"Phil! You're working buddy" Shawn the security guard replied in a bass tone.

"Oh, the guy is a snitch! He gets paid for Snitching. Put some money in my hands and I'll tell you what you really need to hear. He spends all day collecting the building news, from running gums to printing it out in his own daily express newspaper, that the nosey tenants spend all day paying him for the gossip column. He's a building snitch. He told me you two are smashing that's the reason you'll don't want him hanging around the concierge front desk" Aram loudly replied as Shawn burst out in laughter as he grabbed the crotch area of his black pants holding himself. Slowly walking back to his post by the huge brass doors, Shawn the tall muscular African American security guard took out his cell phone, responding to the text messages from his lady Victoria.

"Like Shawn said, Jimmy always yells at the wrong people. Specifically, the blacks" Aram continued to say as

he took off his doorman cap again to wipe the sweat from his forehead.

"That's why there aren't any blacks working here" Max quickly replied.

"Save that one who they hide at night giving the poor guy difficult task they know he's not qualified to handle" Aram softly shared as he put his doorman cap back on his head.

"That's why he's coming for Jamal. His new car doesn't help the situation one bit" Marisol softly responded as she continued sipping on her cup of coffee.

"He's a racist jealous animal" Aram loudly responded as he rushed over to the huge brass lobby doors to open it for the new husband along with his large German Shepherd, that had finished smoking his cigarette in front of the building. Entering the building's lobby, he rushed back upstairs to his apartment.

"All these beautiful models living in here you can get some sex. You don't have to be jealous of me or Jamal because we have got beautiful ladies. I'm telling you he needs to get laid. Jimmy needs some sex" Aram continued to say.

"That's your solution to solving the world's problem. Enjoying some thighs late at night" Marisol loudly asked.

"It beats getting high, late at night. Like my friend who keeps coming downstairs here with that damn large dog" Aram quickly replied.

"I'm glad you noticed" Max quickly responded as he looked at the building's surveillance camera monitors on top of his desk.

"It's the second time already. Why don't you just crack

open a window and smoke from upstairs inside your apartment If you need a cigarette that bad. You pay enough rent to live in this luxury building. I know a lot of tenants who smoke inside of their apartment. Sometimes you can smell it in the hallways as you're walking through the halls" Aram loudly replied as he took his doorman cap off again to wipe away the drops of sweat that fell from his forehead.

"No, the third time he's coming back downstairs in the elevator again. I'm watching him in the surveillance camera monitors now. Oh, wait. He's exiting through the security guard's entrance" Max said as he stood up from sitting on the swivel chair behind the lobby's marble concierge front desk.

"Maybe he's looking for somebody to talk with. The guy doesn't speak to any of us" Aram quickly replied as he stared at Max.

"Maybe he's looking for a model to have sex with" Marisol loudly responded as she sipped on her cup of coffee.

"Ha, Ha not funny Chica! Maybe he's looking for his buddy the Super to talk with. He would do better if he spoke with Jimmy. Maybe he's now looking for Jimmy to talk with" Aram quickly replied.

"Maybe them two are smashing" Max quickly replied as Marisol burst out in laughter.

"Maybe. You will have to allow Phil by your sacred concierge desk to get that specific gossip news column. The guy needs to sex someone. Release some of that built up frustration. Sexy woman or a smokey man with a large dog. If that's your type, get them! Whatever floats your boat buddy" Aram

271

loudly said as he grabbed the crotch of his pants holding himself while bursting out in laughter.

"You're sick! That's your solution to solving the world's problems" Marisol replied as she burst out in laughter.

"That's right vote for me and you won't be horny is my campaign slogan" Aram loudly said as he raised both his hands high up in the air, waving, giving the peace sign on each hand.

"Aram put your hands down, why are you not by the door? It's not time for you to leave yet! Is Kattie in her office? And Where's Jimmy? Did Jake Zapotes arrive yet?" The Super loudly asked as he entered the lobby.

"No sir they didn't arrive yet. Kattie is showing an apartment somewhere in the East Wing and Jimmy was on the twentieth floor with Chong. Jimmy was upset about the electrician not being here sir" Max loudly replied

"Call Cornel and tell him that I said get his butt down here to this building right now! Let Kattie know to meet me on the twentieth floor" The Super quickly responded as he watched the brass door.

"Oh, and sir, Stephanie has a family emergency and has granted access to her family to stay in the penthouse. They will all arrive this evening" Max shared as he sat down in the swivel chair behind the marble concierge desk to drink his bottle of water.

"Why are you letting me know. That should be communicated to security. This young man is standing here at the door in the lobby doing nothing. Shawn should be carrying the signed apartment entry request form to his superiors. What are we paying you for Max" The Super replied.

"Well, that's the thing, Stephanie didn't fill out the entry request form. Her assistant contacted us this afternoon to inform us of the family situation" Max quickly responded.

"Then the assistant is going to have to be here to let the family into Stephanies penthouse apartment if you're uncomfortable with the situation. You must be uneasy since you're just bringing it to my attention. Talk to security Max! I'll be upstairs at twenty. Where the hell is Chong? Did the guys pad the elevator with the palmer pad for Jake. Look at what time it is, and he has not arrived yet. This day is an unsecured disaster. I'm calling a meeting after Thanksgiving Holiday next week, with everybody. Someone might be terminated before Christmas" Jimmy loudly replied as he proceeded towards the upper floor elevators. Aram and Shawn slowly walked back over to the concierge front desk as the elevator chimes sounded.

"Who is Jake?" Aram softly inquired as he took off his doorman cap once again to wipe the sweat off his forehead.

"Jake Zapotes is the Alpine ski racer. Remember his record time at the world cup in Italy, the year two thousand and nine? His family is moving into the tower today from Pennsylvania" Marisol softly replied as she sipped on her cup of coffee.

"Moving in here today, do you see what time in the afternoon it is? I have plans at three o'clock I'm leaving. My hours are from seven to three" Aram the Armenian doorman quickly replied as he put his doorman cap back on his head.

"Do you want to piss Jimmy off any further with you? If Jimmy wants, you to stay then you're staying Aram" Shawn

the muscular African American security guard replied in a bass tone.

"Marisol you better ask Phillip to pad the elevators now. The other guys are too busy with tenant complaints and water leaks. You already know the situation. That will really upset Jimmy if the Super is mad about the elevators not being correct for another athlete that will be living in this famous building" Aram suggested as Marisol arose out of the swivel chair, walked over to the cabinet and picked up the two-way radio from on top of the cabinet to call Phillip.

"I'm listening to their tone; Aram has a point about that fight outside in front of the building earlier, upsetting them. You'll worry about palmer pads on an elevator to protect the glass mirrors from being cracked by boxes and furniture. The penthouse situation is a serious problem that one needs to worry about. You need to call my supervisor now and tell them that there is no tenant signature on the entry request form. Me taking a blank slip downstairs to him is not the answer" Shawn spoke in a bass tone as Aram rushed back over to the huge brass door to open it for the new husband tenant and his giant German Shepherd as they once again for the third time in a row, headed for the upper floor elevators to go upstairs to their apartment.

"Something is not right with that guy. He's nervous about something" Shawn said in a bass tone, as he kept his eyes fascinated on the elevators section.

"That's what they pay you for Shawn" Max quickly replied as he watched the surveillance camera monitors above the concierge desk.

"You see me watching" Shawn quickly responded in

a bass tone as he slowly walked over to the upper floor elevators.

"*That's why I stood up man*" Max replied while watching the building surveillance camera monitor As Phillip slowly entered the lobby.

"*Phil, we need you to pad the elevator. It should have been done already. There's a family moving in today that seems to be running late. It's an Olympic Skier moving in today. The Super is pissed because the elevator isn't padded and I'm leaving on time at three o'clock even if my relief is not here on time to stand at the door*" Aram loudly said as he walked away from the brass door towards Phillip.

"*Take it out on Chong. He's the big mouth boss! He should have had it done or padded the elevator himself. When I was running this building some time ago, we never had these problems. Now there is an issue every day. Yeah, okay Aram. Which elevator you want the palmer pad in Marisol?*" Phillip said while adjusting his uniform pants over his wide belly.

"*The upper floors Phil, thanks so much*" Marisol loudly replied as she sat down in the swivel chair behind the concierge desk to finish sipping on her cup of coffee.

"*You see how I do everything around here without the butt kissing. That's why my Christmas cards look so merry*" Phillip loudly responded as he rushed towards the building's staircase heading downstairs to the maintenance supply room in the basement lower levels.

"*Appreciate you buddy, you're the best*" Aram loudly replied as he took off his doorman uniform cap once again to wipe the sweat from his forehead. "*Hey Shawn, let me ask you, who's the security guard that is getting fired this evening"* Aram softly inquired.

"Didn't I specifically say "don't say anything" Aram? Why then are you repeating something that I mentioned to you in confidence now to the building staff?" Shawn annoyingly replied in a bass tone.

"Come on buddy! Don't be like that. If Phil already knew then half the tenants and the maintenance department already knew. So, who is the security guard buddy?" Aram softly inquired as he placed his doorman cap back on his head.

"True you have point there about Phil" Shawn replied in a bass tone as he burst out in laughter.

"Wait, they're coming back downstairs again with the dog" Marisol spoke as she watched the building surveillance camera monitor over the concierge front desk.

"What's this guy's problem today. Another weirdo that lives here. I'll be glad to leave today. Three o'clock can't come fast enough for me" Aram loudly said as he rushed to the brass doors to open the door for Bradley that entered the lobby.

"They're exiting out of the security guard entrance with the dog again" Marisol loudly shared.

"Back so soon" Max loudly spoke as he drank his bottled water.

"Yes, I'm back Max" Bradley loudly responded entering the luxury building lobby as he slowly walked towards the upper floor elevators. Cornel, the electrician entered the lobby behind Bradley nervously, as Marisol arose out of the swivel chair walking over to the cabinet again to use the two-way radio that was sitting on top

of the wooden cabinet to alert Chong that Cornel was now on the building premises.

"Heard I missed a real battle rumble outside directly in front of the building this morning. A title match fight with Jimmy and the entire delivery squad. A real pay per view special" Cornel the electrician, spoke as he pulled out his cell phone from his jacket pocket. *"Was told there was cops outside in front of the building here, men in handcuffs, guns drawn, all kinds of people arrested and even some blood shed"* Cornel continued to say.

"Yeah man, it was total madness here this morning!" Max quickly replied as the building's office phone rang. Answering the call Max sat down again in the Swivel chair as Marisol made her way back to her chair.

"That means Jimmy is probably not in a good mood" Cornel the electrician spoke as Aram slowly walked over to the front desk taking off his cap and wiping the sweat from off his head.

"When is he not in a bad mood Cornel" Marisol replied as she sat in the swivel chair to finish drinking her cup of coffee.

"Now that's true. Hey, Aram, I heard you was feeling like a heavy weight champion on this morning. Taking on the entire delivery squad. I also see you have your bodyguard security in place here champ" Cornel said as Max hung up the phone and stood up off the swivel chair once again.

"Boss man looking for you and he is not in a friendly mood Cornel" Aram quickly replied.

"That was the Super on the phone, he said for you to head downstairs to the second lower level and that's where

they all will meet you" Max shared, as the new husband tenant stepped on the upper floor elevator again but this time, he was alone, heading back downstairs. Marisol arose out of her swivel chair watching the monitors closely this time. Snapping her fingers signaling to Shawn, she pointed to the monitor behind her desk with her right index finger and then pointed towards the elevator section of the building, with that same index finger. Shawn immediately picking up on Marisol's hand gesture, quickly walked over to the elevators to wait for the new husband tenant to arrive back downstairs in the lobby as Cornel the electrician made his way to the staircase to meet with the Super in the lower levels. Shawn stood by the lower floor's elevator with his right hand in his black pants pocket as the elevator chimes, sounded and the elevator doors opened. Seeing Shawn standing there, the new husband tenant nervously rushed off the upper floor elevator and quickly walked around the large columns to the front lobby. Seeing the new tenant Fastly coming towards him, Aram immediately opened the huge brass door as the new husband tenant took out a cigarette to smoke it as he exited the door and stood outside in front of the luxury tower building. Kattie the rental office manager entered the lobby from the East Wing section of the building with a middle-aged couple that she had shown two studio model apartments to. As the couple exited the building Kattie took out her cell phone to call Herb the property manager.

"*Kattie the Super is looking for you and he's on the lower* levels with Jimmy, Chong and Cornel. There seems to be an electrical problem in the basement" Marisol loudly said.

"What else is new. Everything seems to be a damn problem in this building before Thanksgiving and Christmas holiday. Someone please tell me why the visual announcement board in the hallway by the lobby elevators is not displayed. How are the tenants supposed to be notified about important announcements if there is nothing displayed on the screen" Kattie loudly replied as she ended the call with Herb the property manager.

"That screen has not been on all week. Over the weekend I was informed that the screen was on but there was nothing shown. Jake Zapotes the Olympian skier has not arrived yet either" Max loudly replied.

"From Pennsylvania! What the hell, do you see what time it is? How long does it take to get from Pennsylvania to New York City. I could walk there from here, that doesn't make any damn sense. They were informed of the building's move in times. After five o'clock no elevator should be blocked off from the tenants. I don't care what Olympic record you hold. Let him ski his way upstairs to his new apartment. I've had a long day and I'm exhausted. When Herb gets here from around the corner in the building's management office, tell him I'm not in my rental office" Kattie loudly responded.

"We also have a situation Kattie, that I don't want to involve the security staff. Stephanie has a family emergency, and her entire family is arriving this evening. Her assistant called earlier to notify us that she has granted her family access to stay in the penthouse apartment until further notice" Marisol spoke.

"Let me guess, there is no signed entry request form filled out by Stephanie. Am I the lucky winner in that guessing game" Kattie loudly replied as she turned and looked at Shawn.

"Shawn you're the top cop on duty today I'll contact Stephanie myself and get back to you my friend" Kattie loudly responded.

"Thank you, mam," Shawn the tall muscular African American security guard answered in a bass tone as Kattie walked towards the lower-level staircase to meet with the luxury tower Super. Bradley entered the lobby from the upper floor elevators as Phillip started padding one of the upper floor elevators with the palmer pad to protect the designer wooden, brass and mirrored interior of the elevator from the movers' large boxes.

"Hi Max, did the cleaning services drop off my laundry yet" Bradley inquired as he turned and watched Aram standing at the Brass lobby door. Aram turned around and faced the door looking out of its wide glass window.

"Yes sir, let me get it for you Bradley" Max responded while Marcus entered the building lobby from school, carrying his large bookbag on his back as Aram held the huge brass door wide open for him.

"There's my man" Shawn shouted out as he gave Marcus a high five and a handshake.

"Good afternoon Mr. Watkins you are home early. How was school today?" Marisol loudly inquired.

"We have laundry here for your house as well Marcus" Max shouted out as he handed Bradley the large burgundy bag and went back into the small room

behind concierge desk area to look for the Watkins family laundry bag.

"Hi, Marisol, we were let out of school early today because of the Thanksgiving holiday. My dad and mom know I told them this yesterday that today was the last day of class until the week following Thanksgiving" Marcus quickly replied as he looked at Bradley who was staring at the Brass lobby doors.

"I saw your mom Melonie, earlier in Stephanies apartment, I assume today is her day off from working at the United Nations" Bradley spoke.

"Yes, it is" Marcus loudly responded as Bradley turned and walked away towards the upper floor elevators carrying his laundry bag

"Marcus guess who's moving in today. Another United States athlete, the Alpine ski racer, Olympic record holder Jake Zapotes, from Pennsylvania" Aram said as he removed his doorman cap again wiping the sweat from his head.

"Oh, man that's pretty, awesome. However, I don't follow winter the Olympic sports. Ms. Stephanie, Ms. Danielle and all my mom's close friends are all into going skiing every winter. That's their stuff. I think my older sister Monica follows that ski stuff. I don't. My mom is only into her church stuff praising God, shouting stuff. So, I'm not sure how much skiing she does" Marcus replied as Max handed him the dropped off bag of laundry for his apartment from the building cleaning services around the corner next to the management office located on the other side of the luxury tower building.

"That's all the laundry Marcus and thanks for taking

it. I appreciate you helping us clear out a lot of these tenant items behind our desk. You would be surprised how lazy your neighbors really are. Some of this tenant stuff has been back here in the room behind our desk for over two weeks and still accumulating" Max loudly shared as remained standing keeping his eyes on the brass doors.

"That's because they want door to door service, isn't that right Aram" Marisol quickly replied as she smiled.

"Hey, I don't beg like old man Phil or pretend like busy he's not busy Chong. Everyone in the tower know I'm the man in this building, from the main door to your apartment door. I'm telling you vote for me, and no longer will you be horny" Aram loudly replied as he raised his two hands in the air waving them giving the piece sign with his fingers. As Marcus and Shawn burst out in laughter.

"You are a sick puppy" Marisol replied as she giggled keeping her eyes on the surveillance monitors watching the new husband tenant smoke his cigarette while pacing back and forth in front of the building.

"Well, I hope the Jake ski dude likes it here. I must go upstairs and charge my cell phone the battery completely died on me in class. Talk to you all later or at another time" Marcus replied as he started walking towards the upper floor elevators.

"Marcus, your phone died from watching all that French porn during physics class" Aram jokingly asked as he followed Marcus to the elevators.

"I wish I had porn on my phone Aram" Marcus quickly replied as he continued to laugh at Aram. Herb quickly

entered the lobby, swinging open the huge brass door as Shawn looked down at his cell phone pretending to ignore the property manager.

"Why is Aram never standing on his post at the door when I arrive. You must not like your job" Herb, the property manager shouted as Aram slowly walked back to the door.

"Today is just not your day Aram, man you catching it left and right" Shawn spoke in a bass tone as Herb quickly turned around and stared at Shawn.

"Like I said, my man, three o'clock I'm leaving even if my relief is not here" Aram loudly replied as he adjusted his doorman cap while Shawn stared at him.

CHAPTER 29

GLAD TO BE WITH YOU

As the new Acura sat in front of Louie's Crust, the famous Italian family-owned pizzeria doubled park with its hazard lights blinking, Monica and Jamal embraced each other tightly. Serving each other kisses in between the tight hug, Carlos ordered the large pizza pie for Monica's siblings and his girlfriend Cindy who was sitting at the table playing a hand game with Melody.

"You'll need to stop all this viewer discretion advised crap in front the Judges babies" Kaneesha loudly suggested as her girlfriend burst out in laughter as she grabbed the crotch area of her black sweatpants holding her pants.

"Didn't Cindy tell me that they were just together this morning. Not that much time has past that would warrant all this public indecent exposed lip action" Carlos loudly replied as he grabbed a bunch of napkins out of the napkin holder.

"Don't forget the active tongue Carlos" Kaneesha's girlfriend sarcastically said as she grabbed Kaneesha's hand.

"Too much information for me. Some stuff I don't need to know. I just don't understand why these folks today can't keep their business to themselves. It is not how it used to be. I remember the days when you just had to figure it out" Carlos loudly replied as he burst out in laughter grabbing the crotch area of his blue jeans holding himself.

"Now they want to walk around with red, blue and a purple hickey visibly displayed all over their bodies" Kaneesha loudly sarcastically spoke.

"Oh, wait, I meant to tell you'll one of the reasons it took us so long to return to the elementary school lobby was because I was having a conversation with their vice principal upstairs and tell me why she kept looking at my hickey that you gave me Jamal" Monica loudly shared as she slowly walked over to the pizzeria cashier register counter to pay for the children's large pizza pie that Carlos had ordered.

"Work of art my love. It's the beautiful sign of my love affectionately placed on you Monica, that's all the vice principal was peeping" Jamal said as he put his hands in his skinny jeans pants pocket while slowly walking towards Monica.

"Who's all in the car, Jamal? That's your boys from your block" Kaneesha's girlfriend politely asked as she placed her right hand inside of her sweatpants pocket staring out of the Italian pizza restaurants windows.

"Nah, that's Elder Jackson and another one of our church members who is responsible for having me find this great wave

of peace in my life. I used to be filled with so much confusion. You just wouldn't understand. God's love combined with Monica's lovely personality has calmed my nerves a whole lot. As you can see, I'm riding with the family" Jamal replied as Monica stared at him.

"So, that's why you came for my girl because you're at peace now" Cindy replied as she slowly walked over to them with the three siblings as Monica continued to stare.

"Well whether you are getting the peace that you need or trying to get a piece of what you think you need Jamal from my girl Monica, I'm glad you finally answered our girls stress calls. It was because of you that she was forced into a position to dodge the annoying school guards. I almost had to put my hands on someone for messing with our girl's man Carlos in the cafeteria. I Thought, I was going to have to call my thug brothers to come to the school for some assistance upstairs in the school's cafeteria. I cut out of school early, and will probably be in trouble tomorrow, so your girlfriend won't be by herself while her parents are tripping out. Monica girl I'm out! I'm glad you have your siblings like your parents demanded you to without any trouble. I have a class to attend, and my girlfriend has a class that needs to be tended to. Love you all much and it was good seeing you Jamal" Kaneesha said as she hugged Monica. As they left the restaurant Kaneesha ran over to the new car to say hi to Monica's uncle.

"Yeah, I'm with Kaneesha. Some things are cool, and some things are just not cool at all Monica. Not only the absentee you have to deal with but the hickey on your neck area is going to add fuel to your dad's fire that he already started

with you earlier over the Economics class while we were in Chorus class. Girl, that's not cool. Paul secretly following us around Manhattan is way too much. Call me later if you can. Carlos and I have a little way to travel on the subway girl" Cindy said as she hugged Monica goodbye.

"I'm just happy Jamal's here with me and not with the Supers wife girl" Monica softly whispered in Cindy's ear, as Jamal picked up the large pizza box from off the cashier register counter while Carlos stared at Monica.

CHAPTER 30

THE MANAGER'S ENTRY

"Good afternoon, Herb, Kattie is not upstairs in the model rental apartment office. She's somewhere on the lower levels with Super, Jimmy, Chong and Cornel. There seems to be an electrical problem somewhere in the building" Max loudly said as he stared at Aram and Shawn who stood posted at the lobby's brass door.

"Now what's the problem around here? It's too close to the holidays for serious technical issues. I'm starting to get tired of this. Everyday no compliance. Those water leak complaints are now pouring into my office all day by a lot of the tenants here. Where are the other three rental knuckle heads" Herb the luxury tower's property manager loudly inquired as he turned himself around and stared at Aram.

"Gloria is in the lower-level elevator now on her way downstairs to the lobby from what I can see in the surveillance

camera monitors. The other two fellas must be upstairs in the rental office" Marisol quickly responded.

"Listen Herb, Stephanie has a family emergency and as a result her entire family is on there way here to the luxury tower to stay in the penthouse. Stephanie's assistant called early to notify us of the situation and to give permission for all of them to stay inside her penthouse apartment until further notice" Max shared as Aram opened the huge brass door for the new husband tenant as he hurried himself back upstairs to his apartment on the upper floor elevator.

"Good afternoon, everyone" Tommy the tall muscular Italian doorman, yelled out as he entered the lobby adjusting his uniform overcoat.

"What up buddy. Just in time. It's three o'clock and I have had enough for one day" Aram loudly replied as he walked away from the lobby door heading towards the staircase to the lower-level men's locker room.

"What happened Aram it's not dark yet. There is still a little sunlight left outside. You can still hang around and play with us. Since that's what you been doing anyway" Herb loudly spoke as Aram continued walking to the lower-level staircase ignoring Herb the buildings property management sarcastic comments.

"How are you doing this afternoon Tommy?" Herb loudly asked.

"Feeling like a million bucks their Herb" Tommy loudly replied.

"Sounds like you have a concierge challenge Max. That's your call. I can call Stephanie on her cell phone and speak with her, but I'm not authorized to make that judgement

call if that is what you're asking me. The rules are clear and designed for a reason. If you change the rules, then you will be the person held responsible. No tenant signature on the tenant entry request form than no unauthorized entry by the building's personnel. That's all-security staff included" Herb the luxury tower property manager loudly responded as he turned himself around once again staring at Shawn.

"Kattie said she was going to call Stephanie as well" Max quickly replied.

"Then why are you busting my chops if someone has answered your question already? I have more important things that I must handle at this time" Herb loudly responded.

"He clearly informed you because it's a serious issue. Max personally feels that he shouldn't be liable for this penthouse emergency. Addressing his concern to building managers is the logical thing to do this late in the day. The family members may arrive any minute" Shawn the tall muscular African American security guard loudly responded in a bass tone.

"So, what are you Max attorney? Are you employed as a daytime building security guard and full-time legal representative" Herb loudly replied as he put his hands in his fleece winter jacket.

"That's what he's going to need eventually if he continues taking advice from unknowledgeable shady managers" Shawn boldly replied as Tommy the Italian doorman stared at Herb.

"So, what do you think I should have said to Max, Mr. legal and illegal bodyguard" Herb loudly replied.

"My name is Shawn, but you already knew that before

you shot off with the lip standing here in the lobby this late afternoon almost evening time. I personally feel the matter should be addressed and not by Max at this late hour of the day. Period!" Shawn, loudly responded as Tommy the doorman continued standing still on his post at the brass doors staring at Herb.

"Then you'll handle the penthouse problem when Stephanie family arrives since you have all the answers Shawn. It's the security staff duties to escort the family and unlock the door since they have the master key computer system located in their office anyway. Now it is settled Shawn, the concierge representative will handle that case for you when the evening tenant rush hour crowd returns home from their day-to-day operations. Amid the dozens of deliveries at the same time, now you will be free to fulfill your front desk duties Max and Marisol without any Penthouse worries. No, wait, look at the time your relief will be here within the hour so they will not have to worry about any mixed messages, or any information not being transferred correctly. A whole new evening staff that has not been briefed about the penthouse problem. Which means Shawn will have to be posted here till the midnight hour, patiently waiting, if the family arrives by then. They may come after midnight. Then who will be responsible with the correct information in escorting the family to tenant without the proper apartment request form filled out on the midnight shift" Herb the luxury tower property manager loudly said as he proceeded to walk to the lower-level staircase to meet with Kattie the luxury tower rental office manager.

"Whatever man" Shawn replied in a bass tone as he and Tommy burst out into laughter. Gloria the rental office

worker entered the lobby from the lower floor elevators with a famous female opera singer who wasn't interested in any of the apartments she saw today. As the laundry cleaning service van back-up beeper, loudly sounded, parking directly in front of the building, Tommy pushed open the huge brass door so Gloria along with her French opera singing, world renowned client, could exit the building. Max quickly ran outside in front of the lobby to speak with the manager of the laundry cleaning service about a few of the complaints the tenants had given him concerning the dry cleaning. Aram returned upstairs to the lobby floor out of his doorman uniform, dressed in a stylish designed outfit the model and Alonzo had picked out for him. Entering the lobby to sign out with Marisol, the building office phone begins to ring. Marisol sat down on the concierge swivel chair to answer the phone call.

"Shawn did you let Tommy know that one of your guys is going to be fired tonight" Aram softly spoke as Tommy adjusted his doorman coat uniform.

"Aram did you let Tommy know that the new tenants are acting strange this afternoon and need to be closely observed" Shawn quickly replied.

"Yeah, buddy, I don't understand this guy he and his Russian speaking wife repeatedly come downstairs to smoke a cigarette. With their big four-legged mut! He's a weird guy to begin with. Very antisocial Tommy. Today he's too nervous for me. Looks like you guys are going to have your hands full this evening with the penthouse guest and the Olympic ski racer moving in" Aram shared as they all walked towards the front desk.

"*What happened Marisol why the sudden look of concern on your face*" Tommy asked as Max, Gloria and the laundry cleaning service guys entered the lobby.

"*There is a major flood in the hallways on two of the upper floors. Two of the porters are up there now. I must notify Super*" Marisol loudly replied as Aram took off running in his designer boots to the lower-level staircase to tell Jimmy.

"*Phil, have you finished padding the upper floor elevator? I'm going to need your assistance*" Marisol yelled as a black vehicle slowly pulled up in front of the luxury tower parking in front of the laundry cleaning service van.

"*Philip, take the padded upper floor elevator out of service and switch it to manual, to escort Super upstairs to the flooded floors please*" Marisol loudly spoke as Max returned to his swivel chair behind the concierge desk. As Shawn slowly walked back to his post at the door, he observed the parked black vehicle that had City Parks written on its side doors. Questioning in his mind who would boldly park their vehicle in a loading and unloading zone during the buildings business hours, Shawn stepped out of the lobby through the huge brass doors to observe. Jamal slowly driving his new Acura up the block towards the building, came to a complete stop before the stop sign at the crosswalk, as a large supplies box truck blocked the streets intersection. Patiently waiting for the taxis to move out of his way so he could back his delivery truck into the luxury towers wide block, the box truck driver conversated on his cell phone. Slowly pulling up behind Jamals new vehicle was a large moving truck with two SUV's that followed. The New York police officers who were stationed inside of their police patrol vehicle at the other end of the block of the luxury tower, because of the violent activity that had occurred in front of the luxury tower earlier in the day, observed the traffic build up and stepped out of their police car to patrol the sudden traffic scene around the luxury tower. Walking past the front entrance of the luxury tower, Shawn saluted the two New York police officers by placing his two-way radio over his heart.

"Listen, whoever large van that's double parked across the street near the intersection, must move their vehicle. Not only are they illegally parked but the van is blocking that delivery truck from maneuvering. We already had one fight out here let's avoid another" The New York Police Department officer loudly spoke to Shawn as they continued walking towards the traffic build up. Immediately returning inside of the luxury tower lobby, Shawn went to relay the message to Max and Marisol. Entering the lobby, Shawn walked over to the desk as Aram, Herb and Kattie returned upstairs to the lobby from their meeting on the lower-level floors.

"Max aren't the painters here in the building" Jamal loudly inquired. *"Get in touch with them and tell them the Police said move your vehicle, you are blocking trucks from getting to the building. I also saw the moving truck coming"* Shawn continues to speak.

"Finally, they arrive. Something must have happened to them on the route here because Pennsylvania is not that far" Kattie said as two tall French men stepped out of the parked black SUV that had the words City Park printed on the side doors.

"It depends on how far in Pennsylvania they are traveling from. I go to visit my brother all the time and he lives in Pittsburg which is almost seven hours. When I go skiing in the Poconos mountains, Pennsylvania it takes me three hours. So, it all depends" Harry the laundry dry cleaning services manager replied.

"Listen Harry, we have been getting a lot of complaints about your dry-cleaning services from the tenants" Kattie quickly replied.

"Max spoke to me about it already. You're late. That problem has already been resolved. Instead of worrying about my business, what you and Gloria need to worry about is who's going to open the door for Stephanies family so they can have access to the penthouse apartment since she's at the hospital with her brother Ezra" Harry the laundry dry cleaning services manager, said as his Mexican assistant stood next to him staring at Herb.

"Anything concerning the tenants of this building is our business" Gloria quickly responded.

"Thank you, Gloria, obviously someone has forgot that major point. Like they have recently been forgetting to clean the clothes the tenants in this building daily send them" Kattie quickly responded.

"Like I said that information has been shared with me already, and I will continue to handle my business professionally in the laundry department. The no signature entry request form is a problem that hasn't been resolved and both of you should be

more focused on solving that than any issues my customers have with the services they have already been provided with. Who is going to be liable for the entry of Stephanies penthouse. Who will be responsible for the unauthorized entry of Stephanies very large penthouse apartment. That's a family member we don't know" Harry the laundry dry cleaning services manager loudly responded as Tommy the muscular Italian doorman walked over to the lobby's brass door to open it for the two unidentified French men wearing suits.

"Well, said Harry. I tried to tell them earlier, but Herb smart mouth is going to get him in trouble around here with me" Shawn the African American tall muscular security guard loudly replied in a bass tone as the two French men entered the building's lobby.

"I'll say whatever I feel is necessary to be said and nobody will do anything to me" Harry the laundry dry cleaning services manager quickly replied as Kattie stared at the two French gentlemen as they approached the concierge desk.

"Good afternoon, gentlemen how can I help you today" Marisol politely asked as she arose up from the swivel chair and max walked over to pick up the two-way radio that was on top of the cabinet to contact the painters whose van it belonged to which were painting in the studio apartments in the east wing section of the building.

"Hello Ms. I'm a detective and I'm here to speak with Ivan Vasiliev, is he home" the French man said.

"Yes, Mr. Vasiliev, is home, is he expecting you" Marisol

replied as Shawn and Kattie both stared at the two tall muscular French men.

"Yes, he is" The French man quickly replied as Marisol reached for the luxury tower's intercom phone to contact the new tenant apartment.

"I told the painters to come downstairs to the lobby Shawn to move their double-parked van" Max spoke as he stood at the front desk staring at the two French men.

"No one is picking up the intercom phone. I'll try again" Marisol shared as Tommy, Shawn and Aram walked back over to the front brass door.

"I saw Mr. Vasiliev in the lobby area down here a little while ago Marisol. Did he return upstairs to his apartment?" Herb loudly inquired as Kathy and Gloria stared at the tall muscular French men as they stoically stood at the front desk.

"No, he is upstairs inside of his apartment. He was outside walking their family dog a little while ago, but he is upstairs in his apartment now" Max loudly replied while Marisol tried calling the new tenant's intercom again.

"Call the fire department please" Chong shouted as he stepped off the upper floor elevator. *"Super said for you to call the fire department, there's severe flood damage on the upper level"* Chong loudly shared as he entered the building's lobby.

"I'm sorry but I'm not receiving any answer. Are you sure Mr. Vasiliev is expecting you today" Marisol spoke as Max immediately contacted the New York Fire Department in an emergency to come to the luxury tower. One of the Dutch building painters rushed into the lobby from the East Wing Section, towards the huge brass door.

"Yes, we are sure he is expecting us" the French man quickly replied as Tommy the muscular Italian doorman opened the brass door for the Dutch building painter to exit the building and move his double-parked van so the delivery box truck could have more room to maneuver through the luxury towers block.

"What happened upstairs Chong" Harry the laundry dry cleaning services manager, loudly asked as his Mexican assistant stood next to him staring at the French men.

"Pipe burst. They're going to need to break the wall to get to the problem. There is deep water everywhere. The water is pouring into the hallways. I must get my staff together. No one is going home now. There's going to be a lot of overtime today for the building staff" Chong loudly shared as he quickly headed towards the lower-level staircase to the handyman janitorial room.

"Sorry, I'm still not getting an answer. I know the intercom works because I spoke to Mr. Vasiliev this morning on it" Marisol softly said.

"This is an urgent matter. I'm going to need to speak to him, if you don't mind, we'll just go upstairs and knock on his door" the French man replied as Kattie, Gloria, Herb, Harry and his Mexican assistant stepped away from the concierge desk area, to stand by the sofa furniture in the lobby.

"Once again, I'm sorry but we can't allow you upstairs unless the tenant authorizes it. That's the building's policy" Marisol loudly answered *"I can call Mr. Vasiliev cell phone from the buildings directory when my colleague finishes on*

the building office phone, for you. But I cannot allow you to enter the building any further past this desk without proper authorization" Marisol responded as Max hung the phone from the New York Fire Department.

"Gentlemen good day, what seems to be the trouble" Max loudly inquired as he stood directly in front of the two muscular French men from behind the concierge desk.

"We are detectives that have an appointment to see Mr. Vasiliev" The French man in the suit loudly answered as Marisol tried calling both the new husband and wife tenant on their personal cell phone.

"Do you gentlemen have ID" Max politely inquired as Tommy stepped outside of the building to observe the black SUV that was parked in front of the Harry's laundry dry cleaning service van.

"Listen my friend, he's expecting us. If he doesn't answer the phone then let us go upstairs to knock on his apartment door, so that we could discuss the matters we have been sent here for" the French man responded.

"You listen my friend, this building that you're standing in has rules that are followed and reinforced by the buildings hired staff. I cannot allow you to go upstairs anywhere without the permission of any tenant that lives in this building. Now my colleague has been very helpful in trying to get in contact with the tenant. It seems like they are not expecting you" Max replied.

"You listen my friend. I'm a detective and I have the authority to go past your desk and go upstairs to knock on Ivan Vasiliev's apartment door to talk with him" the French man loudly responded.

"I'll say it again, without valid authorization from the tenant themselves. You cannot go upstairs to any tenant's apartment. You are not allowed past this desk to speak to any tenant without the tenant's authorization. No permission, no entry" Max said as Shawn walked over to the front desk.

"I guess what my partner is trying to say to you is that as Detectives we are authorized to go knock on a tenant's door if we need to. We are just being polite to inform you of our intentions in going upstairs to talk with Ivan since he already knows that we are coming" the other French man said as the sound of pure tone beeps loudly rang outside in front of the luxury tower from the large delivery box truck that was slowly backing up into the block.

"It doesn't matter about your identification or credentials. Without permission from the tenant, you cannot knock on their door. That's the building's policy" Max said as Marisol hung up the desk phone.

"I'm still not getting an answer on the cell phone. I tried both phone numbers that are listed in the building's directory for Mr. Vasiliev. He is upstairs and for some reason chooses not to answer the building's intercom system. That is the best that we can do for you. I'm sorry that it did not work out the way that you two distinguished gentlemen may have planned. As my colleague and I clearly explained, "You cannot go upstairs to knock on any doors" Marisol responded as the two luxury tower concierge reliefs entered the desk area from the back room.

"Good evening, everyone" Lucas spoke as he opened the cabinet to place his bag inside.

"Good evening, guys, I see a moving truck up the

block. Is the truck coming this way?" Athena the female Greek concierge said as she changed the portafilter on the coffee machine to make a fresh pot of coffee.

"Listen just allow us upstairs for a brief minute. If you want, we'll all come back downstairs to the lobby area together" the French man replied as Lucas stopped what he was doing and stared at the two French men.

"I'm going to say this again. You cannot go upstairs to Ivan Vasiliev's apartment without his permission. Period!" Max loudly said as Athena the female Greek concierge slowly walked over to the front desk.

"I'm going to have to ask you gentleman to leave the premises. These men and women have a job to do. If it's that important that you need to talk to Mr. Vasiliev, then I advise you to call him on his cell phone from your SUV that is illegally parked in front of the building. This is a loading and unloading zone and there is a truck as you can hear that needs that space" Shawn loudly spoke in a bass tone as the two French men turned and slowly walked towards the open brass door that was being held open by Tommy to exit the building. Exiting the building Shawn remained posted outside observing the two gentlemen who casually walked to the black SUV with the two words, City Park on the side doors as Tommy closed the building's Brass door.

"Wow What was that all about" Athena asked, putting her pocketbook inside the desk drawer as Herb, Kattie, Gloria, Harry, his Mexican assistant, Aram and Tommy all came and surrounded the concierge front desk.

"The guy is a weirdo! He's been pacing back and forth

in front of the building all afternoon. Upstairs, downstairs, upstairs again and then back downstairs with his wife every five to ten minutes" Aram loudly spoke as Shawn entered the building lobby and remained standing at the brass door.

"This day has been very dramatic. Aram is correct. But I was not letting them go upstairs. I don't care how persistent you want to be. Like Aram earlier this morning outside fighting with the delivery guys, who were trying go upstairs from the building's lobby. The same rules apply for businessmen" Max responded.

"You mean detectives" Herb replied as the large box truck double parked directly in front of the building.

"Those were not detectives" Max quickly replied.

"You're right Max. Not driving a city park car" Shawn loudly said as the sirens of a fire truck loudly sounded outside.

"The fire department is here. There is a pipe bursting upstairs on the upper-level floors. That's where the entire porter staff is right now. Including Phillip, he's running the padded elevator because the Olympic ski racer is moving in this evening" Marisol said.

"Oh, that's the large moving truck that's outside on the next block waiting for the delivery box truck to back in" Athena replied as the loud sound of air brakes released from the large delivery box truck that double parked directly in front of the building.

"You guys have a very busy night ahead of you. That's a lot of trucks outside and the New York Fire department is one of them" Harry, the laundry dry cleaning services

manager loudly replied as he put his left hand on his assistant's broad shoulder.

"The police are outside as well. That's who's now directing the traffic jam, that Athena saw up the block. After the fight earlier outside directly in front of the building, which included the building's Super and his assistant Jimmy, the cops were posted in front of the building. Now the New York Police Department is outside trying to prevent another delivery disagreement from escalating into a brawl. Don't forget about the penthouse situation, regarding Stephanie that there is no proper tenant signed apartment entry request form" Shawn the tall muscular African American security guard loudly responded in a bass tone.

"So, buddy its evening time now and I'm sure the security guy is on the premises. Are you going to answer my question and tell us who the security guard is that they are supposed to terminate tonight" Aram asked.

"That guy Robert was stupid!" Herb the property manager loudly replied. "You'll security guards are the only ones with the master key access. Not only do you have the master key, but it's kept in a computer system that documents every time the key is used for entry to an apartment. The reason for the entry request form, that must be filled out completely by the apartments tenant, and immediately given to the security guard is for you guys to operate the program on the computer. To use the master key, you must log into the systems program with your own personal access code and give detailed authentic reason of why the key should be released by the computer for you to use which is documented, time and date. The master key is the most challenging key to be released to a person than the tenant apartments spare key. However, all the keys must be authorized and unlocked by the computer programs drawer for the security guard to obtain the key. Soon as a key is missing inside the computer key rack, the program alerts all of us managers in detailed emails. So, we all knew who had what key on what days the burglaries occurred. I'm not sure if you knew that one Shawn" Herb continued to say.

"What I couldn't understand is why Robert would sleep in our model apartments every night he's on security duty" Kattie spoke as the box delivery truck driver continued unloading the boxes from off the truck.

"Well, he won't be sleeping in any of those apartments tonight. Straight to jail. Only thing comfortable he's going to be sleeping on is a hard bench behind bars tonight" Harry the laundry dry cleaning services manager loudly responded as the city postal worker, mail carrier arrived in front of the building pushing her Satchel cart. Tommy, the tall muscular Italian doorman quickly rushed over to the huge brass door to let the mailwoman inside of the luxury tower building.

"I'm not sure what time my supervisor is going to notify the New York Police Department, Detective Bureau's Central Robbery Division. I do know it is all going to happen sometime tonight" Shawn replied in a bass tone.

"They're all ex-cops' downstairs in the lower-level security supervisors office. I'm sure they have it all well planned out" Lucas the evening concierge replied as he sat in the swivel chair behind the marble front desk while the mailwoman distributed the building's mail into the tenant's individual mailbox by the elevators.

"I mean, smoking, drinking and masturbating throughout the building is sick! Not only was he wreck less in leaving the computer key system evidence for the Central Robbery Detectives investigation, but Robert was leaving alcohol stains on the apartments carpet, cigarette buds inside trash cans and white stains on the bed linen even in the model apartments. Clear signs of insanity" Gloria, the rental office staff woman spoke as the loud sounds of the fire departments trucks sirens now rang out in front of the building.

"Yeah, the Super's wife and I was talking about that last night. That was stupid, I agree. You wanted to get caught. That was some very expensive items that have been reported missing. We still don't know about items that have not been reported or expensive jewelry that a tenant hasn't recognized is missing" Athena the female Greek concierge shared as the sound of pure tone beeps loudly rang again as one of the fire trucks slowly backed up into the block to also double park in front of the luxury tower building.

"Looks like we're going to be blocked in boss by the wave of trucks backing in front of the building. The dry cleaners service van is now surrounded sir" Harry's laundry dry cleaning service assistant loudly said as the other fire engine truck loudly released the air brakes that was parked on the security office side entrance to the luxury tower. The delivery box truck driver immediately jumped back into his truck to continue reversing his vehicle up further in the block as the New York Police Department officers directed him to do. Loud double sound of pure tone beeps begins to ring in front of the building, as both large vehicles slowly backed into the

block attempting to directly park in front of the luxury tower.

"Here we go again with all the loud sirens and police presence" Aram loudly said as Harry and his assistant exited the building to their van to try and move it out of the fire trucks way.

"The fire fighters are entering the security guard office side of the building. Jimmy just stepped off the upper floor elevator with Phil. He's directing the fire fighters to him" Marisol shared as she watched the surveillance cameras monitor closely.

"No one is going home early today Aram" Super loudly said as he entered the lobby. *"We're all doing overtime tonight. I have a serious emergency, and I need all of you to assist in any way possible. Aram go get your doorman cap and put it on so you can at least look the part. This is the building's evening rush and as you guys can all see, we have a real mess outside that's about to make its way inside here. The crowd of tenants arriving home hasn't even started yet, which is going to make it more congested in the building. The sun is going down, it's after four o'clock and when it gets dark, I have a feeling all hell is going to break loose inside of this luxury tower. We can't put stress on the security guards because alongside their regular duties, patrol tasks, they have to deal with the tenant's food and grocery deliveries. After this morning street fight, I don't want any parts of that. It looks like I see three fire trucks surrounding this entire building. Fire fighters are already heading upstairs with Jimmy. Max, please go open the lounge side door for this delivery guy and have Aram posted there with you at the door. He's bringing in the building supplies*

that Jimmy and the contractors ordered. I'll let security know they're going to need a guard posted at that end of the building. Whatever door is available Jake Zapotes will use for his move in. You still have the Parcel services truck coming. Normally they arrive in the evening to deliver the tenants' packages. It's a circus" Super continued to say as he walked outside exiting through the huge brass door to see the trucks arraying themselves around his apartment building as the fire fighters started walking up the block.

"I'll call Jake Zapotes now and inform him of what Super just expressed" Kattie loudly replied as her and Gloria quickly walked towards the upper elevators to return to the rental office upstairs in the rental model apartment. Herb, the property manager stared at Shawn, the tall muscular African American security guard, as Shawn, stared at Lucas, the evening concierge who was now on duty at the front desk, as the outside sky that hovered over the apartment luxury tower, darkened and the daylight turned to night.

CHAPTER 31

I NEED A CHARGE

As Marcus finished using the large bathroom in his parent's room, he quickly ran out towards the living room to check and see how much the battery percentage was on his cell phone since it had been charging in one of the living room outlets. Picking up the cell phone aiming to cut it on there still was no power on the cell phone. Pressing the side button on his iPhone, Marcus realized that the battery was still on zero percentage.

"All this damn time I was in the bathroom; my phone still didn't charge" Marcus shouted out loud to himself as the large red and blue Macaw parrot rested on top of the cages wooden stick continued to stare at him.

"What are you looking at Roc" Marcus shouted out loud to the Macaw parrot, as he snatched the charger's cord from out the living room wall outlet. Rushing over to the kitchen wall, unplugging the coffee maker,

Marcus shoved the cell phone chargers' cord into the kitchen outlet. No charging symbol appeared on the iPhone display screen. Feeling annoyed he walked over to the refrigerator and opened the refrigerator door, there was no automatic refrigerator light. Running into the living room turning on the light switch, there was no light. Marcus immediately grabbed the remote for the giant flat screen television mounted on the living room wall and there was no power to the television. Not having a cell phone is a tragedy for this teenage boy. Having to sit through midterm exams today was nerve wrecking enough for Marcus. Now he has no outside communication to the entire world. No social media platforms, no music downloaded to his phone and no nudes his eighth-grade classmate sends him every afternoon to make his penis erect. With plans on sexing her, popping that cherry by senior trip and the prom, he cannot miss her nude pics preshow entertainment. Every day she sends him a new angle of her vagina. Now mad and frustrated, Marcus returned to his parents' master bedroom, to get the copy of Stephanie's penthouse key. Melonie called him earlier, explaining to Marcus what happened with Ezra in the post office, and that Monica was in charge until his father, the judge, comes home. Melonie asked her oldest son Marcus to walk Brownie this evening for Stephanie. Disappointed that he had no cell phone he threw his favorite hoodie on and black heavy jacket over it to go upstairs to the penthouse to charge his cell phone. Quickly going inside the main bathroom to wash his hands, Marcus turned on the water faucet and there was no water. Walking out to the kitchen, Marcus turned on the kitchen faucet and there was no water. Minutes ago, using the parent's bathroom there was water, now there is no water and electricity. When he came home from school, there was water in the kitchen. Marcus filled up his parrot's water dish so Roc, wouldn't scrawl all evening long because he was thirsty. Spitting his sunflower seeds on the floor, Roc remained perched on his wooden stick, that was stationed on top of his cage staring at Marcus angrily walking out of the apartment door.

"I'm starting to get worried; Marcus isn't picking up his phone. The call is not even ringing. The phone call is going straight to the voicemail answering service. That's not like my brother Marcus. He always picks up on my calls. I know he's home. Me calling my brother Marcus and going straight to voicemail is not us. I hope he's home for my sake. That wouldn't be funny, the day mom asks me to do something for the family and Marcus goes Rogue" Monica said as Jamal finished sanitizing his hands with the small bottle of hand sanitizer as he opened the large pizza pie box that Elder Jackson had in his hands so the kids could eat.

"That was smart Jamal. With the fire department surrounding the Tower and the police standing out in front, we'll never get to the building. Monica, use my phone to call and see if my nephew answers" Elder Jackson suggested as he rested the box on his lap and passed the cell phone behind him to Derrick who was seated comfortably next to Monica and Melody on her lap.

"All these trucks surrounding us. Delivery trucks, Fire

trucks and a big moving truck parked directly behind me, were not going anywhere any time soon. I can't even go in reverse. Why should the kids suffer. Plus, I want a slice" Jamal replied as he burst out in laughter.

"My G. I meant to ask you are these seats heated cause by butt is feeling warm in this back seat" Derrick inquired as the kids burst out in laughter.

"Yes, they are. I'm still going to fix dinner whenever we get upstairs. Uncle you are staying for dinner?" Monica asked as she dialed her brother Marcus cell phone number on Elder Jacksons phone

"Yup! We all are. Isn't that right Jamal" Elder Jackson loudly replied as Jamal handed Malek, Melody and Makaila slices of peperoni pizza.

"I need to get home and get some sleep. I don't want to make myself sick" Jamal softly responded.

"Guess you're cooking chicken noodle soup tonight in honor of your man" Derrick spoke as the call went to voicemail once again on Elder Jacksons cell phone.

"No Uncle, I'm still getting the voicemail. I'm sorry you'll, I don't mean to sound nervous. I just don't need to get in any more trouble today. My parents are already a little upset with me" Monica spoke as she leaned forward reaching around her baby sister Melody who was smacking her little lips on the hot peperoni pizza, handing her uncle back his cell phone.

"Why sis is daddy and mom mad at you" Malek asked as the cheese from the pizza dripped down off from his lips as he steadies chews his food.

"What I tell you about talking with your mouth full

311

Malek. Chew your food first and then you may speak"
Monica replied as she wrapped her arms around her
baby sister Melody.

*"You'll be careful with that pizza in not getting any of it
on this young man's clean new car"* Elder Jackson spoke as
he dialed his sister Melonie's cell phone.

*"Hear everybody take some napkins. Here Monica please
make sure they have plenty of napkins. Listen my love, I don't
want anything to upset you tonight. As tired as I am I'll climb
up every flight, to make sure your brother Marcus is doing
alright. Tonight, our love has shown and proven to the family
in their eyesight, the intense feeling we have for one another
are truly right"* Jamal softly replied.

"You'll kiss too much for me" Makaila loudly said as
she took another large bite of the peperoni pizza.

"They kiss too much for me too baby girl" Elder Jackson
quickly replied as he took out his Bluetooth earpiece
to connect it with his cell phone, as he made the call
to his sister Melonie who was still at the hospital with
Stephanie.

"Hey Melonie, I have your whole family, they're
safe with me, even little Melody. Don't need for you to
worry, it's my pleasure to be next to my family tree"
Elder Jackson rhythmically said as everyone in the car
burst out in laughter.

"Uncle Jack your mad whack!" Malek jokingly shouted
out as everyone in the car burst out in laughter.

*"Well, praise the Lord, put me on your speaker phone, so
I can hear from all my babies even Monica"* Melonie loudly

replied as Elder Jackson turned off the Bluetooth and pushed the speaker button on his cell phone.

"Hi mommy I love you" Makaila shouted out as she wiped the sauce off her lips with the napkins Jamal handed them. *"Hi mommy luv you"* Melody shouted out as she continued smacking on the slice of pizza.

"Melody what are you smacking on" Melonie loudly asked as Jamal leaned his head back into the butter soft leather heated driver seat while closing his eyes. Derrick and Monica both stared at him.

"Monica brought us pizza mom. Where are you and why did we have to leave school so early today with Monica" Malek inquired as he took another bite of the peperoni pizza slice.

"I'm with Stephanie. Something tragic has happened to her younger brother Ezra. So, mommy is going to need you all to pray in your hearts to God, that the healing power of the great physician, Jesus, will continue to divinely heal Ezra's body here at the emergency room. Monica, Ezra is stationed inside of the Intensive Care Unit. Until the rest of their brother and sisters arrive here to the hospital I'll be with Stephanie" Melonie loudly shared to her family over the cell phone speaker as Jamal dozed off to sleep.

"Okay ma, I'll hold everyone down" Monica quickly replied as the tall west Indian parcel delivery man passed the Acura pushing a dolly loaded with boxes and packages up the street.

"Oh, I know you will. And everything will be done like I asked. We'll talk about what I want to talk to you about when I get home, Ms. Economics" Melonie quickly responded

as the tall west Indian parcel delivery man stopped in the middle of the street directly in front of the new car to speak with the New York Police Department patrol officer.

"Mommy I'm going to pray in my heart to God that you won't be mad at Monica anymore" Melody shouted out as she smacked on the hard crust of the pizza. *"Amen, me too Melody"* Makaila shouted out as she looked over at her sister Monica. *"Amen, Halleluia I'm praying that same prayer in my heart and out loud unto God, Melody"* Malek shouted out as leaned forward to reach inside the pizza box for another slice of peperoni pizza. As Derrick stared at Elder Jackson.

"Hey, Man of God, who's car you have my babies riding inside of this evening" Melonie loudly inquired as Jake Zapotes, the Olympic ski racer slowly walked past the new Acura to speak with the patrol officer who was standing in the middle of the street blocking traffic from moving.

"Jamal's new Acura, sis. There seems to be trouble inside your building. We're being blocked from entering the block of the luxury tower by the police. There are three fire engines surrounding the building. There are fire fighters inside the building and outside as well. There are a lot of trucks, even a moving truck directly behind us. So basically, were stuck here by the intersection, across the street a block up from the entrance of your luxury apartment building, but we are warm and comfy" Elder Jackson replied as Derrick continued to stare at him.

"Yeah, mommy our butts are even being warmed up in the brown seats by the cars heaters" Makaila quickly responded.

"Jamal who, Man of God" Melonie loudly inquired as Jake Zapotes along with the parcel delivery man, pushing the long dolly full of boxes and packages, walked up the block towards the luxury tower.

"One of my new members of the church, my dear sister. A fine young man who you know well. He has been a blessing to my congregation ever since he joined our faith family. He came all the way out to the church in Brooklyn today, to link up with me and the church's porter, so we could pick up some building supplies for the church building. I had to get some pest control things as well. We're having a serious pest problem in our building sis." Elder Jackson cheerfully replied as Derrick continued to stare at him. As the police patrol officer slowly walked towards the new Acura.

"Who is the driver that I know Man of God? Jamal, who" Melonie loudly asked as Monica dropped her head burying her face into the pink hood of her baby sister Melody's coat. As Derrick kept his eyes fixed on Elder Jackson.

"Jamal, your apartment buildings night parking attendant supervisor and my niece's boyfriend sis." Elder Jackson loudly replied as Monica closed her eyes.

"Boyfriend, have you lost your damn mind Niger! You have my babies sitting outside of the warm house that I have provided for them, seated in the cold weather, eating some pizza in some damn car. Take me off speaker damn it!" Melonie shouted as Derrick leaned forward to listen to

the conversation. Jamal immediately woke up from his nap, opening his tired eyes, closing his mouth, slightly turned his head and stared at Elder Jackson with his bedroom eyes.

CHAPTER 32

THE BALCONY VIEW

Opening the penthouse refrigerator, to get a can of eight-ounce cola soda, Marcus reached inside of the refrigerator, pulled out the refrigerator drawer and grabbed a cold can of cola soda to drink while his cell phone was being charged on the penthouse balcony. Glad to know that Stephanies apartment had active electricity, but a little puzzled of what happened to the power downstairs in his apartment, Marcus walked over to the kitchen sink. Turning on the kitchen water faucet he realized that Stephanies apartment didn't have any water either. Realizing that the building's water had been shut off without any prior notice, Marcus ventured back onto the large penthouse balcony. Grabbing some dog treats for his buddy Brownie he walked towards the balcony door. Hearing the elevator chimes sounding from the hallway because of the quietness inside of the penthouse apartment, Marcus glanced over towards the front door, spotting the large box by the carpeted staircase inside of Stephanie's beautifully decorated duplex penthouse apartment, as Marcus eyes looked over the first floor of the duplex apartment. Marcus was always an outdoorsman, since he was a Cub Scout, in the National Boy Scout program. This chilly Fall weather always reminded him of their annual camping trips to New York's famous Bear Mountain. Sleeping outdoors in the cold frigid temperatures, wrapped in a sleeping bag listening out for the Bears, Raccoons and Rattle Snakes was a yearly event the local Boy Scout program participated in. It was an adventure Marcus had grown to love, and every Fall season he looked forward to. Being outside in the forest, wooded areas of the cold mountains with the other Scouts, playing games for badges, learning new skills, competing in crafts for badges, learning archery and building barn fires is Marcus's expertise. That's why Melonie assigned her oldest son the important task of checking on Brownie because she knew Marcus was able to handle the task and execute it with excellence. Sliding open the apartment balcony door as he and brownie went outside on the balcony, Marcus slid the door close behind him. Not wanting the heat to escape the very large apartment upsetting Stephanie any more than she already is. Walking across the balcony to the far end of the large penthouse balcony that circled around Stephanies side of the penthouse floor, of the luxury tower building, Marcus sat on the large, cushioned sofa that was in front of the balcony power outlet. Pulling out his brand-new tablet from his small knapsack, which had sixty-five percent battery left, Marcus connected his Bluetooth earpiece with the new tablet to go online to his favorite teen social media platform. Brownie hopped up on the sofa next to him burying his furry head inside of the two wool blankets Stephanie had on top of the balcony sofa chair. Marcus burst out in laughter knowing that Brownie was afraid of heights. He could jump on a chair with ease but would be scared to jump off because of the height. Looking at his favorite Hip Hop artist, Papose The Goat who was married to Remy Martha Stewart the half African and half Hawaiian rapper that was just released from prison after doing a one year bid in the female correctional facility for tossing the west Indian barbie doll, former pin up bottle girl, now a singer off the Manhattan bridge after beating her up with her thigh high boot from Remy Martha Stewart's fall shoe collection line, for talking about Remy Martha Stewart in a video release party. Marcus adored the couple because Remy Martha Stewart, didn't do serious prison time for almost killing the female singer, after she nearly drowned in the famous New York City, river that surrounded the island of Manhattan, whose only mistake was trying to dis the female beast in her new video. Papose The Goats lyrics were smooth like butter and flowed like the taste of butter on the taste bud of the tongue. Marcus would repeatedly watch his videos on the teen social media platform and recite his lyrics as the video played. As Brownie poked his tiny furry head up for a treat, Marcus tossed him one. Brownie quickly went back under the double wool blankets to chew on his treat, hiding it from the world not to steal his delicious treat. Marcus burst out in laughter again at Brownie's selfishness. As Papose The Goat latest new fire track played on Marcus brand new tablet, Marcus bopped his head back in forth with his hoodie over his head in response to the great beats, taking deep breaths and exhaling like Stephanie taught him how. Brownie poked his head out again but this time growling as his little ears looked towards the other end of the penthouse balcony. Marcus thought it may have been a New York City pigeon that flew on the balcony, because no animal, especially a rodent, couldn't climb up this high in this chilly fall temperatures. Brownie continued to stare at the other end of the penthouse balcony growling periodically. Suddenly one of the bedroom lights came on upstairs on the second floor of the duplex apartment. Marcus immediately looked up towards the second-floor window. What seemed strangely odd was that it was the only light that came on upstairs on the second floor of the duplex penthouse. Looking at the dark window next to it, which was Stephanies master bedroom, Marcus waited for the light to come on that room. After about a minute of waiting and no light came on. Marcus began to think carefully. Knowing that his cell phone was dead, Monica or Melonie, his mom couldn't get in contact with him, if they may have tried to reach him. Marcus perceived Stephanie may have arrived back early to her house.

The only bazar thing about that is, if Stephanie was anywhere on the penthouse floor premises, Brownies, dog senses would have picked it up and his behavior would have been a lot more active. Stephanies dog would be whimpering, wagging his tail uncontrollably and attempting to get off the sofa giving a sign that his master is somewhere on the penthouse premises. Staring at Brownie, Marcus put the tablet down on the sofa as he stood up and slowly walked back around to the other end of the balcony where the door is located. Turning the corner of the apartment's balcony, as he passed the giant artificial tree on the balcony, Marcus saw the reflection of a tall male figure pacing back in forth on the first floor living room area. Suddenly come to a stop, Marcus put his hands in his jacket pocket as he stood completely still, waiting for the unannounced male to turn around so he could identify who was here inside of Stephanies apartment alone with him. As the tall male pulled out a cigarette from box of cigarettes inside of his blazers side pocket walking towards the kitchen area, Marcus nervously stood completely still, staring through the long vertical blinds filled window to see who the unexpected man is.

CHAPTER 33

THE SUPERVISOR ENTRY

As the older white security supervisor with salt and pepper hair, wearing a trench coat who normally drove the building's security car entered the lobby through the huge brass doors, he walked over to Shawn with a two-way radio in his hands.

"This is a circus Shawn, I'm glad you're here with us today. A real boxing match, this morning right outside in front of the building. Man, I thought I was going to knock someone out this morning. These disrespectful guys don't need to be employed by the local diners. Cops and crap yelling at me, I didn't get up from out of my bed for this crap. Now look at this madness. You seen Jimmy" the security supervisor with salt and pepper hair always wearing a trench coat inquired.

"Last time I heard Gary, he was with the New York Fire Department on upper-level floors" Shawn the tall muscular

African American security guard replied in a bass tone. A few tenants entered the building, returning home from a hard day of work.

"*I was told the New York Fire Department went downstairs to the basement level contractor's rooms, to shut off the building's water*" Gary the older white security supervisor with salt and pepper hair, wearing a trench quickly replied.

"*This is crazy! We have the new Olympic ski racing tenant moving in today, his moving truck is stuck up the block and now he's pissed off. He was standing here in the lobby a couple of minutes ago before going upstairs to the model rental apartment office to speak with Kattie. Jake Zapotes, the Alpine ski record holder, was upset because he must pay the movers overtime to sit in their truck and wait. Do you see what time it is they haven't even started unloading the large moving truck*" Shawn loudly responded in a bass tone.

"*Everyone going to get paid overtime tonight. Including you Shawn, I heard about Stephanies best friend Tiffany, calling the concierge desk earlier this afternoon about her brother Ezra who was attacked in the post office this morning*" Gary the older white security supervisor with salt and pepper hair, wearing a trench softly responded.

"*What, oh that's some foul crap there. Are you serious Gary?*" Shawn the tall muscular African American security guard inquired in a bass tone, as he grabbed the crotch of his black pants holding himself.

"*Yup, he's in the Intensive Care Unit at Lenox Hill hospital. I take it the call was to notify the building that Stephanies sibling will be staying with us here tonight as their brother lays critically injured in the hospital"* Gary the older white security supervisor with salt and pepper hair replied as he reached in his trench coat for his cell phone.

"Wow Gary that's messed up. This City can get crazy. Let me ask you who told you? Phil?" Shawn inquired in a bass tone, as Tommy the tall muscular doorman stood at the door staring at Gary.

"Why do you think I'm the apartment building's security supervisor? Nothing gets past me young buck" Gary quickly replied as the loud banging of the New York Fire Department's fire fighters started breaking the walls down upstairs on the upper-level floors to control the massive water leak.

"It's going to be a very long night. They upstairs making a bigger mess around these tenant's home. You know how messy the fire fighters get when they start tearing up stuff. All kinds of Craziness about to happen in this building tonight, Gary. Aram and Max still here, that alone is going to be wild. Aram's freak off parties alone is madness. Now he and Max are stationed together at the other exit by the buildings lounge. You already know this time at night, is delivery time. Nothing like the morning. With the tenant's family's home, everyone orders, and no one cooks. Delivery people are being escorted throughout the building by our security team. Limited elevators with Jake zapotes move in materials. Parcel delivery guy who usually takes the freight elevator upstairs to the apartments, I heard a little while ago over the two-way radio that he must use the main elevators. The craziness about to happen tonight" Shawn the tall security guard shared in a bass tone, as

he grabbed the crotch of his black pants, while holding himself.

"That's why I'm leaving now. After I speak to Jimmy about something" Gary the security supervisor quickly replied as he grabbed the crotch of his grey slacks adjusting himself.

"So, when are they going to fire Roberts dumb butt" Shawn softly asked in a bass tone as he stared into his eyes. As the loud sounds of banging vibrated downstairs to the lobby from the fire fighters trying to gain entry through the wall to reach the leaky pipes.

"Originally it was supposed to be done at four o'clock when he arrived for his security guard shift. After the police episode this morning we decided to do it later when there were less of the tenants entering the building. Now it'll be around midnight, the way things look around here. That's why I'm going home now" Gary replied as he answered a text message on his cell phone.

"You can't leave us now Gary. You know you're in love with us" Shawn loudly responded in a bass tone as he burst out in laughter, grabbing the crotch of his black pants, holding himself.

"Watch me kid" Gary quickly replied as he typed a message on his cell phone. *"Save that love making mess for Aram and his secret private rendezvous all around the building"* Gary the security supervisor continued to say. *"Cornel, the clumsy electrician still here messing up stuff? I heard he cut the power out on three certain apartment lines throughout the building. I think most of the tenants have power, but a few on those three lines don't have power"* Gary

325

the security supervisor inquired as more tenants entered the building slowly from their places of business. As the fire fighters continued loudly banging on the building walls upstairs, trying to gain entry through the hallway to the leaky pipes.

"Yeah, that cat, never came back upstairs. Super and Jimmy were yelling about Cornel the electrician all afternoon, threatening to fire everyone. Gary, its real crazy in this building today. So, what are they going to keep Robert escorting deliveries until they call the New York Police Department, Detective Bureau's Central Robbery Division?" Shawn the muscular tall African American security guard inquired in a bass tone as Tommy stood at the huge brass doors staring at Gary directly in his eyes.

"They assigned him Stephanies penthouse apartment. Since the family will be arriving here to the luxury tower any minute. He's probably hiding in the apartment now. Let me check my emails on my cell phone and see if I received an email from the electronic key filing system about a penthouse key missing" Gary sarcastically said as he lifted his cell phone to start checking his emails. "Shawn, let me ask you about this black SUV with city parks on the door. Who are they?" Gary, the old white security supervisor with salt and pepper hair who always has on a long trench coat, softly inquired.

"Yo, Gary, that was crazy! I never seen Max get heated like that! I thought I was going to have tackle the two big French dudes. Oh, man! They were straight beasting! Trying to go upstairs to see Ivan Vasiliev. Everyone was here in the

326

lobby to witness that one" Shawn loudly replied in a bass tone as he grabbed the crotch of his black pants, holding himself.

"The empty black SUV is parked around the corner in front of the buildings management office next to the laundry dry cleaning service" Gary the older white security supervisor with salt and pepper hair who always wears a long trench coat, quickly replied.

"What! Oh no! Athena, Lucas, I need you to call the police, they're in the building! Call the cops now! The French men are upstairs. Someone call the New York Police Department, the French men are inside of the building" Shawn loudly yelled in a bass tone as he immediately ran towards the security guard entrance of the building to alert the other guards of the situation, while Tommy the tall muscular Italian doorman, remained standing at the huge brass doors lobby entrance, staring at Gary.

CHAPTER 34

MURDER ON THE FLOOR

BOOM! BOOM! BOOM! The loud sounds of banging rocked the hallways of Manhattan's, Highrise, luxury tower, apartment building. As the walls inside each unit vibrated at the loud bangs, coming from the New York Fire Department who were on the premises trying to control a major water leak on two of the upper-level floors of the building. The tenant's dogs barked inside the surrounding floors, at the disturbing banging noise coming from the fire fighters, who were breaking the walls down to get to the leaky pipes. Building Alarms begin to ring because of the sudden activity taking place inside of the building. Shawn, who was also a licensed fire guard, was already posted in the lobby along with Gary who was not only the building's security supervisor, but also a Fire guard. BOOM! BOOM! BOOM! The loud sounds of the fire fighter breaking the hallway and apartments walls trying to get to the leaky pipes.

"It's one of those days here at work today. Any and everything that could possibly happen has occurred on today" Gloria loudly said as Kattie typed up a memo on her desk top computer inside of the model rental apartment office on one of the upper-level floors. As Jake Zapotes stared out of the large living room window, overlooking the scenic view of Manhattan's night skyline, Kattie's cell phone started to ring. Answering the phone call from Herb, the buildings property Manager, Tim the rental office assistant entered the office carrying a tablet.

"Hey, Kattie, that black SUV those two distinguished French men, drove away in earlier is now parked and empty in front of my office. I think you need to get in contact with Shawn and let him know. I tried calling the security supervisor's office, but no one answered my calls" Herb shared. *"Oh, no Herb! I'm going downstairs to alert the authorities. I saw the police outside in front of the building. I'll let the front desk know. They may already be aware. Security normally monitors the cameras. Okay be safe Herb"* Kattie replied as she disconnected the call. *"Tim if you don't mind can you please wait here in the rental office with Jake Zapotes while Gloria and I investigate a building matter. Thanks, my friend"* Kattie professionally spoke as her and Gloria exited the model rental apartment office together. Walking through the loud hallway towards the elevator's, BANG! BANG! BANG! Shots rang out from the staircase. BANG! BANG! BANG! Shots rang again from the building's

stairwell. Kattie took off running toward the apartment building's exit staircase door.

"Wait! Kattie, no! Do not go over there! Come back here" Gloria shouted out, trying to stop Kattie from entering a dangerous situation. As Kattie approached the staircase door and entered the narrow staircase, she ran and leaned over the stairwell banister. BANG! BANG! Shots rang out that struck Kattie, hitting her in the head. Falling back towards the closing door, Kattie's body dropped to the staircase floor as Gloria loudly screamed in a panic reaction. Tim and Jake Zapotes exited the model rental office apartment as Gloria, immediately ran towards the staircase exit door when the hallway lights suddenly went out.

"Oh, my Goodness what happened to the lights" Tim shouted as Gloria stopped in the pitch-black dark hallway. Reaching out her hands to feel the hallway wall, Gloria inched her way to the staircase door that was a little way in front of her.

"There are no lights at all. Is there a blackout" Jake Zapotes loudly inquired as he stood still in the pitch-black hallway.

"Gloria are you okay? Let me take out my cell phone and use the flashlight to see" Tim spoke as he reached in his pants pocket for his cell phone. Jake Zapotes reached in his jacket pocket for his cell phone, to try and use the phone's flashlight.

"Oh no Kattie" Gloria whispered as she slowly reached her wedding fingered right hand out, for the handle of the staircase door in the pitch-black hallway.

Feeling the cold medal handle, Gloria slowly wrapped her right hand around the door handle turning it downward, she begins to apply pressure by pushing the door open when Tim's cell phone flashlight shined on the staircase door as he quickly walked towards Gloria. Shining his flashlight on the door, Gloria tried to open the door, but Kattie's body was laid out against the bottom of the staircase door on the floor. As the cell phone flashlight continued to shine on the door, Tim got closer towards Gloria. Having no success at opening the door, Gloria slowly lifted her sorrowful eyes upward and as her head slowly lifted to the small glass window on the staircase door, she saw the French man staring at her through the stairwell glass. Gloria loudly screamed as Tim quickly ran up to her. Standing completely still with the cell phone flashlight shining on the door, both Tim and Gloria saw the French man staring directly at them through the staircase door's, small glass.

"Tim cut the cell phone light off and let's run back to the office on the count of three" Gloria whispered as her body shook with fear as the French man continued staring at them through the small glass on the staircase door.

"Okay, one" Tim softly whispered as he searched for the flashlight off button on his iPhone, while the French man continued staring at them through small glass on the staircase door.

"Two, two and a half, three" Gloria softly nervously whispered as the cellphone flashlight went out and the hallway turned completely dark. Tim and Gloria quickly ran back down the hallway in a panic towards

Jake Zapotes who was still standing by the model rental office apartment door, texting on his lighted up cellphone. Screaming and yelling as they approached Jake Zapotes, the Olympic ski racer in the completely dark hallway, he turned on his phone's flashlight and shined it on them.

"Go back inside" Tim loudly yelled as the hallway emergency lights turned on. *"There must be a power outage in the building if the emergency lights are on"* Tim continued to say.

"What happened down there" Jake nervously inquired as Tim frantically looked back behind them to see if the French man had entered the hallway floor.

"Kattie has been shot dead. There's a gunman in the building murdering people. Call the police Jake and let them know we have an active shooter in the building" Gloria nervously replied as Tim walked over to the floor elevator to see if the elevators were operating.

"There's a shooter in the building we have to get out of here" Jake Zapotes loudly responded as Tim turned his head and stared at them.

CHAPTER 35

THE FINAL CALL

Standing on the penthouse balcony in the chilly evening air, wearing his hoodie over his head and his favorite jacket, Marcus slowly walked back to the other end of the balcony to get his cellphone and tablet. With the power outage in the building and the lights out in all the luxury tower apartments, the only lights shining were the surrounding buildings in the Manhattan neighborhood. Marcus wasn't sure what just happened in the building, but with no running water in both apartments and as he stood there in the cold, trying to see who the unannounced male was in Stephanies luxury apartment, the lights automatically went out. That meant that he could be visibly seen on the balcony by the array of New York City buildings and skyscraper lights surrounding the luxury tower. Marcus wasn't too sure who the unidentified male was that started smoking his cigarette in Stephanies kitchen, however he didn't want the stranger to know that he was also in the Penthouse. Slowly approaching the sofa chair on the balcony, Marcus quickly picked up his cell phone, turning the power on to contact his older sister Monica for help. He knew the phone had been plugged in the balcony outlet long enough for the cell phone battery to have at least forty percent battery charge. Putting the earpiece back into his right ear, Marcus used his peripheral vision to keep an eye on the left corner of the balcony, just in case the unidentified male stranger stepped out on to the balcony where, the bright lights of New York City keep everything lit, so that a person could see. As the display screen came on, Marcus quickly text Monica alerting her that he was on the balcony of Stephanie's penthouse apartment and there is a strange man inside the house smoking. He wasn't sure what to do. As Marcus pressed her name to make the call, he switched the Bluetooth connection from the tablet device to his cellphone. As the phone rang, Brownie started growling. Marcus immediately knew that meant the stranger stepped out on the balcony. Marcus quickly took Brownie off the sofa as the dog took off barking at the stranger on the balcony.

"Monica, did you get my message? I'm on the penthouse balcony help" Marcus softly whispered as Brownie loudly barked at the unidentified stranger who was now around the corner on the large penthouse balcony.

"Brownie, what are you doing outside here in the cold weather. I didn't know that Stephanie keeps you outside" the

334

strange low range voice sounded as he kneeled down to rub Brownies fur.

"Marcus, I can barely hear you. Knuckle head, did you say penthouse? I see the buildings' lights are out. There seems to be a blackout in our building. We're all in my boyfriend's car. Uncle is here with us. There's a lot of people outside. The New York Fire Department is here, they may have cut off the power. We don't see a fire. I don't see smoke anywhere. Do you smell flames or gas? Is that why you're in the penthouse? Is there a fire inside of the building, that we cannot see Marcus" Monica nervously asked while Jamal, slightly turned around in the driver's seat, as Elder Jackson stared at Jamal with his eyes wide open.

"Monica, wait the guy is out here with me. I can't talk. Don't hang up though" Marcus softly whispered as he quickly went and nervously hid on the floor, on the other side of the sofa throwing the wool blankets over him. Trying his best to listen for the strange voice from the unidentified male. *"Monica, I'm on the carpeted balcony floor hiding behind the long sofa on the other end of Stephanie's balcony. I think they went inside, because I can barely hear Brownie barking. But I can hear Brownie still barking. Who's the stranger sis"* Marcus nervously asked as he hid himself next to the sofa on the large penthouse balcony.

"You said there's a stranger in the penthouse with you and you're hiding Marcus. Don't move we're coming to get you" Monica loudly said as Jamal, Elder Jackson and Derrick immediately hoped out of the new Acura. Elder Jackson through the large pizza box, back inside of the new car as he turned and looked at Derrick.

"No, Jamal you stay here! I need you to stay here in the car with your girlfriend, my nephew and my nieces. Keep your eyes on my family like you have been doing. I trust you man. Continue to keep my family safe. Derrick and I will run up the flight of stairs to the penthouse and get my nephew! Let's go Derrick, I need your help in this building's staircase man. Nobody is going to touch my nephew" Elder Jackson loudly spoke as he and Derrick took off running towards the dark luxury tower apartment building.

"Marcus, uncle is on his way upstairs with one of the young men from the church. I love you, Knucklehead. Stay quiet and stay still I'll remain on the phone with you until your battery dies out again, knucklehead" Monica nervously said as Jamal returned inside of his new car, turning up the volume of the Christian broadcast on his car's stereo.

"Don't call me that. I don't like when you call me that" Marcus angrily replied as he held his knees close to his chest. Breathing in and out through his nose, with his mouth close, under the wool blankets, Marcus hid himself on the balcony.

"I'm sorry little brother. I tried calling you earlier, but I didn't get an answer" Monica replied, as she got out the car and went to the front passenger seat to sit next to Jamal.

"My battery was dead, that's how I ended upstairs here in Stephanies penthouse apartment. I needed to charge my phone. We didn't have any electricity in our apartment. Now the building's lights automatically shut off while the guy was smoking his cigarette in the penthouse kitchen. I just couldn't

see his face. I stood there and watched him through the window. He must be security, because he was wearing a blazer, but honestly, I'm not sure sis." Marcus replied as he remained on the carpeted floor balcony with his knees close to his chest.

"Don't worry just stay where you're at! Uncle is on his way upstairs to you" Monica responded as Jamal grabbed her hand and softly kissed her knuckles with his thick brown lips. As Monica stared at him, Jamal continued to softly kiss her hand. Sitting in the new car nervous and upset Monica continued to stare into Jamal's bedroom eyes. Jamal, rubbing his right hand gently massaging her left knee, quickly glanced up at the passenger side window at the tall male figure standing next to his car staring directly at him. Paul, the six foot, seven inches white male school safety agent took his cell phone out of his right coat pocket and pointed it at the window. As Monica's brother and sisters stared at the school safety agent from the back seat, he gently tapped on the Acura glass window with his cell phone.

"My luv, do you know this clown" Jamal softly asked as Monica turned her head to look and see who it was tapping on the car window. As Paul and Monica locked their eyes, the school safety agent lifted his cell phone to the window so they could see the name of the contact on the phone. As Jamal read Judge Watkins name on Paul's cell phone display screen, Monica took Jamal's right hand with her left hand and placed it on her left breast as she slowly leaned her body towards Jamal. Paul slowly walked off putting the cell phone to his face as

he walked towards the New York Police department officers, that were posted at the corner, in front of the luxury tower.

"That's the school security guard who has been chasing me ever since I entered the school building this morning, after I left you Jamal" Monica softly replied.

"He's still in hot pursuit my luv. I guess no one informed him that you've already been captured by my heart and that embrace no one can undo" Jamal softly answered.

"Hopefully my uncle can assist with my dad Jamal" Monica said.

"Hopefully your uncle doesn't get caught up in his church's dirty porter money laundering scheme. My luv, that's not me anymore. You have helped me walk into a better light. I can't rock with these cats anymore. Today downstairs in my church, as I sacrificed my sleep for your uncle, standing there in front of dirty Derrick, I realized their stupidity isn't a life for me. I'm not going to prison because they just don't care about anyone than themselves. I don't want to risk losing you. Your uncle is a real good dude Monica" Jamal softly spoke as Monica continued to stare into his bedroom eyes.

As Elder Jackson and Derrick loudly explained to the building security and the doormen about his nephew being home alone in the busy tower lobby, Shawn entered the lobby with his two-way radio in his hands. Stopping and looking at Derrick, Shawn grabbed the crotch area of his black pants as Elder Jackson stared at Shawn the tall African American security guard.

"Eastside Niger and what! Stay in the zone all day, stay with the killers and you'll aren't real dealers. You don't want

no smoke with us" Derrick shouted out loud as he threw his gang signs in the air. The super's wife entered the lobby speaking Russian to the detectives, who are now on the luxury tower premises to arrest Robert, the security guard for burglary and criminal trespass. Elder Jackson stopped talking and stared at the detectives as they walked over to Shawn the tall African American security guard.

"Base to patrol pick up! Base, to patrol pick up! We have an active shooter in the building, please be alarm, there is an active shooter somewhere inside the building. Multiple casualties have already been reported. Two white males have been identified as the shooters. Last time seen in the upper level of the tower in the B/C staircase. Please take precautions that shooters are armed and dangerous. Once again shooters are armed and dangerous. Rental office managers are locked inside the model rental office with the Olympic ski racer. New York Police Department officers are now on the premises along with the New York Fire Department. Some floors are flooded. Please take precautions. We have reports of illegal activity in the penthouse" Gary the old white salt and pepper haired that always wore a trench coat reported over the two-way radio to his security guards that were scattered all throughout the pitch-black dark apartment luxury tower building.

"An active shooter, oh man I didn't sign up for this! I'm out of here" Robert shouted out as he put his two-way radio back into his other blazer pocket. Robert turned on his cellphone's flashlight, attempting to make his way to the huge penthouse door, as Brownie continued

to loudly bark, running back to the balcony whose door remained open. Robert, the security guard, ignoring Brownies' noisy barking, began stumbling his way to the front door inside of the large dark penthouse apartment. Being a little intoxicated after drinking the whole 375 bottle of cognac in Stephanies kitchen, Robert proceeded towards the door, when suddenly he heard a key enter the main lock on the huge penthouse door. Brownie continued to loudly bark running back and forth from inside of the house to outside on the balcony, looking at the corner where Marcus was on the other end hiding by the sofa. Robert Stopped in the pitch-black apartment, shining his cellphone light on the huge penthouse door as the key entered the cylinder, turning the locked door to open. Robert slowly backed up as he kept his light shining on the door afraid to see who had access to the penthouse apartment during the building's power outage. Brownie quickly ran to the front door and started barking even louder as Robert continued to slowly step backwards onto the carpeted floor, in the duplex penthouse doorway area. As the penthouse front door swung open to the dark penthouse floor hallway, standing on the decorated doormat in the dark hallway, was Bradley. Robert shined his cellphone flashlight into Bradley's eyes. Bradley quickly raised his gun and fired it one time. Shooting a bullet into the upper chest area of Robert, throwing his limb body backward into the large, tall box that was stationed by the bottom step of the penthouse duplex apartment staircase. As Roberts body dropped from off the tall box, onto the floor, his head hit the edge of a small table by the staircase banister, inside of the pitch-black dark apartment. Roberts body lay out on the carpeted penthouse floor as blood oozed out of Roberts' opened mouth. Bradley walked over to Roberts body and picked up the two-way radio that fell out of his jacket pocket. Bradley slowly walked over to the open balcony door that remained open. Stepping out onto the balcony, Bradley started calling for Brownie, who took off running when he fired his gun.

"Brownie, come here boy. It's your friend buddy. Come here Brownie" Bradley loudly spoke as he snapped his fingers, calling Stephanies pet Shar-pei mixed dog.

"Please don't kill us, my mom works at the United Nations. She will help you get whatever you need here in America. Please we're church going people" Marcus yelled as his entire body nervously shook, while tears slowly fell from his eyes down onto his cheeks. Walking slowly, holding Brownie tightly in his arms, Marcus came from around the corner of the large balcony, which stretched around the entire penthouse duplex apartment.

"Marcus, is that you? What are you doing up here in Steph. Apartment." Bradley loudly responded as Marcus slowly walked towards him nervously shaking. Bradley looked down at Marcus pants, as he moved closer to him. Bradley observed the large wet stained, concluding that in fear of his life, Marcus peed on himself when he heard the gun shots inside of the apartment. Bradley turned and walked back inside of the penthouse apartment towards the front door.

"Marcus take out your cell phone and cut on the flashlight so you can see where you're stepping. I need you to walk towards me, I'm at the front door" Bradley loudly spoke as he picked up Robert's cellphone and shined the light at the front door. Marcus stood in the balcony doorway trembling and nervously shaking.

"Come on son, do what I said, turn on your cellphone's flashlight. No one is going to hurt you and Brownie. I need you to come to me Marcus" Bradley loudly said as Marcus slowly walked over to him through the large penthouse apartment. Passing Roberts body laid out bleeding on the floor, Marcus looked down at the body

"Is he dead" Marcus asked as he shined the flashlight up and down the body.

"I'm afraid so Marcus. I don't know how I'm going to explain this one to Judge Watkins. Hopefully he'll get me out of this one too" Bradley loudly replied as he stood in the doorway of the penthouse duplex apartment. Marcus slowly lifted his head, pointed his cellphone flashlight at Bradley's face and stared at him with his eyes wide open.

THE END